DEADLINE

DEADLINE

A NOVEL

steven cooper

 alyson books
los angeles

Celebrating Twenty-Five Years

MANUFACTURED IN THE UNITED STATES OF AMERICA.

THIS TRADE PAPERBACK ORIGINAL IS PUBLISHED BY ALYSON BOOKS,
P.O. BOX 4371, LOS ANGELES, CALIFORNIA 90078-4371.
DISTRIBUTION IN THE UNITED KINGDOM BY TURNAROUND PUBLISHER SERVICES LTD.,
UNIT 3, OLYMPIA TRADING ESTATE, COBURG ROAD, WOOD GREEN,
LONDON N22 6TZ ENGLAND.

FIRST EDITION: JULY 2005

05 06 07 08 09 a 10 9 8 7 6 5 4 3 2 1

ISBN 1-55583-906-1
ISBN-13 978-1-55583-906-2

LIBRARY OF CONGRESS CATALOGING-IN-PUBLICATION DATA
    COOPER, STEVEN, 1961–
        DEADLINE : A NOVEL / STEVEN COOPER.
        ISBN 1-55583-906-1; ISBN-13 978-1-55583-906-2
        1. JOURNALISTS—CRIMES AGAINST—FICTION. 2. INVESTIGATIVE REPORTING—FICTION. 3. MURDER VICTIMS—FICTION. 4. MASSACHUSETTS—FICTION. 5. GAY MEN—FICTION. I. TITLE.
    PS3603.O583D43 2005
    813'.6—DC22   2005040984

CREDITS
COVER PHOTOGRAPHY BY ALAN THORNTON/STONE/GETTY IMAGES.
COVER DESIGN BY MATT SAMS.

To:
MARTHA, MAURICE, SOPHIE, AND NATHAN
FOUR STARS SHINING BRIGHTLY

I'D SURE LIKE TO KNOW WHO MURDERED ME.

My loved ones would like to know too.

There has been no arrest.

I've been dead for six weeks, and Detective Raul Sanderplaatz of the Massachusetts State Police is still scratching his head trying to figure out who in the world would kill a thirty-five-year-old television reporter who had taken a temporary vow of celibacy, who had regularly ransacked his own apartment to discourage would-be burglars, and who was well-liked by his colleagues, his neighbors, and a fair share of the viewing audience as measured by various focus groups, the Nielsen ratings, and his mother, Marilyn, on the rare occasion when she would not withhold her affection.

Hello?

What about all the people exposed in my investigative reports as scammers, con artists, and embezzlers? There are a lot of people who would have liked to kill me. A lot of people had the motive. Many of them are all too glad that I'm six (actually eight-and-a-half) feet under and no longer a fly in their ointment. Speaking of ointment, no need for Preparation H in heaven. There are no assholes here. Which is a plus.

Detective Raul Sanderplaatz of the Massachusetts State Police swears up and down that he's checked out all of the cretins exposed by my scandalous stories. He says, yes, they all hate my guts and are not sorry that I'm dead but that there is no evidence linking any of them to the crime.

Oh. Evidence?

So that's what this is about.

It's not just means, motive, and opportunity. We need evidence. Now, that's going to be hard. How do I, a dead person, lead Detective Raul Sanderplaatz of the Massachusetts State Police to the evidence he needs to make an arrest? We in the afterlife do not have among our accessories Post-it notes or answering machines. Save for the rare séance or two, we're not called upon all that often for ideas. Which is too bad because we could be a very good resource for many things. I have yet to figure out a way, for example, to tap a living soul on the shoulder and say, "Hey, look, over there, the bloody knife" or "No, don't eat that Pop-Tart. It's full of trans fats," but I'm working on it because I know it can be done. Look, I don't know who killed me. But I do know of one story that almost didn't make it to the airwaves, and that's probably where Detective Raul Sanderplaatz of the Massachusetts State Police needs to begin.

2

THE TRUE STORY OF GINA PARR ALMOST DIDN'T MAKE IT TO
the airwaves because I was too dead to finish it.

On one of those wintry nights when sounds echo steely
through the air and an icy mist fills the gaps between the
houses, the cars, and the people who shuffle in and out of the
cold, Gina's body was found wrapped up in blankets in the
warmth of her bedroom in her fourth-floor apartment.

She had been shot three times.

Twice in the head. Once in the hand, of all places. Why the
hell would you shoot somebody in the hand? I've heard of
shooting someone in the foot to stop the person dead in his
tracks—but shooting someone in the hand? For what? To
stop someone from writing a memoir? From directing traffic?
Giving you the finger?

So, Gina Parr and I were both victims of murder. But the
similarities end there. Except of course that we both worked
in professions generally despised by the masses. She was a
lawyer.

"Fitz, can you come in? We have a breaking story."

I instantly regretted picking up the phone. What could I say?

a) "No, I had planned to write an astonishing debut novel tonight."

b) "No, I don't think I can come in. I'm in the middle of a fantastic masturbation."

"Yeah...sure," I said, instead. "What is it?"

"A murder."

"Oh."

"Up in Spring Hill."

"Spring Hill?" I asked, surprised by the news of such an unsavory crime in such a savory, sumptuous neighborhood.

"Yeah. We called in Johnnie to shoot with you. Do you want to meet him at the scene or come to the station?"

"At the scene."

Ned, the assignment editor, gave me the address. By then I had removed the lotion from my hand and had gathered a pen and something to write on.

"Thanks, Fitz."

"Sure."

3

MY PLAN TO WRITE THAT ASTONISHING DEBUT NOVEL WAS A
direct result of my misadventures in television. Or my disappointment in television. Or my disillusionment, my scratchy
voice, my flyaway hair, my inability to suffer fools like the
ones who gravitate toward management positions in local
news.

I wanted out.

After ten years of "How do you feel about your son's murder?" and "How do you feel about the fire that destroyed
everything you own and singed your eyebrows?" and "How
do feel living next door to a child molester?" I started not to
care at all about the murder, the fire, or the child molester du
jour. I acquired a running mantra beneath my delivery of the
news. You could never hear it. But I'm sure you could see it
in my eyes. It went:

"idontcareidontcareidontcareidontcareidontcare, live in
Boston, Damon Fitzgerald, Channel 11 News."

On really bad nights it went :

"thisisbullshitthisisbullshitthisisbullshit, live in Boston, Damon Fitzgerald, Channel 11 News."

I had come home from work on one of those really bad nights and had unloaded myself on the fat old sofa in the living room and breezed through the mail: bills, bills, an underwear catalog from *International Male* featuring impossibly well-endowed men, a free sample of toothpaste, an issue of *The Advocate,* and the quarterly alumni newsletter from my institution of higher learning and its listing of how much better than me all my classmates were doing. As always, I had flipped immediately to my graduating class to find out who, specifically, had done what, specifically, better than me and whether there were any coattails I could effectively, if not unabashedly, ride. Unable to quickly learn the basics of neurosurgery or the migrating habits of the Africanized honey bee in subtropical climates, I was out of luck. But then I read how Stanford Wells (a pretentious name if there ever was one), one class junior to me (junior to me!), had published his first novel.

"I can do that!" I had cried aloud to my quiet apartment and its quiet furnishings. "That's my ticket out of this bullshit."

Out of the bedroom came the pitter-patter of my dog and the patter-patter of my boyfriend with big feet, Frank. "Damon, is that you?" he asked.

"No, it's Hemingway."

"Hemingway?"

"Get used to it. I'm going to be a great writer."

"A great writer?"

"Yeah."

"What are you going to write?" he asked.

I searched the room for some kind of clue, perhaps, a sign, if you will, of the story waiting to be told. "I don't know."

"You don't know?"

"No. Not yet."

He sat beside me, putting his big hand on my knee. Big hands, big feet, and, yes, big penis, which, despite his desperate plea, did not enter my ass that night. No, I was too preoccupied with my new calling, my sense of purpose, mission, in fact, to find the huge universal theme that had yet to be explored, a plot that would be metaphorical unto itself, paved with poetry and the occasional pedestrian twist, and characters, of course, deep complex characters who could carry it all off, whose lives looked as simple as a day on Main Street but in fact were very troubled.

At that point—the night of the refused penis—Frank and I had been together for three years. I had been working in television for ten years and planning my astonishing debut novel for fifteen minutes. Thank you Stanford Wells! College had finally paid off.

Sadly, the astonishing debut novel would have to wait. Gina Parr had gone and gotten herself murdered and I knew I would be drowning in her death until her killer was apprehended, prosecuted, and convicted. That could take a very long time.

◇ ◇ ◇

I got to the murder scene and did the obligatory live shot.

"Details are sketchy..." I said.

Hmm, thinking about it from up here (heaven, incidentally, is wonderful for perspective) I now realize that if details are "sketchy," they are not, in fact, "details."

Yes, I described a "neighborhood in shock," and lest I should disappoint the viewers at home or the spastic, bloodthirsty neophyte producing the newscast, I did indeed find a neighbor who described Gina as "a quiet type...kept to herself...would never harm a soul."

"Beautifully done," the bloodthirsty neophyte said into my ear when I finished my live report. "Go home and get some sleep."

❖ ❖ ❖

Instead I went home and broke up with Frank and took a vow of celibacy because, after all, it was masturbation this murder interrupted, not mad, passionate lovemaking. So there you have it: masturbation as an element of foreshadowing—a novel idea.

The demise of my relationship with Frank had been coming for a long time—that is, after all, the nature of a demise, is it not? Our interests veered off in different directions. He loved softball and show dogs. My idea of sports was pinball; my idea of pets, taxidermy.

And now I was longing not at all for Frank but, instead, the perfect story around which to build my astonishing debut novel.

"You work ten hours a day in that godforsaken newsroom and then you come home and you want to write a book?"

"I'm writing a novel."

"So far you haven't even turned on your damned computer," he groaned.

"It's the creative process."

"I don't think it's good for this relationship," he declared.

I offered him an indignant glare and said, "What's not good for this relationship is you staring at nineteen-year-old boys."

"I don't stare at nineteen-year-old boys."

"Well, I've never exactly asked their age...but they look barely legal."

"They're legal."

"Oh, so you admit it...you do stare!"

"I do more than stare."

"Fuck you."

"If that was happening, I wouldn't be getting it somewhere else."

The breakup went something like that.

I waited a few months before dating, and when I did I found that, for the most part, my woman friends were not lying when they threw their hands into the air, surrendering to the theory that men, indeed, sucked. I dated a soccer player named Eduardo who, predictably, had incredible legs. He also had a brain that was less active than, say, a brick and I found myself incredibly bored. Then I dated a psychologist named Heaton who insisted on knowing the inner child of every erection. That I could not handle. Then there was Rob—what can go wrong with a guy, a regular ol' guy named Rob? Well, he did have perhaps the worst breath I had ever inhaled and he whined too much about fabric. He hated wool and other rough materials that would itch his skin or just make his eyes water to look at. It seemed obsessive at first, then compulsive. Then I called up Heaton, the psychologist, who told me about Obsessive-Compulsive Disorder. I thanked him hugely for enlightening me, giving me a name to such an odd trait of behavior, and he simply said "anytime" and asked if I might like to grab a cup of coffee the following afternoon.

We grabbed the coffee. And then in the alley behind the coffee shop, as I slipped between two cars on the way to the subway entrance, he grabbed my ass and asked if I'd like to have some psychology-free sex back at his place later on.

"What about Rob?" I asked.

"Oh. That would be great!" he cried. "Never figured you for a three-way. Just warn him about my carpet. It's Berber."

Ugh.

Hence, my celibacy.

Can you blame me? I mean, can you?

4

WHEN YOU DIE YOU BECOME A STAR. IT'S AS SIMPLE AND AS magical and as complicated as that.

As a child I remember turning my young face to the sky, desperately trying to comprehend the meaning of infinity. A friend, Larry Adamson, who was also eight years old at the time, told me he had an uncle who went crazy trying to understand how the sky never ends. I remember identifying completely with that uncle.

Infinity and limitlessness, alas, are concepts that cannot be grasped until death. And then it all makes perfect sense. Human beings always want explanations. They have to know everything about everything and they have to know it IMMEDIATELY!

Well, humans, there are some things that are better left unknown until the time is right. The time is not right until death, which, in my opinion, makes death something to look forward to, not dread. Trust me on that.

So, instead of trying to get your arms around the concept of infinity—or the limitless nature of space—try to understand the *purpose* of infinity and the *purpose* of the limitlessness of space.

There has to be a purpose.

I'll give you an indirect hint. Did you ever wonder if we'd run out of room to bury our loved ones? What happens when we fill all of our cemeteries? Does it really matter?

I REMEMBER THINKING THAT RICHARD NECKINGHAM, THE district attorney, needed the sun badly. Maybe a week on a Caribbean beach. Or an hour on a tanning bed. How could anybody have such a pale face? Even in pilgrimish New England, in the middle of winter, in a conference room with no windows in an office building with fluorescent lights?

"Can we get started?" Neckingham asked the gaggle of reporters and photographers. The one thing you had to like about Neckingham was that he would sit around a conference table for press conferences; for the most part he wouldn't stand at a podium and look like an idiot. The table provided a more intimate dialogue, allowed for more of a discussion and less of a speech. Reporters hate speeches. Despise them. We'd smoke crack during them if we could.

"Sure, let's go..." I said.

Everybody laughed. I shrugged, unable to see the humor.

"All right, if Fitz is ready, then here goes," the district attorney began. "Last night at approximately eleven forty-five Brookline Police responded to a call in the Spring Hill section of the city. Upon arrival, they found the body of Gina Parr, a twenty-seven-year-old Caucasian female. An autopsy on Ms. Parr's body is being performed. Preliminary evidence gathered at the scene suggests a sign of struggle. We believe that Ms. Parr had expired about twenty-four hours before her landlord discovered the open door to her apartment. Ms. Parr worked as an attorney for the Boston law firm Berger, Berger, Cooke, & Langham. She had been on staff there for two years. Her death comes as a shock to the legal community of Suffolk County. An investigation is under way. We are following various leads. Any questions?"

A few raised their hands. I did not. I just asked the damn question, "Rick, you mentioned an open door. Is there evidence of forced entry?"

"No. There is not."

"What about the sign of struggle?" another reporter asked.

"What about it? There are obvious signs of struggle, but the suspect may have gained entry into the apartment without force."

"Are you suggesting Gina Parr knew her assailant?" I asked.

"You know the answer to that, Fitzie. It's always possible that a victim knew his or her assailant."

"I really hate it when you answer my questions like that, Mr. District Attorney. It makes for a shitty sound bite."

"And that is why we are all here, Damon Fitzgerald, to please you."

A snicker rounded the table, finally reached me. I brushed it off with a "Touché, Mr. D.A."

Susan Radwell from *The Boston Globe* asked about the murder weapon. "Has it been recovered?"

"No."

"What kind of law was Gina Parr involved in?" Susan asked.

"I'm not sure. The firm is multipractice. They have about sixty lawyers."

"Did she ever face you in a courtroom?" I asked.

"No."

"So, you can't speak about her personally?" another reporter asked.

"No, I can't."

"Any reason to believe that Gina Parr had made enemies as a result of her work?" I inquired.

"We have no information that would suggest so. But let me stress that this investigation has just begun."

Again, Susan Radwell: "At this point do you have any idea why anyone would want to hurt her?"

"As I stated, the investigation is under way. We hope to know more soon. If that will be all, thank you for coming."

If that will be all?

Who said that will be all?

I hated it when press conferences ended like that. "Well, that was a big helping of nothing," I said to Susan.

"Have you talked to the firm?"

"My next stop."

"Good luck. It's your classic stuffy group of Boston lawyers. A lot of ex-politicians. Very dry, very proper, very..."

"Boring?"

"Exactly."

"Always good to see you, Susan."

"Will you still marry me if you decide to go straight?"

"What will we do about that husband of yours?"

"Kill him..." she said.

"Would we be allowed to cover the press conference?"

"Hope not."

6

We waited about twenty minutes before a young lady in a tight business suit escorted us to the law library at Berger, Berger, Cooke, & Langham. The library occupied a corner of the firm's thirty-second-floor office and offered impressive, almost privileged views of the harbor to the east and the city to the south. The furniture was big, imposing even, and mahogany. Johnnie set up his camera and lined the chairs up just right, and moments later a small man with curly gray hair and little black-bean eyes came in and extended a hand.

"Ross Littleton, senior partner."

"Damon Fitzgerald, thanks for seeing us."

"I don't know how much we can tell you, Damon. We don't want to compromise the investigation."

Johnnie gave me a thumbs-up indicating tape was rolling, and the interview began.

"Tell me about Gina Parr. What kind of person was she?"

The attorney smiled. "First, let me say we at Berger, Berger, Cooke, & Langham are deeply saddened by the untimely death of Gina Parr. Gina came to work for us two years ago as a tax attorney and had, in that short time, built up our client base in that area considerably. She will be greatly missed. Our condolences, of course, to her family."

"Okay, but what was she like?"

"She was smart, determined, hard-working. But she kept her private life mostly to herself. There really isn't anyone in the firm who had a relationship with her outside of work."

"Did she ever discuss any problems she was having in her private life?"

"Like I said, Mr. Fitzgerald, Gina kept her private life private."

"Well, I can't imagine she would have made a lot of enemies doing tax laws..."

A sharp, patronizing laugh. "Uh, no. Probably not."

"Unless she inadvertently screwed something up for someone."

"Unlikely. Will there be anything else?"

"You tell me...What else do you think the public should know about Gina Parr."

"The public should know that we have lost one of the rising stars in the legal community..."

"I didn't realize tax attorneys were on the fast track to stardom—legally speaking."

"Well, we saw a lot of potential in Gina. There's no saying where she could have ended up. Tax law was only a beginning for her. We are all going to miss her."

"Did she have a boyfriend?"

"That would be out of the scope of our knowledge. As I said, she kept her private life private."

"Did she get along with everyone here at Berger, Berger, Cooke, & Langham?"

"Well, yes. She was a valued employee."

Realizing I was not going to get as much as a fart out of the stiff shirt sitting opposite from me, I signaled to Johnnie to shoot cutaways while I wrapped up this fuck of an interview.

"Thanks, Attorney Littleton. Thanks for your time."

"Hope it helped."

Yeah, it helped kill time, I thought with a smile stretched painfully across my face.

❖ ❖ ❖

"And now shocking details about the murder of a young Boston attorney. Damon Fitzgerald joins us now with the latest developments....Damon?"

The audacity of bloodthirsty producers (they're the ones who write the anchor copy) never failed. As the television industry edged closer and closer to the financial shitter, television companies had to trim, trim, trim, and perhaps the best way to trim was to get rid of all your well-paid seasoned journalists and replace them with cheap, inexperienced, precocious college grads who were trained to hype rather than report.

Producers' favorite words: shocking, gruesome, tragic, chilling.

Producers' favorite feature of the English language: alliteration (e.g., midtown murder, holiday heartache, deadly drug deal, mall molester, pampered pets).

But I'm not bitter.

I sat there next to the blow-dried anchors and wondered what the hell exactly were the *shocking* details. And what in the world were the *latest developments*? There were no developments, except for the fact that the district attorney held his obligatory press conference and we captured a few useless sound bites from a very short lawyer in a very big office.

And so the story ran. Video of last night's crime scene. A photograph of the victim (I wouldn't call her pretty, but I wouldn't call her ugly either. She had a mousy little face and straight, unstyled hair. But she did have a pleasant smile. And a hint of a sparkle in her eyes. She was the kind you'd find sitting in that very same study carrel every night in the university library. She had staked her claim and everybody knew it. And you left her alone. Never asked her to get high or if she knew where you could get a Quaalude.) A sound bite from the D.A. A sound bite from Ross Littleton, senior partner. Another sound bite from the D.A.

End of story.

"Thank you, Damon, for that interesting report."

"Yes, thank you, Damon, a very disturbing story."

Yeah, right, anchor shitheads, don't even act like you listened to the report when *I* know you were fixing your make-up and your hair the entire time the video ran. That's what I thought to myself as I smiled at them disingenuously, pained by the charade.

"Nice job," my boss said to me when I came off the set. He had come to the studio to ask the female half of the anchor team to straighten her lapel.

"Thanks," I said. Now, let me go home and write my astonishing debut novel before someone else gets to it first.

❖ ❖ ❖

I returned home at seven-thirty that evening to find Frank packing his things. "Are you sure you want to do this?" he asked. He was wearing rarely worn glasses, as if to tell me that this occasion was worthy of the most serious consideration.

"Yeah. I'm sure, Frank. And I'd lose the glasses before you try hooking up with more nineteen-year-olds."

He shook his head. "I hope you get what you're looking for before you end up old, bitter, and alone."

"The fact is, Frank, I'm not looking for anything. That may be hard for you to understand, but I am not constantly on the lookout for the next best thing—or the next best dick, if you will..."

"Right. All you want to do is stay home and write your novel so you can quit your freakin' job."

"You mean my astonishing debut novel?"

He didn't answer and said nothing more to me, and I only vaguely heard the door kiss the frame when Frank walked out of the apartment and out of my life.

Immediately, I was rewarded with writer's block as big as the Green Monster at Fenway. I dated a baseball player once and contemplated making that relationship the basis for my debut novel, but sitting there across the Charles River from Fenway, in my just-short-of-swanky Cambridge apartment, with Stevie Nicks singing on the stereo about her own strained relationships, the perfectly polished scent of Frank (a delicate blend of sweet, manly aftershave and musky, inoffensive anus) lingering, staring out at the huge canopy of night, I saw not a single possibility out there in the limitlessness (made a mental note of the irony), not even the possibility of conjuring up the enjoyable penis of the baseball player—and I was convinced (still am, in fact) that there's no such thing as a novel, astonishing or not, without a penis. There just isn't. And, with a debut novel, my God, the stakes are even higher. You got to have penis.

7

Have I mentioned that winter sucks?

Sure, you can go on and on about the beauty of fresh-falling snow, the natural jingle of the flakes shaking from the sky—of bluish nights when the moon reflects off the snow and back to the sky, but no matter how you dress it up, it's still winter in New England and it's still frigid cold and the chill still invades you to the spine and you feel like your testicles are just going to freeze up under you.

In the afterlife there is no weather. It just *is*. Kind of like a dream. In the afterlife there is a complete absence of weather reports. No cold fronts. No jet streams. No sensitivity to climate whatsoever. Sure, we have our meteor showers and other galactical events, but they are, quite frankly, for our own amusement.

So, there I was, hating the bone-freezing winter and men in general, when my parents decided to come for a visit from the emotionally frozen state of Connecticut. Marilyn and John Fitzgerald were on tour, making stops at the homes of their seven children, dropping off early Christmas presents to those of us who would fail to show up at Family Headquarters for the annual birthday bash for Jesus Christ.

"The news business doesn't stop for Christmas," I had tried to explain to Marilyn and John year after dreadful year.

"Well, that's something you and the Lord will have to come to terms with," Marilyn once advised me.

"Where's your friend?" my father asked when they arrived, gift bags in hand, at my door.

"Friend" was code for whatever man was attached to the penis that was, at the time, most frequently up my ass.

"He moved out a few days ago."

My mother made a small pout of a frown and gave my shoulder a there-there brush. How comforting, no?

My father searched the room, looking for something he knew was there, trying to remember the place and the things scattered about in the context of me, the second of seven children, the gay one, the one with obviously the best sense of decor. Moments later he found the object of his desire: the liquor cabinet. He fixed himself a scotch and water, gestured to my mother, who waved her hand, no, she was fine. Sober, but fine.

"How long are you in Boston for?" I asked.

"Just till morning," my mother replied. "Then we're off to New Hampshire to see Terrance."

Terrance was the sixth child. I think.

"Where are you staying tonight?"

"At the Marriott, Long Wharf."

"You know, there's room for you folks here." I just had to say it so it could be said, though, of course, they would never stay because that might somehow suggest that they approved.

The approval.

It had nothing to do with my sexuality. They never stayed at any of my (two) brothers' or (four) sisters' homes. They didn't approve of any of us—each in our own way, I suppose.

"We hope you haven't eaten, Damon. We were hoping to take you to dinner," John said.

"That would be nice," I told him.

Mother smiled.

"How's the news business?" my father asked.

"Interesting."

"I bet," he said.

"Have you covered any good stories?" my mother wanted to know.

"Most good stories are bad stories," I told her. "If you know what I mean."

"I do," she said evenly

Dinner was uneventful. I don't even remember where we ate. I just remember a softly lit corner booth and how awkward my parents looked when confronted with the intimacy.

"Is Terrance your last stop?"

"Yes," my mother said.

I don't think my parents had huge sums of money, although they would try valiantly to prove the blueness of their blood. They vacationed in Palm Beach. They golfed at fine country clubs and both drove Volvos. They gave generous gifts and kept stiff upper lips even around the comic antics of their six grandchildren. John, my father, was a mid-level executive at a huge insurance company where mid-level executives landed in the same maze of cubicles as did the throngs of secretaries assigned to them. He looked a bit like Ted Kennedy, somewhat thinner, though, and he lacked that true Kennedy quality—that political smile that had charmed generations of Democrats. You wouldn't describe John Fitzgerald (how's that for Kennedy quality?), a third-generation American, as charming. No, you might describe him as quiet, aloof even, with indifference fairly constant in his eyes. As for my mother, I believe Marilyn never lost her love of playing dress-up. Even as an adult, she always looked like she had raided someone else's closet and had stood in front of a mirror for hours, maybe, admiring the transformation. She favored pillbox hats and waist-length jackets—a smart look. Her hair was wavy and coiffed, styled away from her face to capitalize on her enviable bone structure, her wide-eyed affectations. She worked at the town library. She never talked about her job, dismissing it as something that simply kept her busy. Occasionally, Marilyn would even talk about her work as if it were philanthropic, as if she were, perhaps, donating her time to the library. "Literacy," she would say, "is everything."

After dinner we smiled and kissed, or kissed and smiled—I'm not sure of the order—and said "stay warm." They hopped into a cab and drove away. I walked home. Across the Mass Avenue Bridge from Boston into Cambridge, turning left at Memorial Drive and onward into the night's ever-hanging mist. I was then at the point in my career when every night felt like Sunday, when the thick dread of Monday coagulated at the very opening of my psyche and my soul. I had tried drinking to anaesthetize the pain, but the truth was I was not in pain, so the drinking did nothing but fill my bladder.

If not pain, then what?

Could it not be possible that I had simply turned off the TV of my life? That I had tuned out?

No cliff-hanger.

No drama.

No sequel.

Could it not be possible that, despite all the consultant-driven, out-of-the-box, flashy, splashy thinking, television was boring me senseless?

I really thought an astonishing debut novel would do the trick, so that evening I sat in front of my PC once again and struggled to come up with a meaningful story with universal implications.

My main character's name would be Luke. Or Carter. Yeah, last names made for good first names. And he'd be an art critic, or a music critic, or perhaps a media critic. Yes, that would work. He could be a media critic and through him I could unleash the truth about the news business—how manipulative it was, how phony it was, how news stations across the country engaged in myth-telling every day, pumping up copy for the sake of drama, forsaking the truth in search of ratings. And there would be conflict. Because his boyfriend, or girlfriend—sexuality, at this point, undecided—would be a well-known and well-liked broadcaster and their jobs would be hopelessly opposed to one another. And there would be a house somewhere that would be symbolic of something.

And a lot of rain.

And emotional baggage.

8

THREE WEEKS LATER, AS I SAT AT MY DESK FEIGNING enthusiasm for my boss who had stopped by to ask about my upcoming projects (February sweeps was only two months away, and my boss, Lloyd Lasser, would want to let corporate know what stories we were planning that could be counted on to scare the shit out of our viewers), my phone rang. I regarded the ring with a dubious stare, but then Lloyd made a gesture with his hand indicating it would be fine to answer the phone, which I did, while Lloyd looked on and feigned interest in my end of the conversation.

"There's been an arrest in the Gina Parr murder," I told him after I hung up with the caller.

"Who was that?" he asked, never trusting of any source.

"The PIO from the D.A.'s office."

"Is this something that you can put together tonight?"

I scrunched up my face and said, "Well, if I don't, one of our competitors will."

"Go talk to a producer. I want it in one of the early shows."

I then followed his instructions and approached the producers of the 5 P.M., 5:30 P.M., and 6 P.M. newscasts. I don't think any of them had been out of college for more than a minute, but they were very valuable employees when you considered their utter lack of experience commanded an utter lack of salary and left the conglomerate that owned us rolling in even more pig-in-shit-dough than it would be rolling in had the producing staff actually finished puberty.

"But is it a lead?" one of them asked.

"Uh, yuh, I think so," I said. "What's your lead now?"

"We're leading with the state budget in one show and with weather in the other two..."

"The weather?" I asked.

"Yeah...the big storm," one of the producers squeaked. "It's supposed to wipe us out!"

"Wipe us out," I repeated. "That's amazing. So, what about the arrest?"

"Can we do it in two shows?" the 5 P.M. producer asked. "You know, once in my show and then again at six?"

The 5:30 P.M. producer rolled her eyes and made a snitful sound with her nose.

"You mean repeat the story in more than one newscast?" I asked.

They all nodded, why, yes, of course.

"Sure. Why break from the norm?" I said and retreated to my office.

Did my attitude suck?

Absolutely.

Was I beyond the point of no return?

Absolutely not. All I needed was a news executive with a vision and a brain (the combination, I hear, is outstanding), a seasoned management staff (with people skills at no extra charge), and colleagues who embraced the idea of *reporting* rather than SHOUTING the news at our viewers—or posing coyly in front of a darkened city hall hours after the feisty budget battle ended.

All I needed was for the world to stop spinning for just a second so I could have a word with God and maybe make a deal to be a better person if he could just see to a few housekeeping items. Like firing the assholes. Stopping the violence. Pulling the plug on Britney Spears and this entire generation of pop-until-you-drop stars.

Johnnie and I departed for the courthouse.

"A press conference?" he asked with dread in his voice.

"No. An assistant D.A. is taking the case and will do a quick one-on-one."

"Mug shot?"

"I should hope so," I replied.

"Hey, did you hear about the big storm coming?"

"Yeah. I heard it's going to wipe us out. Are you prepared?"

"Prepared? How the hell am I supposed to prepare?"

"Tune in tonight at six. I'm sure there'll be some tips. You know, something you've never thought of, like stock up on canned goods. Or have candles ready."

"What about extra blankets?"

"If you have to be out driving," I said. "But we suggest you stay off the roads unless you absolutely must go out."

Johnnie Fanahan grew up in South Boston and sounded it for the lack of *r*'s in his speech and the way he went on and on about the Celtics and this one being a "*stinkah*" and how the new "*Hahbah* Tunnel" was a joke. He had strawberry-blond hair and a generous share of freckles. He was thirty, thirty-one, maybe. He still lived in Southie and always tried to get me to go drinking at the real Irish pubs. I rarely went, not being predisposed to the ubiquitous smell of ancient smoke and urine. Johnnie had a long, lanky build, which aided us often in our pursuit of stories. A clusterfuck of photographers and microphone-wielding reporters never caused Johnnie to miss a shot. His height raised our camera above all others. Occasionally you'd see the back of another reporter's head, but that didn't bother me unless it was Mitch Colombo, Boston's answer to Geraldo Rivera but, hard as it is to believe, more obnoxious. Like Geraldo, Mitch adored *being* the story rather than *telling* the story. Like Geraldo, he regarded self-promotion as a favorable lifestyle choice but claimed rather stridently that he was *born* with a healthy ego, that it wasn't a *choice*.

Okay. Neither is leprosy.

Turns out Neckingham himself did the interview, decided at the last minute to front the case to the media rather than hand it off to an assistant. Which was fine with me. Neckingham knew how to punch out a good sound bite, knew how to give you the facts in a concise and orderly manner. Everything about the man was precise. His pointed collars, fitted suits, manicured hands. About the only thing that was not precise was his age. Hard to guess. His light brown hair receded fairly far beyond his forehead, but his features were youthful, his face free of lines, so I would guess forty-five, maybe. Like I said, hard to tell.

Neckingham handed me a picture of the suspect as Johnnie set up his gear. The guy's name was Roberto Cruz. I've seen the face before. A thousand times. And that's not hyperbole—when you figure I was a television reporter for ten years, that's a few thousand stories which, just by the sheer odds of TV news alone, had more to do with villains than heroes. No, Cruz did not look familiar to me in the sense that, hey, I know that guy, he's the same one who got busted for cocaine trafficking last week or he's the same one who raped a librarian ten years ago, just familiar in the way he reminded me of all the other downtrodden, sunken-shouldered, dark and dangerous creatures who had paraded along this road of prosecution before. They were almost always dark—so many blacks and Hispanics who had no chance in hell of finding a good lawyer. They were always left exposed to the camera lens. White criminals could usually picket-fence themselves in a garden of lovely flowers with really terrific attorneys at the gate.

You just knew Roberto Cruz, guilty or not, was a poor sucker. A fucking loser.

Tape rolled.

"Mr. Cruz was arrested this morning on an unrelated charge. Upon further investigation, police discovered key evidence linking him to the murder of Gina Parr."

"Please characterize the unrelated charge. What prompted the arrest of Mr. Cruz..."

"Boston Police received a report of a man exposing himself from the window of his apartment. A female neighbor of Mr. Cruz had reported that Mr. Cruz was knocking on the glass to get attention and then grabbing his genitals when someone looked."

"So, he was arrested, initially, for indecent exposure?"

"And lewd and lascivious conduct."

"Was he masturbating?"

"He was."

"Is there more than one witness?" I asked.

"There are several."

"Why did this arrest prompt further investigation?"

"Initially, it didn't. Police were handcuffing the suspect when they noticed a few items in his apartment that matched items taken from the home of Ms. Parr."

"This is the first I'm hearing of articles stolen from Gina Parr's apartment. On the day following the murder, you stated that there were no signs of forced entry. I don't believe you mentioned robbery as a motive."

"That's correct, Damon," Neckingham said. "At that time we were unaware of missing items. It was not until Ms. Parr's family visited the murder scene days later that we were told about a TV and several pieces of missing jewelry. Those items were subsequently identified at the apartment of Roberto Cruz."

"So, you're suggesting one of the officers arresting Mr. Cruz actually recognized the TV and the jewelry and immediately made the connection?"

"It would appear that way."

"How many calls does the average officer respond to in a day?"

The district attorney did not move his face but distinctly moved his eyes from the paperwork in front of him and fixed his stare at me. "I don't know. Many, I suspect."

"And was it common knowledge in the law enforcement community that Ms. Parr had been robbed?"

"I can't speak for the whole law enforcement community. But most officers were following the developments in this case closely. When the family identified the items as stolen, that information was distributed to every working officer. We're grateful that the officer at the scene this morning had the presence of mind to make the connection. I should add he's a rookie who has made a very favorable impression on this department already. Besides, Damon, the TV was sitting on the floor, unplugged, without as much as a cable attached. And as well as the officers could conclude Mr. Cruz is a single man, living alone, which made the presence of two bags of women's jewelry fairly suspicious."

"Where was the jewelry found?"

"On the floor next to the TV."

"Has it been positively identified as belonging to the victim?"

"Yes."

"Mr. District Attorney, doesn't it seem odd that weeks after the crime, the suspect would still have items stolen from the scene sitting on the floor of his apartment?"

"Not if he was getting set to sell them on the street. The officers believe Mr. Cruz was planning to leave the apartment momentarily with the items...to look for a buyer, perhaps."

"Upon completion of the task at hand, so to speak..."

Neckingham wrinkled his otherwise smooth and shiny brow. "I don't follow..."

"You allege that Mr. Cruz was on his way out to dump the merchandise. I'm simply indicating that his masturbation seemed to be first on his dubious list of priorities."

"Yes, it would appear that way," the district attorney said with a smirk, as if we were two old buddies from college—which we were not. "Now if that will be all...."

"Have you walked the suspect?"

"We're not walking him. But you're free to cover the arraignment. It's scheduled for four this afternoon."

Great. That's fucking great. A late afternoon arraignment which would leave me—on a good day—with twenty minutes to turn the story.

Twenty minutes. To write, edit, and jump in front of a live camera and make sense of the freak show to the viewers at home who, in the bigger picture, would go on and live their lives completely unaffected by the murder of the moment.

"I need a live truck," I told the executive producer. Gretchen, that was her name, was the woman in charge of the day-care center we called the producing pool. She was typical of producers in the business who had been in the business too long. She had clawed her way to the top of middle management (which is still not the *top*, if you ask me) ripping peoples eyes out on the way, forsaking sex for the real orgasm of an exclusive story, drinking way too much coffee and smoking her lungs into oblivion. She was single and over thirty and not half-bad looking if you like a kind of catatonic quality in your women.

"Where?" she asked.

I told her.

"Are we the only ones with it?"

"I think so."

"You think so?"

"Yeah. I don't exactly have the time to call all the other newsrooms in town to see if they have the story or not, but I think my tip was exclusive."

"Exclusive," she said softly, reflectively, as if remembering one of her more pleasant, less spastic orgasms.

"Then again," I cautioned her, "I expect the district attorney's office is preparing a press release right now to fax to all the other media announcing the arrest."

"Whatever," she said abruptly. "You're there. The arraignment is in twenty-five minutes. No one else will get there in time. We're sending a truck."

Funny. That's all I asked for in the first place.

✧ ✧ ✧

The courthouse is not known for its ambient lighting. Few of the courtrooms have windows. The arraignment was in one such chamber. Dimly lit, a yellow-orange glow from recessed ceiling lights; long shadows on faces. A box of a room, really.

Roberto Cruz looked worse in person, which is really quite an accomplishment when you consider how unflattering mug shots are. His skin was dark, Latin, but somehow jaundiced.

He did no talking.

Instead a clerk read the charges. The state-appointed attorney entered a plea of not guilty on behalf of his client. The judge ordered Cruz held pending a bail hearing.

Very standard. Nothing unusual.

Though you would never have known that from the way our newscast opened that evening.

"Dramatic moments in a Suffolk County courthouse late today, as the alleged killer of a young Boston lawyer is arraigned. Damon Fitzgerald is standing by with the shocking details...."

Jesus Fucking Christ.

SPEAKING OF JESUS CHRIST, I HAVE NOT SEEN HIM HERE IN the afterlife. But that does not mean that he does not exist. You have to remember the afterlife is a very big place and he could be anywhere, really. There are sightings all the time, much like there are sightings of Elvis.

What about that bright light? Won't he be waiting for you in the bright light?

Well, maybe. He is known to travel in extremely luminous circles and some souls here do communicate the experience of seeing Jesus at the pinnacle of the light. And that is really wonderful to know, isn't it? But, you should also know that other souls communicate the experience of seeing Sammy Davis Jr., John F. Kennedy, and Agatha Christie.

Weird, I know.

But I can tell you this: It's common knowledge here in the afterlife that Mr. Christ is not at all pleased with all the hype about him on Earth. He doesn't much care for the bumper stickers. And he hates being used for political gain of any sort. Enough said.

For now.

Let's talk about the bright-light thing.

It's true.

You will see the bright light. You will head toward it.

The bright light is your star. The heavenly body your soul will inhabit. There's one for everyone. After all, there are infinite stars in infinite solar systems in infinite galaxies.

Let me tell you that life as a star is gorgeous.

And yet some people waste so much of their earthly lives striving for the other kind of stardom, the famous kind. That kind of stardom seems so attractive. You get the big homes, the A-list parties, the limos, and you get to throw tantrums. But that, sadly, is not stardom. In fact, here in the afterlife we laugh at that manifestation of stardom. It is false and thin and desperate when you compare it to the ultimately democratic process of stardom in the afterlife.

Stardom is different here. It's about transformation and energies and bliss.

Why do you think they call it heaven?

You don't have to understand everything about science and astronomy to understand the existential meaning of space. You don't even have to understand existentialism. I remember an old boyfriend of mine who had an unquenchable thirst for all things scientific. We sat one evening on a Florida beach under a canopy of stars and he explained the unexplainable to me. He explained the size of stars (very, very big), the relation of planets to solar systems, solar systems to galaxies, galaxies to the one known universe. He said there had to be a trillion stars in one galaxy alone. And I came away from that evening not with an encyclopedic knowledge of astronomy but rather a strange and very real belief in the possibility of anything and everything. I mean, if this world could contain such powerful and illusive realities, if the Earth is really just the tiniest of tiny dots in a much bigger schematic, if distance is true, if space is endless, then anything and everything is possible if not probable.

I'm glad for that evening. It opened my mind to a god-size helping of faith and spirituality. It prepared me well for my journey in the afterlife. Go sit under a dome of night. That's what you should do. Consider everything above you, really consider it—then close your eyes and feel the impossibility of it. Wait. Then open your eyes and see who's right.

If you're lucky you might find someone like my old boyfriend Tristan, who can enlighten your intellect while your spirit soars.

ALMOST FEBRUARY. SWEEPS HAD A WAY OF STARING YOU down with the arrogance of a Canadian cold front coming after Boston. Reporters and producers who loved their jobs were ready to confront any intimidation the next season of ratings might bring; they braced themselves for the torture, pumping their psyches with robust adrenaline that warmed them from the inside out. Their blood thickened. They salivated like a team of winning huskies. I, on the other hand, wanted to pull the blankets over my head and disappear for a few months.

I envied bears and the permission they were granted to hibernate. Surely after a decade in the news business I had earned a hiatus, hadn't I?

Apparently I had not. We sat in the pitch meeting. Three reporters and six managers (you do the math) went round and round and round and round hashing out the big stories for February.

"I think automatic doors at Home Depot are killing people," a manager said.

"Killing?" I asked.

"That's what I hear," he replied.

"So people are dying at Home Depot fairly regularly," I persisted.

"Well, I know of a case in Cleveland."

"Oh."

"They close on people," Gretchen interjected. "You know, they don't sense dark colors and a lot of African-Americans are getting jammed in the doors."

Fryer Rant, the one black manager in the room rolled his big brown eyes until all you could see were two scary bulbs of white on his otherwise dark face.

Donna Donovan, a fellow reporter, sighed, cleared her throat, and tried to poke her voice through the white noise in the room. "What about New England Savings?"

"What about it?" the Home Depot genius asked.

"Well, it's about to go down the tubes, and I have some really good inside information about who's behind the failure."

"Too dry," Gretchen concluded. "People don't watch bank stories. We can't sell bank stories."

"No," Donna conceded. "But we can sell corruption stories. And I have some very good sources that will lead in that direction."

Todd Murphy, the special-projects producer in charge of the entire slate of February stories, yawned heartily. "Sorry," he said. "But multiply that yawn by 5 million viewers and you get our ratings picture for the New England Savings story."

Donna muttered "asshole" audibly enough for my ears and no one else's.

"What about you, Damon?" Fryer Rant said, turning to me, his eyes now dislodged from the back of his head. "We haven't heard from you."

"Well," I fumbled. "I have a few stories in the works. But nothing I can really talk about with any authority right now."

Which, I thought, was a very authoritative way of saying I don't have a fucking idea and doubt that I will anytime soon.

"What about Gina Parr?" Lloyd Lasser, the news director, asked me.

"Still dead," I replied.

The room of pseudo-jaded journalists tittered for a brief moment with laughter. There was nothing like a good, cold corpse to lighten those heavy moments of in-the-trenches news reporting.

"Yes," Lloyd continued, "but I'm wondering if there isn't a bigger story there."

"No bigger than any other garden-variety murder," I told him.

"You're not hearing anything on the streets, Damon, that would suggest otherwise?" Lloyd asked.

"Nothing. I do find it weird how this Cruz guy was picked up, though. I don't think it merits a lengthy investigation, but I just think it's strange that, boom, all of a sudden they arrest this guy for jerking off and, boom, all of Gina Parr's stuff is in his apartment."

"I'm with Damon," Gretchen said, which of course made me nervous for a moment and in fact made me shudder and made me rethink the story because it was dangerous, I felt, to be in agreement with Gretchen on anything save for, say, the best thing to do with testicles during a blow job (we discussed it once and both agreed that a gentle tug was nice). "There's probably no story there and I'd hate to see him weighed down on a murder that most of us will forget by next week. What about transvestite teachers? I've been dying to do that story since that football coach in Somerville had a sex change."

"Far be it for me to speak as an authority on cross-dressing," I began, noting as I did the various elevations of eyebrows in the room, "but I don't think transsexualism is the same things as transvestitism."

"Boy that was a mouthful," Donna jabbed.

Everyone else laughed nervously. Like, maybe it was too close to home to have the avowed homosexual on staff instructing his colleagues on the delicate distinction between genital-swapping and singing Judy Garland.

"Tranvestite teachers! I still like the idea," Gretchen insisted. You see, once a producer, at any level, gets alliteration in her head, it sticks there like bonded cement. "Or what about following around municipal workers to see if they wear their seat belts?"

Jon Schmidt, the third reporter to face this panel of fools, emerged from a self-induced sleep and said, "that's hardly a story."

Lloyd Lasser shrugged, indicating, quite accurately, that this meeting was going nowhere.

"Well," Gretchen continued, "I think if the state is going to crack down on drivers who don't wear seat belts, then the state should practice what it preaches and *insist* that its employees use seat belts in government vehicles."

"With all due respect, Gretchen," I said delicately, "I give that a bigger yawn than the banking story."

"Totally disagree," she retorted. "Totally. Who cares if a bank fails? But I can hear the cries of injustice now when people realize their tax dollars are going to state workers who don't obey state law."

"No," I told her. "Those are not the cries of injustice you hear. Those are the cries of our stockholders when they see how much money we're losing on stories like that."

"Well folks," Lloyd said, standing, "I think that's enough for today. Obviously we have a lot to think about. Let's give it a week and meet again. I'll want a more complete list by then."

He left.

We sat and looked at one another, our eyes searching the room for some meaningful conclusion. I put my hands in the air as if to juggle the possibilities but shrugged them to my side just as quickly. "Does anyone know where the nearest Home Depot is?"

✧ ✧ ✧

What I did not share with my colleagues and dubious collection of managers was that, actually, I had several stories stuffed up my February sleeves but had learned that the best if not only way to produce the stories was to work on them quietly, massage them slowly, and spring 'em on the newsroom at the last minute, when it was too late to analyze the material to death, research the audience, consult with the consultants, or ask for a presidential pardon.

Here are some examples of how recent stories made it to the airwaves:

"Hey, I just uncovered evidence of radon gas at the statehouse...."

Before you could say "This Just In...," I was on the air with my six-month investigation, which Gretchen promptly titled "Lethal Legislature" (you can't win every battle; at least it got on the air).

Oh, yes, and there was my mad dash into the newsroom last November with this: "Hey, I have evidence of drug use among commercial flight crews!"

Yup—in exactly seven minutes I was on the air presenting my eight-month investigation: "Pothead Pilots."

I was, in fact, planning hard for February. First, there was my expose of politicians taking kickbacks on all kinds of contracts (everything from solid-waste removal to the vendor in charge of the tampon machines in the statehouse). Then there was my investigation into college professors at some of Boston's most prestigious universities faking their credentials on their CVs. And, finally, there was my favorite story...the one about drag queens laundering money for illegal arms dealers from the Sudan. The kickback story was all but done.

Johnnie and I had interviewed two insiders and we had conducted heavy surveillance of the state legislators involved. Research for the college professor story was done, as well, but I still had to confront the individuals implicated. The drag queen story was, well, another story altogether. It started as a tip from Patrick O'Hare, a well-known, highly placed political consultant in town. He saw me one night at a Back Bay bar; he had been drinking and he started introducing me to all his friends as his "good buddy from Channel 11." People were impressed and this pleased Patrick, puffed him up a bit, loosened his lips about the Collins brothers, two Waspy boys from Brookline who admired the Mafia and all but owned the entire nightclub circuit in Boston. There were always problems in the underbellies of the brothers' businesses. There was tax evasion. A drug bust. Widely spread and widely believed but unsubstantiated rumors of prostitution. The brothers, two fairly good-looking men in their thirties with twin paunches of success and glamorous women dangling from their arms, were no strangers to the glare of television cameras and the ink of newsprint. But, somehow, the stories would disappear almost as quickly as they had surfaced. Another Collins club in trouble...and the Collins organization would spin the trouble away with the polish of, well, a highly placed political consultant.

Which is where Patrick O'Hare came in. His association with the Collins brothers was circumstantial at best, but in Massachusetts you could convict on circumstantial evidence, so suffice it to say that Patrick O'Hare, doughy and pink-faced Patrick O'Hare, was guilty by association. So, naturally, I was highly suspicious when Patrick dragged me into an alley behind that Back Bay bar to tell me something "highly confidential." I remember saying a quick prayer to God that this was not a request for a blow job. Straight men always seemed to me to be under the misguided impression that gay boys scheduled their days around fellating heterosexuals.

What the hell is that? They find out you're gay and suddenly you want to suck their dick! It's like their penis instantly sees this as an opportunity and all brain matter, all normal processes of the cranium go out the window when there is a blow job at stake.

Thankfully, Patrick O'Hare kept his penis to himself that night, didn't even reference the fact that I was homosexual and he had a penis to imply the inevitability of a blow job; he instead told me about Gerard DeKashonni, the owner of Rendezvous, a gay bar–slash–drag bar in the heart of Boston's theater district. Of course, the skeptical reporter in me had to wonder about a man with such close ties to the Collins brothers trying to discredit the owner of another venue, but I found the story intriguing if nothing else. And, for damn sure, it was better than going anywhere near his scrotum. O'Hare told me how DeKashonni was working with arms dealers selling illegal weapons to Sudanese rebels. He said DeKashonni was laundering money through Rendezvous.

"How?" I asked my informant.

"Not sure, Damon. But I figured you could spend some time there and check it out."

"Spend some time there?"

"Well, it *is* a gay bar," he explained.

"Yes, but you're assuming I spend my free time in gay bars, Patrick. Which, you must realize, is a heinous generalization."

"I'm sorry, Damon. You *are* the famous gay reporter in town. And you probably end up in gay bars more often than I do."

"The Collins brothers ought to give gay bars a try..."

"Too much of a drug scene."

"Oh, please. The Collins's clubs are a virtual pipeline to the fucking Cali cartel."

"I can give the story to another reporter, Damon. Do you want it or not? I can't stand out here with you all night," he insisted. "It's bitching cold; besides, everyone will think you're giving me a blow job out here."

Okay, so maybe he did reference the fact that I was a homosexual and he had a penis to imply fellatio's inevitability. "Then you need to tell everyone that I wouldn't suck your dick for all the sand in the Sudan."

"So, you want the story?"

"I'll call you in a day or two. Sit on it until you hear from me."

Truth to tell, Patrick O'Hare was not all that bad-looking. He had meaningful, pretty eyes and, when he was at his most political, a fetching smile. He could be disarming with a handshake and a pat on the back. And, despite his thickening middle, he seemed sturdy in the former football player kind of way. My guess was that he drank too much beer and despite all the upwardly mobile trappings still had a lousy diet. Not that it mattered.

Straight men aren't my thing. I could never understand the gay fascination with straight men. They are not known for their fine treatment of women; why would they treat a homo any better?

They don't always smell the best.

Or make the bed.

So, why?

II

THE THING ABOUT ANGELS IS THAT THEY DO EXIST TO SOME extent but not in the sense that most earthlings imagine. Angels are not winged cherubs. No, angels and stars are one and the same. Centuries of artists gave you winged cherubs. Great artists long ago looked up at the sky and saw star-shaped creatures and they created angels, because, when you think about it, a five-pointed star could very easily, with a sprinkle of imagination, take on the appearance of a graceful winged creature. So, yes, when you die you become a star and join the other angels of heaven. That which you radiate sheds love and grace and, ultimately, light to your loved ones on Earth below. It's a beautiful thing, really.

All you can do is face the sky on a clear purple night and say to us, "I love you" or "Thank you" or "I miss your kiss-es" and we'll be, at once, gratified and renewed.

This is hard to grasp. But go find an explanation that isn't.

Understanding the heavens takes an inordinate amount of faith. And if it's hard to find your faith in a house of worship, that's okay. God says you can find him (her...God is really unisex, I should tell you) within yourself. You are but a vessel of soul and spirit that has the capacity for self-inspection. Actually to *not* self-inspect is to waste one of the most important qualities of the vessel you've been given. Sounds crazy, I know. But it works. The good thing is that your vessel never leaves you (that would be quite a feat!) and allows you to find faith whenever, wherever, however, on your own time, in your own time. You probably didn't even realize that you were born with such God-given freedoms. It's your own personal constitution.

Remember...Earth may have its finite capacity somewhere in the very, very distant future, but the infinity of space allows for the infinity of heaven and, thus, no cap on the number of souls welcome here in the afterlife. There's room for everyone.

Even your eighth-grade algebra teacher you thought was such a bitch.

And, yes, even your dog, Sassy, who genuinely was a bitch.

Even lawyers.

Hard to believe, but yes, lawyers have souls too. But, lucky for us, their television commercials are strictly forbidden in heaven. Personal injury? Medical malpractice? Slip 'n' fall? It's entirely too late for that up here.

12

New Year's Eve. I'm the anti-New Year. I don't get the whole fascination with throwing away a perfectly good year and celebrating a whole new one before you know what kind of angst it's going to bring. I'm just not into the whole New Year's buildup. It leads to anticlimax, which often leads to medication.

Suddenly single and suddenly bored, I did the unthinkable. I went out.

I had called my dear friend Louise who had only recently admitted to herself that the gold band on her boyfriend's finger was indeed a wedding ring and had (you go girl, you got the power) shaken him loose, and I asked her if she'd like to join me for an evening atypical of both of us. Fun.

"Fun?" she asked. "My idea of fun these days normally requires a D battery."

"Then you'll go?"

"Where?"

"Rendezvous."

"You want to spend New Year's Eve with a bunch of drag queens?"

"It's almost guaranteed we won't wake up with a stranger."

"Hmm. I'm tempted. I don't know. I'll think about it."

"Fine," I said. "You have twenty-four hours."

In the ensuing twenty-four hours I got my haircut, bought a new pair of denim jeans, and studied my friend Karl's new penis.

"Unbelievable," I said as he shimmied his briefs to the floor and his fleshy cock flopped in my face. "How much did that thing cost?"

"Five thousand."

"Five thousand!"

My friend Karl was blond, azure-eyed, and dating an Air Force pilot stationed somewhere in the Pacific. Karl was beautifully muscular and conscious of all things aesthetic, which would explain his physique and the hours he spent at the South End gym to maintain it. It would also explain the penile enlargement he had recently acquired on a trip to Los Angeles. You can have all the muscles in the world; you can kick Charles Atlas in the ass...you can serve drinks off your firm, bubble butt, but a small penis is still a small penis and for people to whom that matters, well, muscles don't compensate and neither do sports cars or Rolex watches or a nice pair of Bally shoes. Karl had them all and, despite his material trappings, I loved him. He was the best friend a gay man could have, and when you consider the bitchiness and cattiness that characterize so many gay friendships, that is saying a lot. We met one summer during college. I had been turned away from a pissy gay bar on Boylston Street because I had not yet turned twenty-one. I was embarrassed and humiliated and Karl was two people behind me in line, observing. When I turned from the doorway disgraced (but exceptionally well-dressed in my preppy Harvard sweater), he stepped out of line and put his hand on my shoulder. "Don't feel bad, buddy," he said. "I just turned twenty-one last week. I know what it's like."

I smiled sheepishly. "Thanks."

I looked back at the line and was instantly grateful that if any man had chosen to make a move on me in that utterly vulnerable moment, it was such a fine, clean-shaven, well-mannered young man. "My name is Karl," he said, extending a hand.

We shook.

"Damon Fitzgerald."

"Damon? That's a very dramatic name."

"Dramatic?"

"You know, like a soap-opera name."

"Thanks a lot."

He laughed softly. "I'm sorry. I didn't mean anything by it."

"I don't think my parents did either," I told him and gestured again to the line for the bar. "You better get back in line. Or you'll never get in."

He sunk back a bit. "Well, if you don't mind, I'd rather go for a walk."

"Really?"

"Really."

You know when initial moments and chance encounters are imbued with the chemistry of promise and potential. You just know it. It's as if you can feel your soul salivating or something. Well, this did not happen between Karl and me. And as attractive as he was, I am glad—for he became a much, much better friend to me than he ever could have been as a lover.

Our walk took us into the sunrise the following morning over the Charles River. From there we wandered into weekends of cycling, nights of studying (he attended Boston University, across the river), days and days of conspiring, confiding, mentoring, and the occasional over-indulgence in drinking.

"Are you happy with it?" I asked him as he put his member in his hands, still seemingly amazed himself.

"Uh, yes, I guess so."

"You guess so? Your penis is easily four inches longer than it used to be, and you *guess* so?"

"Well, would you like to see it erect?"

I rolled my eyes and shook my head. "No, Karl. I can do the math. Thank you."

"I haven't taken it for a test drive, so to speak. Jeff won't be home on leave until April."

"Hmm. That's four months. Ever hear of masturbation?"

"Oh, yes. I know it well. And I have gone for *that* test drive."

"And?"

"And nothing. I didn't notice any real difference. But I do like what I see when I look in the mirror and that's all that really matters. It boosts my confidence."

"I appreciate your honesty, Karl."

He scrunched his face and bent over, pulling his briefs from the floor. Stashing his cock in his underwear he asked, "how do you mean?"

"I just love that you know yourself. So few people do. What are you doing New Year's Eve?"

He smiled. "Probably another test drive."

I laughed. "Then that settles it. You'll come—er—go to Rendezvous with Louise and me."

"Oh, fuck, then. I better get to the gym. I love it when the drag queens pull me up onstage and show off my muscles to the crowd."

I shook my head. "You're incorrigible."

"Love you," he said, heading for the door. "Thanks for checking out my dick."

And he was gone.

I called Louise and told her that her deadline had come and gone and that, by default, she was spending New Year's Eve with Karl and me.

"But he's prettier than me," she whined.

"He's prettier than everybody," I told her. "We can't all stay home."

And we didn't.

Rendezvous was packed. Fucking teeming with generations of people. So ironic, if you think about it. Here was a place that would be frowned upon by those who couldn't embrace the idea of diversity and yet here was a place where there was no judgment at all, but instead celebration of itself. How sad that so many horrified people missed out on something so joyful.

Even the layers of smoke seemed to swirl joyfully above the crowd. The music was loud. The drag queens were louder. Crass, crude, but touching, at times. Fucking hilarious, really. We had a table to the side of the stage, along the runway.

A twinkie of a waiter came by for drink orders and the man with the new penis bought the first round.

"You can see it later tonight," he told Louise.

She snorted and rolled her head the way black women do and said, "I am not going near another penis unless it has a money-back guarantee."

I looked at her compassionately, figured here was a woman in need of a compliment, deserving of praise, and I just bore my eyes into hers and said, "Honey, in that gold head wrap of yours, you look an African queen tonight."

"Aphrodite?" Karl asked.

Louise and I cackled, grabbing each other's hands, stomping our feet, even. "No, you dumb shit," I said to Karl, "Nefertiti."

"Sorry," he said with a woeful look. "Black is beautiful."

At this point the music had become so loud, the crowd so rowdy, that is was hard to hear each other without screaming, so we sipped on the first round and watched men become women and women become divas and everyone become intoxicated by the performance.

It wasn't long before a line formed at the end of the stage and the performers dipped lovingly for tips.

Karl held up a dollar and waved it at Louise, who shook her head no adamantly. She would not be leaving her seat. Karl rose to his feet, arranged his package so it presented its bounty to all those who desired such a glimpse, and made his way to the line.

I scanned the room for would-be arms dealers and no one came across my radar. It's hard to say exactly what I was looking for. Shadowy figures? Distant eyes? Contraband? The show bar was dark, of course, so I didn't have a lot of advantage in my furtive endeavors and, craning my neck that way, I was beginning to look obvious if not stricken with some kind of palsy.

I gave up and turned my attention to Karl, who was approaching the head of the line and waving dollar bills toward an enormous drag queen clad in only a pink leotard and belting out Aretha's anthem "Respect." I smiled as the performer bent over and offered her highway of a cleavage to Karl who, without as much as a flinch, deposited his money, offered a kiss, and made way for the next adoring fan.

I bought the next round of drinks. Louise excused herself to pee.

"I love you, Damon," Karl shouted at me.

"I love you too man."

"No. I mean I really love you."

"I mean it too."

He shook his head and reached for me. "You are such a dear friend."

"I sure hope you haven't taken that ecstasy shit."

"Never!" he cried.

"Well, I suspect there's plenty of it going around here tonight."

"That and every other illegal substance, I suppose," he said. "You know me better than that Damon. My body is a temple. A great huge house of worship. I would never fuck with my temple. I just wanted you to know how much you mean to me. I don't know what I'd do without you."

"Likewise."

He leaned forward and planted a generous kiss on my lips. Louise appeared just as the kiss retreated and she said, "Lord ha' mercy. I don't need this tonight."

"Sit your ass down," I told her. "It was just a kiss of friendship."

She tsked and said, "I'm not talking about that, boys. Some chick just asked me to go have a drink with her in the dance bar."

"Oh," I said. "Sorry. Feel flattered."

"She was wearing a wedding ring!" Louise cried.

"Oh, come on! You can't be serious," I begged.

She did her black-lady roll of the head thing again and I knew for certain that she was serious. "We need to find you a fucking convent," I told her.

"Oxymoron," she retorted and I laughed. "A regular, non-fucking convent would be just fine," she added.

Louise was ready for another drink, which I gladly landed for her.

We decided to stay in the show bar until after midnight, figured nobody was going to ring in the New Year with more of a bang than the cast of drag queens, and I observed that the closer we got to midnight the bigger the tips handed to the performers. They were really vamping it up, hamming it up, and the denominations of those bills escalated with the energy and euphoria of the evening. By midnight, it was common to see tens, twenties, even fifties making the vibrant, nasty change of hands.

It became the very opposite of a silent auction. People made a spectacle of their appreciation, planting bills in the obvious cleavage, stuffing still more cash into boots, waistbands, panties. The bidding went astronomical, a shower of money and celebration and abandon.

Just before midnight a not-so-bad Whitney Houston (actually a better Whitney Houston than Whitney Houston) pulled Karl onstage and fulfilled his needs for the evening. She ran her hands across his muscular physique and taunted the audience with her discoveries. She convinced him to remove his tiny shirt from his massive body and there he stood in the spotlight, a gorgeous, almost sinfully delicious example of perfection.

Ultimately, the audience was too inebriated to notice, so Karl returned to the table at the height of anticlimax and waited for the countdown.

Ten.

I remember a fleeting moment of regret about Frank.

Nine.

Then, an about-face. An affirmation, really.

Eight.

And yet a longing for penis.

Seven.

Predicated by Chinese food.

Six.

No MSG.

Five.

Not a single person in the crowd looked even remotely Sudanese.

Four.

Three.

The number of times Gina Parr had been shot.

Two.

You never, ever know just how long you have.

One.

Definitive pandemonium.

And so began another year which in its humbling way

would be just another micromoment in history. The tiniest, tiniest microscopic life-form on the lens of time.

And I kissed Louise. And she kissed me. And Louise kissed Karl. And he kissed her back. And Karl and I kissed again and I was glad that the taste was waxy and brotherly, not sweet and complicated.

13

A FEW DAYS LATER, THE SHOW AT RENDEZVOUS A PLEASANT
memory, Gretchen stormed into my office not unlike an out-
raged drag queen and tore into my unsuspecting hide. "Are
you sleeping on the fucking job, Fitz? This totally sucks!"

Before I could say "What totally sucks, you spitting cunt?"
she threw a newspaper across my desk. It landed in my lap.

"Did you read the paper this morning, Damon? Or would
that have cut into your time flirting with Ernesto?"

"Ernesto?"

She shook her head and folded her spastic arms across her
chest. She offered me a patronizing grin of perfect orthodon-
tics and said, "It's obvious you want to fuck him."

I leaned forward and said, "Gretchen, whether or not I
want to fuck the tape librarian is really not your business and
certainly not an issue that is keeping me from my work. Now,
if you have some kind of problem with me, just give it up."

"*The Boston Globe* is reporting a new lead in the Gina
Parr murder. It's in this morning's paper and we're appalled
that you dropped the ball."

I scanned the article and learned that keys to Gina Parr's BMW had been found in Roberto Cruz's apartment. I looked up from the paper and my instinctive reaction was to reach for a chloroform-soaked rag to wipe the vindicated look from Gretchen's face. In the absence of such a rag, I chose to exasperate the woman instead. "So?" I asked. "What's your point?"

"My point?"

"Well, I'm not sure what the story is here..."

"What the story is?" she huffed. "More evidence linking Roberto Cruz to the murder."

"But the man has already been arrested and arraigned. He's probably been fitted for his very own jail-issued tennis shoes by now. Do you really want me chasing down every little bit of discovery the state is gathering to prosecute this guy?"

She twisted her head. "Well, yeah, if it's relevant."

"So, I'm on the murder beat?"

She stomped her foot (really, she did) and said, "We don't have a murder beat!"

"Well, you better establish one with a separate team of reporters if you want us to follow every nuance of every murder in Boston."

Now the hands went on her hips (what there were of hips, that is, on her otherwise skeletal frame) and she said, "You make it seem like you have something better going on."

"Maybe I do. But I can guarantee you I will not have any stories for February if you want me to camp out at Hotel Gina."

"Just don't miss anything big, Damon. This is a warning." And she left.

I assessed the damage. No deaths, no injuries, no destruction to property.

"What the fuck was that about?" Donna Donovan asked, rolling in her chair from her office to mine.

Donna was probably forty and had straight salt-and-pepper hair that reached her shoulders. She was pretty in an I've-been-around-the-block-a-few-times sort of way. She had a way of meeting your eyes with immutable interest even while her hardened face told you she had heard it all before—first as a street reporter for *The Boston Globe,* then as a public information officer for the Boston Police Department, and most recently, lured back into reporting by the ridiculous money in television, as a member of the investigative team at Channel 11. She still drank with her cop buddies and still caroused with her *Globe* pals, all of whom dismissed television news as shallow and weak when compared to the *real* reporting that went on at the *Globe*—and, for the most part, she agreed with them and never really tried to hide the fact that she found the way television packaged the news completely asinine. She would routinely say so at news meetings, in a cigarette-scarred voice that made you only respect her more. She took shit from virtually no one and told me she liked me because I took almost as little. She once told me I was a little too pretty to be taken seriously but she considered me a good reporter, and coming from her, that was praise.

Truth to tell, I had my pretty days. When I was eighteen, for instance, and smuggled into gay bars and ogled by anyone with eyesight. But *every* gay boy is pretty at eighteen even if he is otherwise ugly. By the time I hit my mid thirties I had settled quite comfortably into my average frame, topped by my average face and my average desire to be anything but an average guy. It was with pity that I read about the circuit parties, the washboard stomachs, the trips to Ibiza. It was with resignation that I looked into the mirror at my pale Irish skin, my blue-gray eyes, my sandy, thinning hair. People still told me my smile was winning, my shoulders strong, my bone structure enviable. And when you think about it, that's what being gay is truly about: bone structure. And pretentious apartments. Chiseled cheekbones, a great jaw, a doorman and a city view. "Look," Louise would tell me, "your looks landed you in television. No one's gonna put a moose on the air."

"Gee," I would reply. "I thought my reporting skills landed me in television."

She would merely snicker. Then, getting no reaction from me but a glare, laugh heartily.

I told Donna about Gretchen's beef with the *Globe* story. She shook her head. "As someone who worked in newspaper, I can tell you that story is nothing but filler."

"Kind of what I suspected."

"Go with your gut."

"Always do."

She put her feet up on my desk. "I mean I can't fault the paper for wanting to keep the story alive," she said. "They ran the story because they had to fill space today—not on its merits alone."

"What are you working on?"

"The banking thing..."

I smiled. "They actually gave you the green light? That story didn't exactly go over that well in the pitch meeting."

"Like a fart at the opera." She pronounced "fart" *fahht* and it sounded so properly Bostonian. I had to laugh.

"Lloyd's going to let you do it?"

"Yeah. We went out for a drink..."

"Say no more. Stories sound so much better when you mix in a double martini."

"I think it was between his second and third when he mentioned you."

My eyes, which had wandered to the calendar in front of me in search of a dental appointment, returned to hers. "Oh?"

I studied her hard. "Yes," she said. "He wanted to know if you were all right."

"All right?"

"Thinks you've lost your fire."

"Hmm."

"Have you?" she asked, leveling her tone to one that was mutual and safe.

"What do you think?" I asked her.

"I think you don't want to become the Gina Parr reporter."

I shrugged. "Is that such a bad thing?"

"That depends on whether you think it's a big story or not, or whether you're too bored to know the difference."

I leaned forward. Sighed audibly. "Let's just cut to the chase, Donna. Do you think it's a big story and do you think I should be covering it better?"

Her feet came off the desk. She sat up. "We won't know if it's a big story if we don't look into it. And if it is, then, yes, you should be covering it better."

I shook my head. "You just told me an overwhelming amount of nothing."

The phone rang. I let it go to voice-mail.

"Do you think Roberto Cruz killed her?" she asked me.

"I'm not sure."

"Why aren't you sure?"

"I dunno. I guess something just bothers me about the so-called evidence. Like, I think they got him on very little."

She smiled. "Then, why don't you, like, go with that, Fitzie?"

I cocked my head to one side. "Is there something you're not telling me? Are your cop buddies leaking you information?"

"Give Raleigh Dean a call."

"Raleigh Dean?"

"Cruz's attorney. The public defender assigned to the case. You were at the arraignment, Damon. Didn't you get his card?"

Fuck. I was sure I had. It had to be somewhere in my notes or in my files. Perhaps tucked between Malaise and

Disinterest. Or filed under Boredom. Maybe they all were right. Maybe I had dropped the ball. Obviously, at that moment, I looked to Donna Donovan like a man who had dropped not only a ball but his entire scrotal sac as well, because she just looked at me and said, "He's in the phone book. Give him a call and ask him about the car keys."

I nodded then turned away because I didn't want my colleague to see the flush of self-disgust rising in my cheeks. "Thank you," I called to her as she wheeled herself out of my office and across the hall.

I checked my voice-mail before I dialed Raleigh Dean. It was a message from my mother. "Your father has prostate cancer," she said. "Call when you have a chance."

Quintessential Marilyn. Passive. Aggressive. Passive-aggressive. To the point to make a point.

I considered the crisis. Dad had prostate cancer. And, ultimately, I'd have to put on my reporter's hat to get the details. Like, when the hell did this come up? When did he have that fateful appointment with the physician and first learn he'd have to take a camera and other assorted probes up the ass? When did that ass-probing take place? Was he scared? Indifferent? Indignant? How long did he have to wait for the results? How much did they know when they breezed through town with Christmas gifts and obligatory affection?

Damn them. And then some.

For some reason an image of my father as a young newlywed came to mind. I had seen those dusty black and whites of him leaning against his '57 Chevy—slim-waisted in blue jeans and white T-shirt—and had realized that the older I got the more I became an astounding image of him. But in those photos there was a man so different from me. He was tough and steely. He had an Eddie Haskell quality to him that made me wonder what intentions he had for his new bride. Was she just the latest woman to discover the mischief of his penis? Would he do right by her? How odd it was to consider the man who would father me in his years before fatherhood. I tried to communicate with that image for a moment, to instruct him in some way, guide him much the way all those New Agers prescribed connecting with your *inner child,* and I had to laugh because the expression on his face, the expression that stayed with him through three jobs, six promotions, seven children, a mortgage, and three weddings was, after all, his trademark caption: I don't need *anyone* for *anything.*

I dialed. No one answered. I left a message. "It's Damon. I got Mother's message. I'm concerned about the news. Please call."

Then I flipped through the Boston phone directory and found the number for Raleigh Dean.

A lazy-sounding secretary put me on hold for what seemed like fifteen or twenty minutes but was, in reality, probably a much shorter time. Then I heard the fast-talking, almost desperate voice of Raleigh Dean. "If you want to come by my office, today would be no good because I have to be back in court. I'm in court tomorrow too, but only in the morning. How about Wednesday? No, wait a minute, Wednesday is full. Shit, where the hell is that file?"

"Uh, Attorney Dean, I can do this over the phone."

He cleared his throat and I could tell he was a smoker because he hacked a bit like Donna Donovan and it was then I realized I'd probably have to meet the guy after work one night and buy him a beer. But it would be a cheap beer in a neighborhood bar. A *real* neighborhood bar in a *real* neighborhood, not some imposter place that placated the well-heeled attorneys from the stuffy firms who fancied themselves good old boys, good enough, in fact, to come when they wanted, leave when they needed to, and only reveal to the most perceptive their patronizing attempt at slumming.

"We can do this over the phone," he barked, "if you only want to talk about the keys."

"And you have more to talk about?"

"That depends..."

"On what?"

"On how much you want to hear."

I felt all at once the weight of a thousand court cases heaved at me, landing on my chest. I swallowed hard and tasted what could have been a mouthful of worms fresh from a whole new can, a whole new story peeled open and pouring down my throat. I shook my head at the misery of it all, of getting fucking waist-deep in another case, and I pushed hard with resistance. The elevator doors were closing and I couldn't decide if I wanted in or I wanted out. But either way my head was stuck and my arms didn't know what the fuck to do.

We decided on Kelly's Toe, a godforsaken pub which resided somehow fittingly in a basement hole below the Salvation Army in Porter Square. Sucky area if you ask me.

"Tomorrow night," the wheezing attorney said.

"Yeah. Around eight."

14

THE PEOPLE AT WORK ARE STILL DEBATING A MEMORIAL service, as if my funeral wasn't enough of an ordeal.

My funeral:

The church service was long and dreadful. The family priest said remarkable things about me and unremarkable things about my death. Yes, he called it tragic and senseless.

When is the last time you heard of a murder that wasn't tragic? Or that made perfect sense? We have turned into a culture programmed by the discourse of TV news, which, as is obvious by my description of the daily operations at Channel 11, is in the dubious hands of children and the morons who manage them.

People cried. One of my sisters threw up at the cemetery. My brother punched a tree. Throughout it all, during the service at the church and later at my grave site, my parents wept openly. Then they drank just as openly as mourners came to pay their condolences at the family home. Among the mourners, Karl and Louise, who sobbed operatic sobs throughout the day and, frankly, embarrassed themselves,

but they touched my soul deeply in a way that no other
mortal could have mustered. They were truly despairing,
rocking in each other's arms. Staring up at the sky, searching for answers, they seemed to beg God for an explanation. How had this happened? Why had I been taken? They
shook their heads in resignation. They cursed the unfairness of it all. Louise smoked an entire pack of cigarettes.

There were three limousines and not one famous person
in any of them.

The day started gray and raw, a true late winter chill, its
icy grip unlikely to relinquish its hold in time for spring.
Just as the burial service began the clouds parted and people quickly remarked at the magnificence of the timing,
that somehow I must be in heaven shining down on them,
giving them a sign that I was at peace. Actually, it was just
a break in the cold front and a momentary change in the
weather, which was fairly typical for New England, and
most of the mourners on the rolling, gauzy green hills of
the cemetery below probably knew that but didn't want to
spoil the banality of what others had assumed was a poet-
ic and glorious occurrence.

It's not that we don't give signs from here in the afterlife. We do. It's just that we don't control the weather. A
higher power handles the weather and has never shown any
indication of relinquishing control of it. And, besides, who
wants that responsibility, anyway? Too much cleanup. Very
high-maintenance. The higher power has it down to a science. Think about it.

Anyway, the signs we give from the afterlife *cannot* be
tracked by even the most advanced super-duper Doppler-
radar systems employed by your local geeky meteorologist
(actually geeky isn't fair, as I have fucked my fair share of
weathermen).

The signs we give are more subtle.

Remember that light you thought you had turned off in

the den? Or the cereal you thought you had put away?

What about all those missing socks? All those socks that go into the wash as pairs but come out of the dryer as singles?

We love messing with socks. We do it all the time.

Actually, we're responsible for a lot of things that go missing in life.

RALEIGH DEAN HAD A DISTINCTLY UNIRONED LOOK ABOUT him. He looked like a rumple of a man, wrapped up in that old shapeless raincoat of his. Scuffs marred the leather of his shoes—as if everything had been an arduous climb for him, as if nothing came easy. He seemed intense, the way he talked so fast, practically spat words at you. He looked fifty but was probably five years younger. He didn't tell me much about himself. I just guessed, from looking at him, that the stress of the system had aged him—that he was overwrought by the caseload he had to maintain just to keep his one-man practice running. This was not a man with a fancy office. I pictured him holed up in a two-room suite with mint-green walls, linoleum floors, institutional furniture. He had a bench for waiting clients and a secretary who gave them no reason to hope for good representation. That was just the impression that I got from him, a micromoment of assumption as we settled at the end of the bar and ordered the house draft.

He took one sip and said, "Her car was torched two weeks before the murder."

"Gina Parr's car was torched?"

"Yes."

"And you know this how?"

"I have a private investigator who's looking into her background."

"Okay," I said. "And the significance of the torched car?"

He reached for something in his pocket, withdrew a pack of cigarettes, and lit one. "The significance? You don't know what it means when a car is torched?"

"Well, it's usually a warning of sorts."

He smiled. "Exactly."

"And you think someone was giving Gina Parr a warning?"

"It's textbook. I think someone wanted her dead, Mr. Fitzgerald."

"Well, someone succeeded."

"And it wasn't my client."

"Then who was it?"

He laughed. "You understand the judicial system well enough to know that it is not my job to do the police work, here. I don't have to find the suspect. I just have to prove that the state has no case against my client."

"And how do you intend to do that?"

"The torched car suggests a hit. Someone was warning Ms. Parr that she was in deep trouble. It is my assertion that the same person who torched her car also killed her."

I had a sip of beer. Swallowed hard. "Okay, let's say I buy that much. You still haven't shown me why your client couldn't be the guy. Why does the torched car absolve him?"

He studied me hard, like maybe I was demented or slow and needed to be walked through this gingerly. I tried to disarm his patronizing stare to no avail. "My client may be a thug, Mr. Fitzgerald. Roberto Cruz is not going to be named citizen of the fucking year. But what kind of beef could a lowlife like him have with a up-and-coming attorney like her?"

"Maybe she liked nasty men. Maybe she had a thing with him and then scorned him. Maybe he went into a rage."

He shook his head, emphatically. "I'm *telling* you, he and Ms. Parr were strangers. They were not known to each other in any way whatsoever."

"How did he end up with her car keys?" I asked, growing a bit tired of this verbal tug of war. I had done countless murder investigations and the black-and-white crime-caper quality of human misdeeds no longer intrigued me.

"I can't tell you right now how he came to possess those keys. But let's assume for a moment that I'm right about the person who torched the car also being the murderer. What use would that person have with the keys? In fact, you don't need keys to torch a car. And if you do set a car on fire, chances are you're not going to hold on to the keys…"

"And you're hoping that I can create a news story around this theory and cast doubt about the arrest of your client. Nice job, Attorney Dean. I know what it's like to be used. That turnip truck that just rounded the corner did not exactly dump me off in the gutter."

He exhaled a puff of smoke and a puff of disgust. "Figured this would be a waste of time. But I thought you sounded sincere on the phone."

"If anyone is being disingenuous, Attorney Dean, it's you. You can't expect me to entertain your theory on one hand, and then, on the other hand, let you walk away without explaining—in your words—how he came to possess those keys. I think you have a credibility problem." I gulped the last of my beer.

"First of all, call me Raleigh. None of this *Attorney Dean* shit. And second of all, you *will* find out why he had the woman's keys. Just not now. I never said I wouldn't tell you. I only said I couldn't tell you now."

"Understood."

"I'm not sure you do. You're quick to dismiss any notion

of a story here. And I think you have something perfectly good to go on, Damon. I'll give you the date Ms. Parr's vehicle was found. Go pull the police report. You might want to ask the district attorney why this bit of information hasn't surfaced—why it isn't relevant to the case. Maybe it's because the district attorney can't link my client to the first crime involving Gina Parr. Ain't that inconvenient?"

At that moment his sick smile reminded me of a Cheshire cat and I knew that I would not have another beer with the man. But it was not lost on me that the poor slob had a point.

❖ ❖ ❖

How astonishing would it be for my debut novel to open with the torching of an automobile?

Not very astonishing, I decided, as I wrestled once again with an excessive amount of bad ideas. Couldn't the blackened auto be a metaphor for something? Anything?

It could not.

There I sat brooding over my elusive novel and all the pretentious prose that somebody else was busy writing, trying to give Raleigh Dean the benefit of the doubt, anticipating the spin the D.A. would offer.

The blank screen stared me down, chastised me, it seemed, with its glare.

"You have nothing to offer, Damon Fitzgerald," it whispered to me. "Stick to reporting. The story tells itself."

I typed F-U-C-K Y-O-U.

The retort felt triumphant.

And that was all I typed that evening.

I went to bed with the taste of beer still on my lips. I hadn't had dinner. My appetite had not kicked in. I thought about my meeting with Raleigh Dean and wished he had been cleaner-shaven and less ragged. It would have made his arguments more compelling. Isn't that awful? To dismiss the work of a man's mind on the basis of his raincoat? It was no wonder then that evening I dreamt of rain. A hard, falling, slanting rain that came in off the ocean and doused my dog, Prostate, and me as we walked along a deserted boardwalk. Cut to Millie's luncheonette in the seaside town of Hull where the locals talked about the *weathuh* and no one balked at the sight of my sopping canine. The waitress offered me a menu and smiled at Prostate. She wore a name tag.

It said: GINA.

The smell of fresh cold cuts and grease wafted through the diner. Gina disappeared and never came back.

Prostate made a puddle of pee beside the table. I spilled some apple juice—it was just there—for camouflage.

I looked outside through the steamy windows and saw the rain had taken on a yellowish hue and concluded that God was pissed.

The locals agreed.

I DROVE TO CONNECTICUT FOR THE WEEKEND TO CHECK IN on my father.

"He's not dying," my mother said as she swung the door open and planted a kiss on my face.

"But it's cancer," I said removing my jacket.

"He's going to be fine. He doesn't want a lot of fuss."

And neither did she. It was obvious when she asked, "How long are you staying?" before I had even tossed my keys on the hope chest in the front foyer.

"Till tomorrow," I replied.

The house was empty, felt empty, like a shell. There were, of course, no kids left teeming through the place, banging up and down the stairs, making the normal ruckus picked up by parental radar. The house dated back to the late 1800s and was well cared for. The wood floors glowed with the sheen of a preserved landmark. The moldings had been freshly painted. There were two bedrooms downstairs and three upstairs. I could smell something baking in the kitchen. It smelled like a comfort meal. Roast chicken, maybe. Sweet potatoes.

"He's reading in his den," my mother told me.

I had for the slightest instant forgotten why I had come. "Oh...right."

The den resided in one of the downstairs bedrooms. It had been my brother's room, where Cal, who was taller than all of us, had been caught fucking his high-school sweetheart in his bed below the window. His height was evidently not in proportion to the size of his brain. In some way I suspect Cal knew when my parents would get home that Saturday afternoon. He had always been so perfect and there had always been such huge expectations of him and when he didn't get into Harvard he spent the rest of that senior year proving to everyone why he was such a fuck-up. Or something like that. I never actually talked to him about it. I was three years younger and, besides, I was more interested in how big his dick was and whether my mother and father got to see it.

"Hi, Dad."

"Damon!"

"I'm glad to hear you're doing well."

"Relatively speaking."

"And you're my relative," I quipped hopelessly.

"Will you stay for dinner?" he asked.

"Actually, I'm here until tomorrow," I told him.

"Of course. I don't know what I was thinking."

He looked pale but not sickly so, just paler than normal, perhaps tired. I didn't want to ask too many questions about his cancer. My reticence was twofold. First, I didn't know enough about prostate cancer to ask intelligent questions, and, undoubtedly, my questions would not matter to my father as much as the intelligence of them. Secondly, I didn't really *need* to know. What could I do with the information? I had become extremely discriminating, I realized, about the kinds of information I would seek. Being a news reporter I was always flooded with torrents of information, some of it useful to some people, none of it useful to everyone. I had become an information machine. Ingest, digest, shit it out to the masses. I had become afraid the hard drive of my brain would run out of space.

I took things on a need-to-know, need-to-report basis.

And I really didn't need to know the exacting details of my father's prostate. There was, after all, nothing I could do about it.

I was powerless.

I had learned the beauty of powerlessness from my friend Louise. She was working a twelve-step program. Her addiction was food.

"I'm a big, fat black woman who can't sing. Of what use am I?" she'd ask me.

"You're a big, fat black woman with beautiful skin, delicious eyes, and the best fucking laugh I know," I'd tell her.

She would have none of my praise, save for a slight breeze of gratitude, but she would continually remind me that she was not, in fact, powerless over food, but powerless over the insanity that made her seek food as a drug. The insanity of her job, her hateful mother, her jailed ex-husband. "When I accept that I am powerless over that shit, I don't need the fix of a Twinkie."

"Surely, Twinkies aren't your drug of choice."

"No," she had told me. "But there are eight to a box."

My father put his book on his lap and folded his arms across his chest. "Did you want to talk about something, son?"

I heard the clank of pans in the kitchen, the running of water. "Uh, well, no...nothing in particular. I just wanted to see how you're doing."

"And how am I doing?"

"Dad, if you would rather not be disturbed..."

He shook his head. His lips were chapped. "You're not disturbing me, Damon. I was simply asking your opinion. How am I doing? Do I *look* like I have cancer?"

"You look tired."

"A euphemism for 'You look like you have cancer.'"

"Not really."

He smiled a thin smile that seemed to take the effort of his entire face. "Fine, then. I look tired because I am tired. I just wanted a layman's opinion, what with all the doctors and their prognosticating."

"Which is...?"

"I'm not going to die. That's the general consensus."

"Ever? You're not going to die ever?"

He lifted his book, preparing to read again. "Don't be a wiseass," he told me, peering over the edges of two Grishams ago.

"Well, you have to admit that would be one hell of a prognosis."

His eyes pretended to follow the text in front of him as he made this aside, "Nobody *wants* to die, Damon."

"Life is so grand nobody wants to give it up."

"Said so ironically, son."

"For all we know death is even grander."

"Why don't you see if your mother needs help in the kitchen?"

I left the room, amused by the bareness of the truth: When you're an adult your parents can't punish you, but they can dismiss you and they usually will in a manner consistent with your childhood.

I called my home to check my messages, thinking maybe I would reconnect with the threads of my own life—having been this unraveled in only forty minutes of their life—and there were two calls.

"Hi, honey. It's Karl. Where are you? I want to cook for you. Have you gone to Connecticut? I hope you haven't. You know, they haven't found an antidote for Connecticut. Come home. Love you."

Then, "Hey, Damon. It's me, Donna. Sorry to bother you

at home, but I have another tip about Gina Parr. Call if you can. If not, see you Monday."

I sat at dinner that evening fearful that if the room got any more quiet I would hear my father's cancer metastasizing. My father chewed lazily. That was very noticeable. He usually attacked his food with the vigor of a gladiator. Not tonight. No, he just chewed somewhat slack-jawed and careless. Disinterested in the morsels that traveled from his plate to his mouth. My eyes met my mother's and we smiled halcyon smiles. Forks and knives clinked, competing for precision, it seemed, with the ticking of the kitchen clock.

And so passed the seconds and the minutes and the hours of my visit. I did get big hugs, though, when I left the next day. And two "wonderful to see you"s. My father offered an extra slap on the back as I finally turned for the door.

"Drive safe," my mother told me.

I assured her I would.

That sense of safety seemed to comfort her.

17

Most of my colleagues tried to impress each other with chat about NPR's *Morning Edition*. "Did you hear the story about deforestation?" "Or the one about venereal disease on the Ivory Coast?" "Did you hear the interview with Deepak Chopra?"

No.

But I did listen to the Howard Stern show on my way into work. And it was fucking hilarious.

The thing I liked so much about the King of All Media was his ability to see celebrity for what it was: a cultural obsession, a shallow grave of wannabes, soon-to-be-has-beens, and silicon breast implants. Howard Stern was the middle finger flipped at Hollywood, network television, and anything else that fed the American audience with empty calories of no-talent writers and actors and Paris Hiltons.

"Did you hear?" Johnnie asked me, entering my office, carrying a camera battery in one hand, Starbucks in the other.

"Hear what?"

He sat at the corner of my desk. "About Charlaine?"

"No. What about her?"

"They're not renewing her contract."

Charlaine Williams was our main anchor, a beauty-queen blond who wouldn't know a hot news tip from a hot curling iron and who had a horrible habit of pronouncing Massachusetts *Massachuzetts*. A terrible black eye on her credibility, often the fodder for talk-radio roasting. Our anchor desk was not known for its stability. Compared to the other anchor teams in town, our desk was known for its revolving door of blow-dried, perfectly chiseled, flashy-trashy Kens and Barbies. So, it was no surprise. Charlaine had anchored for two years, the average life span for Channel 11. Not that it would be any great loss to put Charlaine out to fluffier pastures, but her firing was yet another indication of the moronic management in television news. We need another rating point, let's get another anchor! Let's confuse the viewers one more time! Let's force our audience to familiarize themselves to yet another face, another pronunciation of Massachusetts.

"She'll turn up on *Inside Edition*," I told Johnnie. "Or the Travel Channel."

Johnnie hacked a resonant cough then sneezed.

"Maybe you should be drinking tea," I told him.

He shrugged, maybe. "What are we shooting today?"

"More on the diploma mill."

"Uh...right. I had forgotten about that story. I need to find a couple of batteries. Be back in a sec."

On his way out he collided with Donna Donovan who punched his arm. His coffee cup quivered but did not spill. Donna called him a "spaz" and turned to me smiling, and it was then I recognized the flirtation between them. I didn't say anything. Nothing needed to be said. Donna knew I noticed. You could see it in the coy movement of her eyes, the mischievous smirk on her face. I figured they had common ground. Had the same South Boston roots and the Irish freckles to prove it.

"Did you get my message?" she asked me.

"Yeah. Got in too late to call you. Went to Connecticut."

"Oh," she said indifferently. "You need to call Raleigh Dean."

"Do I?"

She sat down, put her feet up on my desk. "Okay, so I'm out this weekend with some guys. And they tell me that detectives on the Gina Parr case are pouring over the shit they took from her apartment. They collected all kinds of evidence, including a diary, or a journal, and there's all this shit in there about this guy. Turns out she broke off with the guy two weeks before the murder."

"Broke off?"

"They were engaged."

"Oh. Well, I guess that would make him a suspect."

"Maybe. Maybe not. You should call Dean and ask him. If that evidence hasn't been turned over to the defense, it will be soon."

"Does this fiancé have a name?"

"I didn't get that," she replied. "Sorry. Let's just say he probably had a motive."

"Her car was torched," I told Donna.

"No shit! Talk about a lover scorned."

"Well, I don't know. If your car gets torched chances are the mob is after you, not a brokenhearted lover."

"You need to talk to Neckingham about it."

I sat back quietly for a moment and wondered why, suddenly, I felt imposed upon. Or second-guessed. Outmaneuvered. "Donna, do you want this story?" I asked.

She bristled. "Absolutely not, Damon. If you want me to stay out of it, I will. I just thought you should know some of the scuttlebutt going around."

"I appreciate that. But you do seem more enthusiastic about the case than I do."

"Not really. It's just my nature to stick my nose in where it doesn't belong."

I laughed. "Well, that's what makes you such a darn good reporter. I wouldn't want you investigating *me*."

"And vice-versa."

As she was leaving my office she turned and said, "Another one bites the dust."

"Huh?"

"Charlaine. Did you hear?"

"Yeah. Johnnie told me."

"And I told him," she said.

"I bet you did."

She flipped me her middle finger and disappeared into the hallway.

❖ ❖ ❖

I talked to Raleigh Dean's secretary. She seemed heavily sedated or hungover when she told me Dean would not be in all day. "He's in court."

"Which court?"

"County. Suffolk."

"That's a big courthouse. Is he on a pager, or can I call his cell?"

"No."

"Which one?"

"He is not on a pager and, no, you can't call his cell."

"Jesus..."

"You can't call him either," she said dryly.

"Actually, that was very funny," I told her.

She hung up without saying another word.

Queer. No?

I flipped through my notes and found the information about Gina Parr's car. Raleigh Dean had given me the date it was found. I dialed police headquarters and asked for the report to be pulled. I ushered Johnnie to the car.

"Boston P.D.?" he asked.

"Yeah."

"What about the diploma mill?"

"On hold for now."

I explained why.

"Her car was torched?" he asked. Not waiting for an answer, he added, "That's generally organized crime. You know that, right?"

"That's why they pay me the big bucks. Do you want to fuck Donna Donovan?"

Perhaps I should have delayed the question until we rounded the corner because I found myself flung abruptly against the window by his sudden hard turn. "What? What the hell are you talking about?"

"I thought I sensed a flirtation."

"Please..."

Johnnie recovered nicely from the sudden jerk of the vehicle.

"What? What's so wrong with Donna?" I asked. "She's attractive. She's smart."

"Not my type."

"You wouldn't know it from your body language."

"Huh? What body language?"

"It was obvious."

He looked at me. "I don't need you watching my body language," he said.

"Keep your eyes on the road," I told him. "I just thought I noticed something. And if you're not interested, be prepared to fend her off. She has that 'fuck me' look in her eyes whenever you're around."

He feigned a sigh of disgust. "Stick to reporting, Damon. You're not a good matchmaker."

We rode silently until we reached the police department. Johnnie waited in the car while I went in for the report. When I returned he was sipping on a hot cup of Starbucks, his head wagging lazily to rock 'n' roll angst playing on the radio. I interrupted his rhythm, it seemed, his moment of Zen. I apologized, but he ignored me and pulled away from the curb.

"Let's go get video of the scene."

"The scene?"

"Where the car was found." I gave him an address.

"Probably just an empty lot," he said.

"Probably."

"What about the car?"

"We're cleared to shoot it at the impound lot."

His eyes widened happily. "No shit?"

"No shit."

❖ ❖ ❖

According to the police report, Gina Parr's automobile was a 2001 BMW 5 Series.

You would never know it to look at it.

I recognized the ghost of the BMW emblem on the hood. Other than that, I saw nothing but a blackened shell. The car was hopelessly gutted. Obliterated as though a bomb had actually celebrated its explosiveness. Perhaps it's because the roof was ripped open, like a cork popped through foil, the metal shredded upward as the car blew itself to the sky. Fuck.

I suddenly felt sympathy for Gina Parr. It puzzled me that I should not have felt any emotion until now, seeing this, the precursor to the crime. Johnnie shot from all the angles he could find. At one point he looked at me with an ironic smile, as if to say, *You work hard, determined to drive a Beamer, and, poof, it's all up in ugly smoke.*

Okay, maybe not *poof.* Johnnie is not the *poof* kind of guy. As I watched him more closely I could see what he was thinking, his interpretation lodged in his eyes. "Man, it was, like, *bang,* and what a fucking mess!"

I did a stand-up that our producers and promotion writers would salivate over. It went:

"Coming up on Channel 11 News: Does this burned-out automobile hold the key to a shocking murder? I'm Damon Fitzgerald. Stay tuned for that story."

Johnnie nodded his approval and we left.

As I suspected, there was much salivation. Producers practically tripped over each other trying to seize the story.

"I want it for my show."

"No, I want it for *my* show."

"Wouldn't it make more sense to run it in my show and tease it throughout both of your shows?"

"Yeah," Gretchen said. "Let's *milk* this thing."

And so it was milked. And so it appeared on Channel 11 News. Exclusive new details into the shocking murder of a Boston attorney.

Damon Fitzgerald has the exclusive on the Bombed Beamer.

Damon Fitzgerald makes a grisly discovery.

Damon Fitzgerald uncovers the *unthinkable*!

Damon Fitzgerald, in truth, wanted to throw up.

But I did not. Instead I retired to my office after my report and waited for the phone to ring. It did.

"Hey, it's Raleigh Dean. Saw your story."

"Yeah, and?"

"And I think we should talk."

"So do I. Do you know anything about a broken engagement?"

"No," he said.

"Well, I do. Are you in your office tomorrow?"

"No, I have court again all day."

"While you're there why don't you ask the D.A. about the boyfriend..."

He hesitated. I heard a fart, maybe, in the background. Then Raleigh Dean said, "Good enough."

"Can I speak to one of your P.I.s?" I asked him.

"Not without me being present. How about next week?"

"You want me to sit on this until next week?" I groaned.

"Hey, Damon. This ain't going to trial for a year. What's the hurry?"

February ratings. That was the hurry. Can't let that pesky judicial process get in the way of a good, highly promotable, *shocking* and *exclusive* story.

❖ ❖ ❖

Later that evening I struggled. Really struggled to identify the demon standing in the way of my astonishing debut novel. The demon pissed metaphorically in my face. Just stood there on my white screen and aimed his triple-headed penis of fire at me and let me have it.

Very hard to write with demon urine dripping down your chin. Very hard. So I walked away. And then, to my amazement, I heard a clicking sound coming from my apartment door. I left my computer room and followed the insistent noise and asked, "Who's there? Anybody there?" Perhaps the demon had come for a visit in the flesh. Maybe this time he'd defecate on me. I hoped he wouldn't. I had already felt duly defecated upon by Channel 11 News. There's only so much shit one man can be expected to take.

From across the room I saw the doorknob twisting and dashed immediately for the peephole. Nothing. I heard the quick padding of getaway footsteps and, in fact, when I opened the door and surveyed the hallway there was nobody there.

That was probably the first sign that someone had been unhappy with my discovery of Gina Parr's charred automobile. That someone had seen my report and had acted quickly to thwart any further investigation. It was probably the first sign, but it was a sign I missed when I simply dismissed the intrusion as a drunken, partying neighbor (one of the Eurotrash-hip-glamo college students whose Euro-daddies were footing the bill for an American education, an upscale apartment, and the necessary intoxicants) who got off the elevator on the wrong floor.

Or, of course, it could have been the demon. And he could have been constipated. Unable to defecate on me or anyone else. Buh-bye.

I did not watch the late news. I watched *The Daily Show* on Comedy Central. I cheered on the mock-reporters as they mocked the news with dead-ringing and humbling accuracy. And, oh yeah, I had a beer. Two, in fact.

They tasted good. Really, like a Jacuzzi for the mouth and the throat. Mmm. I loved that. A good beer (or two) in the self-indulgence of celibacy and solitude. Beer never tasted better.

Then I watched two episodes of *I Love Lucy*.

And contemplated the lovemaking of Lucy and Ricky. It must have been hot and dramatic. Passionate and powerful. Despite the single beds, of course. I could hear a lot of guttural cries, primal moans. Yes, that was it, primal and guttural and good for everyone involved. In fact their sex was so good its essence permeated the whole set and everyone, even the grips, felt satiated the next day.

Vivian Vance, however, was a bit resentful. She was hornier than hell. And not very pleased with her lover at the moment.

I must have fallen asleep at some point during the third episode of *I Love Lucy*. I dreamt about Havana. Ricky Ricardo in a BMW. Lucy with a gun. Ethel with a tampon.

Go figure.

I woke up the following morning to the obvious headline: DEAD ATTORNEY'S CAR FOUND TORCHED. And, yes, I'll concede it was gratifying to watch the other media outlets scramble for the story I broke a day earlier. Gratifying, but still not motivating or inspiring. I still hated like hell to go to work.

When I got there I was surrounded by praise about breaking the BIG story. Even Gretchen retracted the teeth of her vagina to tell me about a "job well done." Lloyd Lasser gave me a pat on the back. Literally. A real good ol' boy even-though-you're-a-homo pat on the back.

You would have thought I had restored Helen Keller's eyesight with all the fuss they were making. Or found a cure for halitosis.

I sank into my chair and tried to muster up the interest to move the story forward, find a new angle, or rehash an old angle in a very new way because, according to our consultants, the viewers really didn't give a shit as long as you made them *feel* a sense of urgency. Which is why I once peed on the foot of one of those consultants just as he was packing up his things to head back to the home office in Dubuque. I followed him into the men's room and pulled out my dick just as he was cozying up to a urinal. Then I let him have it.

"What the hell was that for?" he begged, incredulously.

"Sense of urgency, sir. I had to go real bad."

Turns out I didn't have to contemplate my next angle for very long before the phone rang and an assistant for the district attorney invited me to a press briefing about the Gina Parr case.

"Does this have anything to do with my report last night about the car?" I asked.

"Could be," the woman said.

"Damage control," I explained to Johnnie as we motored out to the D.A.'s office.

"Neckingham must hate you," he said.

You wouldn't think so by the greeting we received. Neckingham offered a full, man-size handshake. A big smile and sweep of the arms begging us to enter his conference room. It was then that I realized the man had higher political ambitions. He would not be a D.A. for life. He was eyeing the office of state attorney general, or governor, perhaps. I just knew it. I was, at first, surprised he would face the press so quickly after the story of the torched car broke. A press conference would only raise difficult, awkward questions and perhaps even doubt about the guilt of Roberto Cruz. But seeing Neckingham greedily welcome us, gathering the rest of the media as though we had come for a campfire and a few rounds of "Kumbaya," I could see this was a whistle stop on his campaign. It had little to do with the case. All to do with his face.

"Some of you have learned of an incident involving a vehicle owned by Gina Parr," he began. "Let us assure you that this department knew about that incident but has no evidence whatsoever linking it to her murder."

The reporters looked at each other dumbfounded. We eyed each other carefully, as if to confirm that, no, we did not look like a cluster of idiots.

"We are investigating the incident as malicious destruction of property."

"You think her car was *vandalized*?" I asked.

"Malicious destruction of property carries stiffer penalties than common vandalism," he replied.

Susan Radwell from *The Boston Globe* bristled. "Come on, Rich," she said to the D.A., "you know that an automobile left like that means something. It means someone is after you and it's a warning. Two weeks later the woman is dead. And you expect us to believe it's a coincidence?"

Neckingham smiled coyly. "I'm not asking you to believe anything. I'm just trying to clear the air here and tell you we have no evidence that it's connected to the murder."

I badly, so badly it hurt, wanted to ask Neckingham about Gina's boyfriend and whether the breakup might have led to her murder. But that would have been showing my hand to the other reporters in the room and, as I could see by the way they sized me up in their own coy flashes of recognition, they were already hot on my trail.

"So, you're saying Roberto Cruz was not involved in the destruction of Gina Parr's BMW?" I asked.

"That's what I'm saying," the district attorney replied.

"Were the keys still in the car when it was located?" I asked.

"Yes," Neckingham said. "They were still in the ignition."

"So, it's safe to assume that the set found in Mr. Cruz's apartment was a separate set? And that Mr. Cruz had no knowledge of the car being torched two weeks prior?" I persisted.

"That's precisely what we've concluded. That Mr. Cruz intended to locate the woman's car in the adjacent parking lot and steal it."

"Okay," I continued, "but wouldn't you also conclude that if, in fact, the torched car was a warning and that whoever left her the warning is also responsible for her death, that would eliminate Mr. Cruz as a suspect..."

Neckingham scowled. "That's awfully abstract and theoretical. We don't deal in the abstract, Damon. We deal with the evidence and the facts. And the fact is," he continued, "and let me make this very clear, we have *no* evidence that the incident with the car is related to the murder."

"Do you have any evidence that it's not?" Susan asked.

"I think that's enough for today," the D.A. said, getting to his feet. He gestured broadly toward the door, as if we should all leave en masse. "We just wanted to respond to all the reports about the car. We hoped to clear up any speculation."

I looked at Johnnie and shrugged. "Let's go. Pack it up."

18

I USED THE NEXT FEW DAYS TO WRAP UP LOOSE ENDS ON other stories. The diploma-mill investigation had really paid off. We confronted four "professors" at area colleges and questioned them about their degrees. Guilt does amazing things. It seeps out in your sweat and flushes like a red page turning across your face. One of the "professors" tried to dodge our camera by ducking into a restroom. It was a ladies' restroom. He was not a lady. Another "professor" jumped into her SUV and sped away, taking the FACULTY PARKING sign with her. The third acted dumbfounded. "What do you mean American College of Arts & Sciences doesn't exist? How can that be? I have a long history with that institution."

"And the campus is where?" I asked.

"It's a very nontraditional campus."

"There is no campus," I suggested.

"Not in the traditional sense."

"Is it a correspondence school?" I asked.

"I corresponded with the administration regularly."

"But there is no administration. We checked."

"Uh...I see. Guess I've been hoodwinked."

"Is that it, sir? You're the victim here?"

"Precisely."

"Will you resign as a result of these revelations?"

Then the man, a fortyish oaf with stringy hair and fat hands, lunged at me. He pushed me aside and aimed for the camera. A lot of people aimed for the camera. A lot of people felt compelled to give us that hand-over-the-lens shot to somehow thwart us in our attempt to reveal the truth. The truth is a hand-over-the-lens is simply a hand-over-the-lens and generally it finds its way into the story and generally makes the person attached to that hand look, well, unilaterally guilty.

I immediately recovered and stepped between the man and the camera and effectively guarded Johnnie until he could achieve some distance. The man lunged for me again and I resolved to go home that evening and not only begin my astonishing debut novel but finish it, in fact, because I was tired of meeting up with every idiot who stumbled into the glaring spotlight of investigative journalism.

"A lot of people use literature to escape," Karl told me a few nights later. "But not to escape from their profession."

"I hate my profession."

"Please, you're one of the best reporters I know."

"I'm the only reporter you know."

"You know what I mean."

Karl had stopped by with hot soup and had maneuvered around the clutter of my kitchen, finding a bowl, serving it to me. I was getting a cold. A typical New England middle-of-winter smack in the head, sore in the joints, fire in the throat kind of cold. He had heard me sniffle a few hours earlier and had insisted on bringing me the soup. I had written two horrendous chapters of drivel and had realized there was not an astounding metaphor among them. Karl said I was trying too hard. Two slurps into the soup, I heard the shrill of my pager.

I grabbed it from the counter. *Call the station.*

Marcus, our night-shift assignment editor, told me the district attorney had been trying to call me for hours.

"Neckingham?"

"Yep."

"What does he want?"

"Said he was trying to return your call."

"My call?"

"That's what he said."

"I never called him."

"Whatever," Marcus said. "He left his cell number."

I apologized to Karl and dialed the district attorney. He answered on the second ring.

"It's Damon Fitzgerald."

"Hey, Fitz. I'm sorry it's taken a while to get back to you."

"No need to apologize. There must be some misunderstanding. I haven't called you lately."

"Huh...maybe my office got it wrong."

"Maybe."

"Well, it was someone from Channel 11. Someone called looking for me. Assumed it was you."

"No," I told him. "But since I have you on the phone, Rick, I'd like to ask you something about the Gina Parr case."

He laughed. "Like I even thought I would get off the phone without some kind of inquiry..."

"Call me an opportunist. I need to ask you about Gina's fiancé. Do you know anything about him?"

"Of course. We interviewed him."

"Did he tell you about their breakup?"

"Yes."

"Is he a suspect?"

A sigh of disgust, subtle, but disgust nonetheless. "He *was* a suspect, Damon. Everyone *was* a suspect. But we have our man. You know that. When the heck are you going to get out of the conspiracy game and wait for this thing to come to trial?"

"That would be no fun," I told the district attorney.

"I'm afraid the facts are no fun."

"Sometimes they are," I needled him.

"Since when is reporting about fun?"

"When cases begin to resemble puzzles, Rick, that's when I sit down with all the pieces and start to play."

"Oh boy, Fitzie. You just better be sure you're playing on the right team."

I let the conversation pause there for a moment, considering the implications of his comment. It was no secret I played on the Homo Team. But I don't think he was talking about that kind of team. No, I think Neckingham was one of those entrenched politicians who truly but misguidedly believed that it was the media's job to support, bolster, never question their mission.

"Hey, Rick, how about a lead to the fiancé..."

"Not if you're going on a manhunt, Damon."

"Maybe I just want to talk to the guy, you know, to ask him more about Gina. Maybe I'm just trying to get a better sense of who she was...put a face to a name, that sort of thing."

The D.A. surrendered with yet another sigh. "Okay, enough already. My secretary will call you tomorrow with a name and a number. It's all public record."

"Yes," I told him. "It is."

Karl and I finished the soup and watched a rerun of *The Love Boat*. Karl reminisced about the gay cruise (the redundancy, it seems, was lost on him) he went on the preceding winter. "Not a chest hair on the entire boat!" he sang in delight.

NECKINGHAM KEPT HIS WORD. MOMENTS INTO MY MORNING
(not even a "hello" from Johnnie or an appearance from
Donna) I had a call from the D.A.'s office and the woman
caller offered me a name and a phone number.

Sam Young.

I dialed the number and reached voice-mail. I left a message and went on to other matters. I'll admit it: I did call a
few more times to listen to the fiancé's recorded voice, to analyze for myself whether it was the voice of a killer. What does
a killer's voice sound like, you may ask? It sounds tentative.
Or deliberate. Menacing or gentle. Thin or diaphragm-deep.
Hard to tell. Killers don't have a distinctive voice as much as
a distinctive mind. But it never hurts to analyze. To listen
carefully.

Gretchen spun into my office and asked about the diploma mill story. I told her it was done and she clapped. That's
right, she fucking clapped.

Then the phone rang. Hoping it was Sam Young but certain it wasn't, I lunged for the phone, capitalizing on the

opportunity to avoid a prolonged encounter with Gretchen.

It was Patrick O'Hare. He asked if I was still interested in the money laundering at Rendezvous. I told him I was. "But I'm real wrapped up in some other stories right now," I explained. "Is something going down soon? Or can this hold?"

He snickered. A very straight-white-boy arrogant snicker. "Yes, the crime of the century will hold for the reporter of the century."

"Don't be an ass."

"Seriously, Damon. I have some good tips. I'll come by tonight. We'll go out for a drink. I can give you some dates and some places and you can decide what to do from there."

I acquiesced. "Fine. Be here at six-thirty."

Finally, Donna Donovan shot across the hallway from her office to mine once again, saddled in her chair. "Hey, Damon...good morning."

"Morning..."

"Coffee?"

"No, thanks."

"I need a favor, Damon."

"You and the rest of the world."

She smiled. Her face softened a bit and I took notice of this departure from her usual steely expression. "Can you go over my banking script with me today?"

I shrugged. "I guess. Is there a problem?"

"Oh, no," she replied. "I just want another pair of eyes on it before I bring it to Lloyd."

"You've been doing this longer than I have," I told her. "I don't know what I could possibly suggest."

"You can tell me if it's sucky TV."

"If it's on TV, Donna, it's sucky. Trust me on that. It's a given."

"Any progress on Gina Parr."

"No," I told her.

I had no way of knowing that two hours later Sam Young would return my call and agree to meet with me. He seemed completely unfazed. "Yeah, I figured it was only a matter of time before the press caught up with me," he said.

I heard the sound of my own salivation and knew that it was a turnoff to those I was strapping in for an interview. I tried to conceal my excitement. "Well, we can do this at your convenience," I told him.

"Tomorrow," he said. "I don't know how much I can tell you. I mean, I don't know if I'll be any help."

"No pressure," I told him, and like a coed on her first night at the fraternity house, he believed me.

I had every intention of pressuring his ass into a jackhammering mind-fuck session. And it would be fun.

Johnnie had slipped into the office while I had Sam Young on the phone. At one point he simply shrugged at me as if to say: "Like, hey, dude, what's up..." I shrugged back. Like, nothing, dude, okay?

He sipped on Starbucks and when I got off the phone asked, "What are we shooting today?"

"Some interviews on the kickbacks at the statehouse."

"Boring."

"Sorry, Johnnie, I realize it's my job to keep you amused. Go load up your gear. We leave in twenty minutes."

He grunted and left. Something about that grunt made me think of Frank and his audible pleasure at coming all over my chest and face. Did I miss him? No. Not in the sense that I recognized a void or an emptiness. But celibacy was not agreeing with me. My chest, my face, yes, even my heart, were too young to forsake completely the occasional well-aimed spurt of warm semen.

I started to consider Ernesto, the tape librarian, and whether there was potential.

For sex, yes.

For anything more, no.

I was pretty sure he did not speak English. Which would leave only sex.

I was never a Sex-Only kind of guy.

I was a Sex-and-a-Movie, or Sex-and-Starbucks, or better yet, Sex-and-a-Baseball-Game kind of guy.

Sex and follow-up. Perhaps that came from my experience as a journalist. A story had to be bigger than itself. There had to be context and, by God, there had to be follow-up. It had to be more than *wham, bam, smile for the cam.*

There had to be new developments.

A bigger purpose.

A broader scope.

And a neck massage always helped too.

Johnnie was right. The statehouse interviews bored me nearly to tears. There, under the famous gold dome atop Beacon Hill, I inhaled generations of boring policy-making, overzealous lobbying, flesh-pressing, ass-kissing, loopholing, filibustering, political favor–repaying government dysfunction. The smell was old and musty in places, starchy elsewhere, like all the shirts of the good old boys who rounded the corners of those venerated hallways with the whisper of propriety following closely behind, buzzing at their ears like pesky mosquitoes in the middle of a good night's dream.

The story would be good, though. The state had fucked up in the contractor bidding process. And we had proof. We also had some red-faced legislators promising, on tape, to rectify the situation immediately. It wasn't Watergate, or even Enron, but on a local level it was big enough. A black eye, as the producers would inevitably describe it, on state government.

Whatever.

Truth is, it would fill two minutes of airtime and that's all they really cared about.

I was not out the door two seconds that evening when I heard my name coming from a dark automobile at the corner of the parking lot. I didn't recognize the car or the silhouette of the man sitting in the driver's seat.

"You're not going home, are you?" the man called to me.

Shit. I had forgotten. Patrick O'Hare.

I crossed the parking lot and apologized. "This is a really busy time, Patrick. It slipped my mind."

"Can you spare an hour?"

"Yeah. Sure."

"Get in."

I did and we drove over to Copley Square and ducked into a bar on Newbury Street.

He told me about a federal agent who had infiltrated an illegal arms ring and had linked the money to Rendezvous.

I smiled.

"What's so funny?" Patrick asked me.

"I just don't see it. Drag queens and contraband."

"It's probably more common than you think."

"Please..."

We ordered beer.

He refused to reveal the agent's name but told me that the man was leaking critical information to a friend of a friend of the Collins brothers.

"How convenient. Next thing, you'll tell me the Collins are looking to get Rendezvous at a good price."

"I'm not going to lie to you. The guys tried to buy that whole block about five years ago. They lost the deal. And if this weapons thing shuts the club down, then so be it."

I shook my head. "Right. And I, the celebrated TV homosexual, will be responsible for the shutdown of Boston's premier gay bar."

He laughed. "So, you told me you weren't into the bar scene."

"Maybe not. But I don't want to alienate myself from the whole community. I'll never get a date."

"Too much information."

"Patrick, if you're going to roll up your sleeves with the fags, you better get educated."

"Are you in?" he asked.

I said nothing.

"Look," he persisted, "if you break this story, you'll win all kinds of awards and you can get that network job."

"The networks are overrated, Patrick. They're a fucking nightmare."

"Are you in?"

"What if I am?"

The waitress arrived with two tall glasses brimming with brew.

"If you're in, Damon Fitzgerald, I have a time and a place for you and your camera."

Suddenly, I was more interested and said so with wider eyes and a deliberate lean across the table. "Where? When?"

He gave me an address in Rhode Island. Said I needed to be there next Thursday night.

"You guys have to be very, very careful," he warned me. "You cannot blow the agent's cover. You must be stealth."

I laughed. "Stealth?"

"I'm serious."

"Then don't say such silly things."

He took a gulp of beer. I could tell he was distressed with me by the way he nearly slammed the glass back to the table. "Damon, I'm serious. Too many things are at stake here."

"I see."

"You guys drive in an unmarked car, right?"

"Yes."

"Good. You'll need to keep at a distance. You cannot be spotted."

"Understood."

"You can call me from the site if you need to."

I shrugged. "Don't think that will be necessary."

"You'll want to follow the blue van back to Boston."

"The blue van."

"Yeah."

I finished my beer, declined another. Patrick drove me back to Channel 11.

I dashed into the building to empty my bladder of the rising beer tide and Johnnie stopped me in the hallway.

"What are you doing here?" I asked him.

"They needed someone to edit for Donna tonight and I needed the overtime, so..."

"Fuck, Donna..."

He smiled. "Already told you she's not my type."

"No, no, no," I said. "I told her I'd go over one of her scripts today and totally forgot about it. Did you edit her banking story?"

He shook his head. "No. She says that's not airing for a week."

"Good. I need to print out the script and read it tonight."

"I'm outta here," he said. "Regular time tomorrow?"

"Yeah. Regular time."

He left. I went directly to my office and logged into Newstar and found that Donna had mailed me her script and had, in fact, mailed me a note later in the day to remind me to read it—and then one more time presumably before she left for the evening mailed to ask me "what the hell is it going to take to get you to read the damn script, Damon?"

Feeling sufficiently reprimanded and ashamed, I printed out the script and took it with me when I left the building.

Unfortunately, I had been diverted from my original plan and nearly wet myself on the short ride home.

20

THE TRUTH IS, IT WASN'T FRANK'S PENIS I MISSED AS MUCH AS it was his cooking. Nights like this made that truth quite pronounced as the wedge of light from my refrigerator revealed few if any choices for a meal. There were eggs. And there were remnants of pizza circa late November. The freezer offered up a Lean Cuisine. It took me less than ten minutes to heat it *and* eat it. That was sad.

Even sadder, the story of New England Savings. I began to pore over Donna's script. I could tell from the beginning that it would run too long for television. A whopping three minutes. Consultants to the news business had done intense research and had discovered that the attention span of the average American is forty-seven seconds. If stories ran longer than forty-seven seconds, they had better have the bells and whistles to keep the viewer glued to the screen. If not, we risked losing that viewer to reruns of *Diff'rent Strokes*. My first note to Donna: cut, cut, cut. Or incur the wrath of our attention-deficit-disordered producing staff.

Cut.

But it was a good, compelling story. A banking institution collapses because its officers approved hundreds of millions of dollars in bad loans to friends and associates. The loans would never be paid back, but enough of the money would be kicked back to those officers as incentive to look the other way. And look the other way they did; in fact they laughed all the way to another bank down the street where they ultimately deposited all their kickback millions.

Nice work, Donna! This is great shit!

Seems that six bank officials pocketed some $40 million each before getting caught—before a seventh turned against them and spilled it for the feds. And then called a friend who called a friend who called Donna Donovan.

Now, according to her script, the attention would turn to an outside law firm that drew up the loan deals. Was the firm getting a kickback too? Had the firm subverted the law for its own financial gain?

More, in part two of "Breaking the Bank."

Seeing copy was not enough. I had to see the story, the edited piece. I could not imagine how Donna could tell this story with, I guessed, no more than four shots of the bank amid the towers of the city's financial district. Limited video killed you. Then I thought about Enron and how many times I had seen that pathetic *E* spinning around the company's entry plaza. New England Savings was Boston's Enron. And Donna had unraveled the story beautifully.

I called her to say so.

"Thanks," she said in a groggy, post-martini voice.

"But what the hell are you going to do for pictures?"

"Lot of money shots. Close-ups of cash. We have video of the houses these guys bought, their boats. One stashed a helicopter away on the Cape."

"No shit."

"No shit," she confirmed.

"More white men who think they're entitled to the mother lode."

"So to speak," she said.

"Just like Enron," I continued. "A bunch of middle-aged white men who thought the money was theirs for the taking. That only they had a right to get rich."

"Wait till you see part two," she said.

I stretched out on the couch, rested my head on the arm. "Yeah, you only sent me the script for the first part."

"I'm working on the rest tomorrow."

"Which firm?"

"Firm?"

"Yeah, the one that drew up the loans."

"Oh, right," she said. "Berger, Berger, Cooke, & Langham."

I bolted up, suffered a momentary head rush, gripped the sofa firmly, and said, "What?"

"Berger, Berger, Cooke, & Langham."

"No fucking shit!" I cried.

Donna laughed.

My skin went clammy, a cold sweat dampened and chilled me. "This isn't funny, Donna," I told her. "That's where Gina Parr worked. That was her firm."

21

OF COURSE I DID NOT SLEEP WELL THAT EVENING. I TOSSED and turned and composed a theme song for Gina's death. Could it be that she was in on the scandal from the beginning? Could it be that she pissed somebody off?

Obviously, she pissed somebody off. She was, after all, shot three times. Her Beamer was toasted.

All night I drew up scenarios, complete with dramatic sound bites, to tell the story of an impressionable Gina Parr, a young, eager attorney sucked into a web of deceit and betrayal. I twisted in my bed sheets, chastising myself for ordering up the obvious clichés. I wondered who had approached Gina first. Which of the bankers? Was there sex involved? There probably was sex involved. Those same middle-aged white men who felt entitled to windfalls of cash undoubtedly felt entitled to mistresses as well.

Fuck, what a story!

All night I heard arguments and counterarguments and press conferences and grandstanding and screaming headlines and blistering editorials and indignant rebuttals and spinning, spiraling, sobering resignation.

Could the television audience digest all this information?

Could one populace handle all this drama?

It's no wonder I only slept for an hour or two. It's even less wonder that I stumbled out of bed thirty minutes after the alarm fingernailed the chalkboard of my brief serenity, that I skipped breakfast, had a cursory shower, and locked myself out of the apartment when I left for work.

Damn.

No, make that *Fuck*.

I lunged into my briefcase and fished desperately for my keys, knowing quite well I would not find them. They would be splayed across the very same breakfast counter I had forsaken in my rush to get out the door.

I did find my cell phone, though. I dialed work and asked for Johnnie. He had not arrived yet. I tried calling him in the car but was immediately transferred to voice-mail because, I suspected, Johnnie was either listening to his music too loudly or standing in line at Starbucks. I called the station again and asked for Donna.

"Please," I begged her, "go into my office and check my desk for my spare key."

"Car key?"

"Apartment key. It's in the middle drawer, in that little tray where most people keep their paper clips."

She tsked and told me to hold on. She returned a few moments later and said, yes, the key was there. "Do you want me to bring it to you?" she asked.

"No, no," I replied. "Thanks, but as long as I know it's there, I'll take a cab to work."

"Are you sure?"

"Yeah. I'll be there in a few. Brew some coffee. I'll need it."

"How will you get home tonight?"

I paused. "Johnnie. Or you...or a cab..."

"You're pathetic," she said before hanging up. She was right. I was pathetic. In my sleep-deprived desperation I sounded pathetic.

✧ ✧ ✧

The cab driver told me he once worked for the CIA. I rolled my eyes and thought, *Yes, and I once fucked George Stephanopoulos.* There was a time when you could rely on a cab driver to bounce you swiftly through the city, defy the laws of gravity, break every rule of chiropractic care, and get you to your destination without a family history. But now everyone had a story. And as soon as the driver recognized me as "that kid from Channel 11" he launched right into his autobiography. I ignored most of it, save for that short vignette about his circle jerk with Fidel Castro. We arrived at Channel 11. I paid him, tipped him generously, and sent him on his way.

Donna was waiting for me in my office. She had perched herself on the corner of my desk, sipping her inevitable cup of morning coffee. "Well?"

"Well, what?" I asked her.

"Do you think Gina Parr was in on this banking scandal?"

I was almost breathless at the mention of it. "Of course. This is no coincidence, Donna."

"Then somehow you're going to have to prove she was getting a kickback."

"Yes, I know that, Donna. Maybe she was holding out for more money and maybe that pissed off someone at the bank."

"Or someone getting the loans."

"It makes sense," I said.

"But first you have to prove that she had something, anything to do with those loans," my colleague added.

"Yes, I know that," I told her, sensing immediately the horrendous amount of work cut out for me at that moment.

A terrible thing when all you really want to do is mail it in.

"I think it's a two-person job," Donna said with a purpose and confidence I found convincing, not threatening.

"Hey, a joint investigation," I concluded.

"I don't want to step on your story, Damon," she told me. "But I think we can pull off an amazing thing here."

Like a self-dividing cell, half of my horrendous amount of work seemed to split away and drift into her office. I liked that.

Later in the day when I met with Sam Young I was quite preoccupied with my latest theory linking Gina Parr to New England Savings, and I decided to see the hapless fellow as more of an informant and less of a suspect. Though I must say, his short frame (maybe five-foot-six), dark eyes, and unkempt hair would have been perfect for a mug shot. And when he mentioned, rather quickly, that he had taught Gina how to shoot a gun, well, that momentarily forced me back from the plate like a curve ball.

"Shoot a gun?" I asked.

"She said it was for self-defense, but I didn't really believe her. She hated guns and would have more easily signed up for karate, I think."

We had met at a small diner just down the road from Channel 11. There was so much noise in the air (waitresses yelling orders, the griddle sizzling, fat men loudly lunching with one another) that no one could hear the confessions of Sam Young in his dusty flannel shirt and corduroys. He had some growth on his chin that straggled from his face like hairy drool. Somehow I couldn't place Gina and he as lovers. She, the young lawyer on the rise, and he, the disheveled young nobody.

"What do you do?" I asked him.

"I'm a substitute teacher."

"Substitute?"

"Yeah. Math and science."

"Not looking for anything full-time?"

"No," he replied directly. "I'm working on a novel."

I suppressed a smile and a laugh. "Okay, then," I continued, "why do you think Gina wanted target practice?"

"No idea. She had a very private side to her that was even hard for me to get at. That's kind of what ended it for us."

"Her privacy?"

"Well, yes," he said. "But, over time, I began to think of it as secrecy, not privacy. I hate secrecy. You know, it damages trust."

"Of course," I said, knowing if I sat there with eager eyes and said little he would continue. Which he did.

"I think she was keeping something from me," he said. "Like maybe she was having an affair."

An affair? Oh, please, spare me this cliché, spare me your machismo conclusions, I begged silently. Did not a woman have any other ambitions outside of an otherwise happy relationship besides the ambition to fuck?

Disappointed, I waited for more.

"Of course, I never did prove she was having an affair, Mr. Fitzgerald. But her secrecy and my accusations eventually put a strain on things and drew us apart."

"I see..." Actually, I did not see, and did not buy it, but knew the only way I would get on the inside was to stay on the outside.

"I figured the gun was for self-protection. You know, in case the guy's wife came after her."

I tilted my head a bit. "So you not only felt she was having an affair but you thought she was doing it with a married man?"

He looked at me as if I'd never seen a Lifetime Original Movie. "Of course," he said. "What would be the point of fucking around with just another guy? There had to be something different from what I was offering her. There had to be something more to it."

"So you think the wife eventually found out and killed her?"

"It's in line with my theory," he replied.

"That's some theory, Mr. Young."

"Yeah, maybe," he conceded. "But you walk in on a crime scene like that and some things just jump out at you, stay with you. You know, first impressions..."

"You walked in on the crime scene?"

He hesitated. "Well, not exactly. I came to identify her."

"You ID'd the body?"

"Yeah." He looked away. His eyes filled with tears. His voice shook nervously when he turned back to me and said, "I'll never get that image out of my mind. You see someone like that in their final moment and you just can't imagine their soul at peace."

"Hmm...that must be hard."

He shook his head, as if to cast the image away for the moment. "Anyway," he said, "I don't believe that Cruz guy killed her. Maybe my theory is too much of a cliché for you, but I think it's more credible than what the authorities have come up with."

I did not. But, suddenly, as a man, as a witness, as an informant, Sam Young became quite credible himself. All I needed to know was that he doubted the involvement of Roberto Cruz and I felt he was enough of an ally for the moment. And I would exploit that alliance. Without shame.

"You know," he continued, "the super in Gina's building says her door was unlocked and slightly ajar for a few days before her body was found."

"Yes," I told him, "that's what the district attorney has said. He says the open door explains why there are no signs of forced entry."

"No," Sam Young said instantly above the noise of the splattering diner. "There is no way she would have opened that door to a strange man. She was a cautious girl. She wouldn't have done that."

"Did it ever occur to you that maybe Roberto Cruz was the man with whom she was having the affair?"

He laughed. So did I. Neither one of us believed that as a real possibility. The laughter, though, was well-timed, as it gave us a moment to pause, re-collect ourselves, sip our coffee, nibble at the sandwiches, and check our watches as people often do when a moment becomes awkward.

Sam Young had returned the remnants of his sandwich to the plate, but I was still in midchew when he said, "Look, I think it's perfectly reasonable to assume that Cruz saw an open door and saw an opportunity to steal some things without knowing about Gina's dead body in the bedroom."

I nodded emphatically, enjoying this hint of like-mindedness, and said, "Well, yes, I have been thinking the same scenario for some time now."

"It makes sense," Sam Young assured me.

"It does," I said, reminding myself to be cautious, though, to always stay one step ahead of my informant, to never stride at exactly the same pace. "Did she ever talk to you about work?"

"My work?"

"No, Sam. Her work. At the firm?"

"Well, of course we talked about it. She pretty much hated it. Thought that most of the senior attorneys were these blowhard white guys who walked around with drilling rights to everyone's ass."

"Very vivid," I told him.

"I'm working on a novel," he reminded me.

"Yes, of course," I said, knowing that the fucker was a metaphor ahead of me already. "Why did she have such a low opinion of them?" I asked.

"First, you have to know Gina. She was amazingly intelligent, but she was all too aware of her brilliance. In other words, she knew she was smarter than most people and hated taking directions from supervisors she deemed intellectually inferior."

"Wow," I said. "She sounds rather elitist and smug."

He smiled. "Oh, she could be, indeed. She had names for everyone at the firm. There was Beef Jerky, Hammerhead, Dickless, Ass-Stain, and, let me think....Nazi Goldberg. Those were the partners."

"Nazi Goldberg?"

"A self-hating Jew," he whispered.

"That's terrible," I said.

"Well, she also had names for the various secretaries and assistants. I can't remember them all. They're all in her journal, but, let's see, there was Big Hair, Vaginetta, Lulu, and Goody Proctor. She was not happy at the firm. She was thinking of quitting."

"She talked about quitting?"

"All the time," the fiancé replied.

"Right before the murder?"

He hesitated. "Uh...yes. For probably two or three months before the murder."

"You mentioned a journal." I felt myself salivating and tried to divert his attention by taking one last dive at my sandwich.

"Yes. Her sister has it. It was just a bunch of ramblings about work. The stupid tax cases she was working on, how bored she was, the idiots in the office. That kind of thing. She used to e-mail her sister all the time with stories of office politics and she used all those fictitious names and her sister absolutely loved it."

"Did she e-mail her sister from her office computer?"

Sam Young, the substitute teacher/aspiring writer, looked at me like I'd just emerged from the Idiot Hall of Fame. "No, of course not," he said. "From her home computer."

"Do you think her sister will talk to me?"

He shrugged. "I don't know. You could try."

"Can you..."

"Give you her number?"

I looked him squarely in the eyes, a marriage of confident closure and delight in mine, and said "Yes, can you give me her number?"

He folded his hands under his chin, diverting from my stare not for a moment, and said, "Yes."

22

"*The universe burst into something from absolutely nothing—zero, nada. And as it got bigger, it became filled with even more stuff that came from absolutely nowhere. How is that possible?*"

—*Discover* magazine, April 2002

A STAR IS TEN BILLION TIMES BRIGHTER THAN A PLANET. That's a fact. So if you think death is the end of your radiance, your brilliance, and your energy here in the cosmos that is life and the afterlife, you have a big enormous surprise waiting for you.

How many times have you seen Hollywood depict death and departure as a "walk toward the light"? It is fantasy based on hypotheses based on speculation based on wonder and the latitude of religion. It is also fairly close to the truth. The "light," as it were, is the afterlife that awaits you. The light is brighter, of course, than anything your living eyes have ever seen, because this is the light you will become. This is the light your soul will inhabit. This is your star. So, yes, when it is your time, you must go toward the light and become one with the light as you would become one with the Lord. Your death is nothing more than the birth of your star.

And it is beautiful. And breathtaking. And, ultimately, peaceful. You cannot imagine this peace. When someone dies and you say they are "resting in peace," you have no clue just how right you are. The peace is God-given. It is a peace you can only know once your star is born. Happy birthday and all that.

To become a guiding light of the universe is nothing to sneeze at. It is, ultimately, the best birthday celebration you will ever know.

I don't know much about science. I do know that scientists the world over are trying to analyze stars and their relationship to planets. They try to estimate the age of stars and the planets they support. When you die you will not figure this all out. You will not receive a doctorate in astrophysics. So don't expect one. Your state of bliss will transcend any scientific explanation of stars and planets, galaxies, and their implications for the universe. You will witness God or some godlike higher power sweeping magical and immeasurable doses of meaning your way. Your soul will absorb this and it will feel easy and uncomplicated and you will understand that your lifelong faith has led you to this ultimate serenity.

Pretty cool, no?

Perhaps the closest thing you can find in your earthbound life to this pure serenity is a meditative state where you achieve a higher level of consciousness through the self-hypnosis of your conscious thought. The most successful meditators can reach this so-called nirvana—and it is lovely, really, but still, it is only a whisper of what awaits you on your trip through stardom.

I didn't hear back from Jessica Parr for probably three days. I had left a message on what I assumed was her home answering machine, though I wasn't sure because her outgoing announcement seemed quite formal, clipped even. Perhaps she ran a business out of her home. I would never know because Jessica Parr, quite formally, in the same clipped voice, told me, when she returned that call, that she would under no circumstances meet with me to discuss the death of her sister.

"Surely you understand that meeting with you, Mr. Fitzgerald, will do no good for anyone. We are not interested in sensationalizing Gina's death."

"Yes," I said. "Of course. I am not interested in sensationalizing her death either. But I believe there may be unanswered questions, Ms. Parr. How convinced are you that the suspect in custody is the man responsible for your sister's death?"

"We're leaving that to the prosecutors, Mr. Fitzgerald.

My family is not in the position to second-guess the investigation."

"No," I told her, "but with all due respect, the media is."

"Then second-guess all you'd like. We can't stop you. But we have chosen since Gina's murder not to meet with the media because we see no good coming out of it."

"I see."

"Will that be all?" the woman asked. She spoke with the efficiency and sterile inflection of a librarian and I was having a hard time in that moment feeling any compassion for her, though I wanted to.

"I understand Gina was unhappy at work..."

Much to my surprise my remark was met with a tiny albeit unmistakable laugh. Then a sigh. Then another naked laugh. "That's an understatement, Mr. Fitzgerald."

"Please, call me Damon," I told her, begging solicitously for more time. "She made up names for her coworkers."

"How do you know that?" she asked quickly.

"Sam Young."

"Oh."

"He said she kept a journal."

"She did."

"Do you know the whereabouts of that journal now?"

I heard her inhale deeply and I listened to a protracted silence that gave me pause to wonder on her physicality. What could she possibly look like? It was only then that I realized I had assigned her Gina's face, Gina's features, Gina's personality perhaps, as if mere association to Gina's blood and genes made Jessica dissolve into some kind of assumption of sibling likeness, that I had, in fact, superimposed an identity on her that was not her own.

Finally she said, "The prosecutors have it, as far as I know."

"Did you have a chance to look at it?" I asked.

"I'm not liking the direction this is heading," she replied. "Suffice it to say that if I have read it, I would, in no way, betray my sister by sharing her private thoughts with a reporter."

"I'm sorry."

Then the muffled, quivering sound of her tears. What had I done? Other than act like a complete buffoon and become for yet another moment every Geraldo Rivera I had ever hated. She sniffled and said, "Mr. Fitzgerald, I can't be of any help to you. But I think you should worry less about Gina's journal and more about the legal files that she had taken from the office."

"Legal files."

"They, too, are in the hands of the prosecutors. Good luck."

"I'm not sure I understand."

"Neither do we," the woman said. "We do know she was unhappy with her job. We think she may have gotten involved with something questionable."

"Questionable?"

"We don't know. But it's just a feeling we get."

"And those files?"

"Those files are either evidence that Gina was doing something wrong, or that she knew something wrong was going on."

"What do the authorities tell you?"

"About the files?"

"Yes."

"Not much. We've asked. But our questions have been evaded. If you really want to make any sense of my sister's murder, you need to find out what was in that box of files a lot more urgently than you need to interview her grieving family."

She was a smart woman. Perhaps, like her sister, she too thought herself smarter than most others. She had summed up my intentions and my needs and what my telephone call had represented so cogently it embarrassed me, even then, when I really thought I didn't give a shit anymore about my job and all its tentacles.

"Thank you, Ms. Parr," I said. "I'll do what I can. Should you change your mind about meeting with me..."

But it was too late. She had hung up the phone. Not abruptly, however. The phone just seemed to slip casually into its cradle and leave me unceremoniously on the outside of one family's secrets—where I belonged.

✧ ✧ ✧

I called Raleigh Dean later than afternoon, hours later, when I figured he'd be packing it in after a fruitless day of lawyering among the other rumpled public defenders, that he'd be just an arm's reach away from his dusty overcoat when the phone rang. And he was. "I was just getting set to leave," he said.

I asked him about the box of legal files. He said he knew about it and was waiting for it to be turned over as evidence.

"Does it sound suspicious to you?" I asked him.

I heard a gruff murmur of dismissal, the same gruff murmur that probably put limitations on his career, keeping him out of the gilded law firms—if he ever really cared. "Not particularly," he replied. "A lot of young hotshots take their work home with them, Damon. Not unusual."

"Would you feel differently if I told you that her firm was connected to the collapse of New England Savings?"

Dead silence. Not even a breath. I heard sirens in the background whizzing by his office, predicated by the sound of bodily function—flatulence again, I guessed.

"Raleigh?"

"I'm here, Damon. Do you mind telling me how the hell

you uncovered *that* connection?"

"I do mind, Raleigh. I can't put that on the table just yet."

"Even off the record?"

"Even off the record," I told him. "Let's just say you have the information. You can put your P.I. on it, okay?"

"Yeah, whatever."

I laughed. I don't know why exactly, but I laughed. Perhaps it was the race of endorphins that, despite my reluctance and reticence, proved, on the brink of a sexy deal, that I was still a journalist. "Look, you review that evidence. Let me see what's in that box, and I'll tell you what we know about New England Savings."

"So, now you don't think my investigator can handle the case himself?"

"No. I welcome as much information as possible from him as well."

"Do you owe me a beer?" the attorney asked.

"No," I replied. "I don't."

We agreed to talk again in a few days and left it at that.

✧ ✧ ✧

Over the next few days, Gretchen came probing like a proctologist, her finger poking at the anus of my story arsenal and Donna's as well. We made a huge mistake and told her about the connection between the bank and the law firm and she immediately succumbed to one of her sensational TV-gasms and, salivating like a horny dog in Miami, announced that we would pull the story together and get it on the air the first day of February sweeps.

"It might not be ready," Donna told her.

"C'mon, you guys," she begged. "You can make it ready. We'll blow everybody out of the water."

She was always resorting to naval images, battles at sea,

wreckage on the ocean. And while we admired her com-
petitive spirit, her love of strategy, we had to insist on a
more judicious approach. "When we've checked all our
sources, and double-checked all our facts, and when we
really have the story nailed down, we'll let you know and
we'll be glad to do it in tandem," I said.

She backed against the wall, as if she had sustained a
blow to her abdomen, so stunned was she by this demon-
stration of journalistic integrity.

Donna tried to comfort the woman. "Right now,
Gretchen, it's all speculation. We don't want to get sued
over speculation."

"You people are always threatening me with lawsuits!"
she cried.

We looked at her, puzzled. "We're not going to sue you,
Gretchen," I explained.

She snorted back in disgust. "I know that, Damon! But
you guys are always threatening me with the *threat* of lawsuits."

I took the crazy woman by the hand, wished I could
have inconspicuously dropped her forty milligrams of
Prozac, and said, "Well, we won't do that anymore,
Gretchen. We won't make you worry like that."

She left and Donna and I rolled our eyes and sighed in
perfect harmony. That's not hyperbole. Our sighs reached
a mutual pitch, a symbiotic utterance of deep understanding, laced with deep disappointment yet tempered with a
cadence of resigned bemusement.

✧ ✧ ✧

I must admit that later that evening when starting my car
in the Channel 11 parking lot I jumped out of my seat
when a hand rapped at my window. Maybe it was all the
dark secrets lingering about the Gina Parr murder, the

bank collapse, the box of files, the open door, I don't know, but I was surprised at how easily I was startled.

I peered through the frost-covered window and could only see a small shadow of a figure. I didn't recognize the outline of the person, not that I should have been able to, so I hesitated to lower the window. Instead I blasted the defroster, hoping the window would clear fast enough to reveal the shadow's identity. It did not. The hand rapped again. And again. Harder.

Fuck, I said to myself. Then I acquiesced and cracked the window, preparing my left temple for a bullet and the explosion of my brain, and I felt somewhat relieved and liberated by the prospect of death (I wouldn't have to worry about Gretchen, February sweeps, my father's prostate, or cleaning my bathroom).

Sam Young smiled at me.

"Oh, hi," I said.

"Hello. There's one more thing I wanted to tell you."

I lowered the window even more. "Yes?"

"I should have told you the other day."

"Do I need a notebook?"

"No," he said. "I'm bisexual and I have a very big penis."

I laughed abruptly. "And I'm homosexual and do not."

"Well," he said, his warm breath escaping in small clouds to the chilly air, "I knew you were gay, Damon."

"Of course you did," I said flatly. "I'm the famous gay reporter in Boston. Everybody knows and who the hell cares. But what does this have to do with Gina's murder? Did she find out about one of your gay lovers and try to kill you? Did you murder her in self-defense? Is this a con-fession?"

He looked at me horrified. "Of course not!"

"I'm sorry. I didn't mean to offend you."

His eyes started to fill with little bulbs of water. "No, I

never cheated on her. But she knew that I was turned on by some men."

"But why do I need to know this?" I asked and turned the ignition, indicating my imminent departure.

"Thought you might want to fool around, you know."

I laughed. "Are you serious?"

"I'm psychic," he said.

I shook my head, then rested it on the steering wheel. *Why*, I begged the universe in silent distress, *did the freaks always pick me out of the crowd?*

I looked at my visitor again. "So, you had a vision that we had sex?"

"No," he replied. "But I have imagined it, Damon. And enjoyed it."

"You're making me uncomfortable, Sam."

"Nervous?" he asked with a thin smile.

"No. Just uncomfortable," I lied.

"Well, you don't have to sleep with me to know the truth. I won't withhold it from you."

"Really?" I said, racing the engine now..

"This investigation is going to kill you," he said.

"Yeah, I know, Sam. It's already giving me an ulcer."

He rested a hand on the window's edge. "No, I mean it's really going to kill you, Damon. If you keep at this, you're going to die."

"Okay..."

"But I will channel you when you're gone."

I laughed openly now, if not to deflect my uneasiness, then certainly to enjoy for a moment the whimsy of this encounter. "Channel me?"

"I channel."

"Let me tell you something, Sam. I work at *Channel* 11 now. I have worked for several *channel*s in my life. Television has taken its toll on me and my life. There will be no *channeling* of any kind when I'm dead."

"I just thought you should know," he said. "Have a good night." Then he turned and walked away. Got into his car, I presumed. But I didn't hang around long enough to see.

24

"You're a shining star,
No matter who you are
Shining bright to see
What you can truly be."
—Earth, Wind & Fire

YOU MUST UNDERSTAND THE PAIN AND GRIEF OF LOSING
someone is nothing more than a function of survival. The living long for another moment with the one who passed away.
The living cannot bear the separation. The living cannot fath-
om life without that familiar face, and touch, and voice.
Because survival is so harrowing, the living have become
acquainted with the *tragedy* of death, the *unfairness*, the
untimeliness; the living assume that death is the darkest irony
of life. Yet it is not. It is merely another chapter in the best
mystery never published.

If the living knew how astonishingly beautiful and magical
death is, they would grieve less, celebrate more. Yes, they
would *miss* the person terribly, but that *missing* would be

mitigated by the knowledge that their loved one was shining down on them with an intensity unimaginable but believable. After all, scientists know for sure that most of the luminous matter in the universe is in the form of stars.

God knows, I paid my dues as a cub reporter, and most of those dues were paid interviewing the grieving survivors of homicide victims or anyone else who died an unusual death. There is an unwritten rule in news reporting: GET THE FAMILY. If there is a dead person, there *has* to be a grieving family member. There *must* be tears. If the dead person is Hispanic, there may even be a vigil. The rule requires the television reporter to stick a microphone into the face of a sobbing human being and ask "How does it feel?"

I had my own rules. I never asked, "How does it feel?" I said, "Please, tell me a little about [insert dead person's name here]."

Grieving people like to talk about the deceased. And they need little encouragement. And you can usually count on several very good sound bites to pick and choose from.

The worst, of course: interviewing grieving parents. A dead child is heartbreak like no other. But the heartbreak, the horrendous feeling of loss, is, again, a function of survival. The survivors simply cannot understand the blessing in the skies above, that this young soul has been granted early entry into the luminescence of the heavens. We mourn a *life cut short*. We grieve the loss of such a young life, full of such potential. It is the living who have hopes and dreams for the younger generations, and thus the dashed hopes and broken dreams belong to those survivors. And the death of a young person leaves them feeling cheated. And, yes, to some extent they are cheated. But the only reason death is a bad thing is because it is bad for the living.

If people knew the best thing about life is the *afterlife,* there'd be a whole new attitude about funerals.

❖ ❖ ❖

Let me confess a few things:

I have used my energy to play with Karl and Louise.

I shine on them, and in this cosmic blend of light and heat and matter that matters I allow for a little mischief. I have lightened Louise's makeup a shade or two. I think people respond to her better now. I have presided over a few of Karl's wet dreams. He wakes up in a massive puddle of joy and knows he will never come like that with a partner or even during a very aggressive session of masturbation. I have also hid his dildo several times because I don't think he needs as much ass-probing as he thinks he does. A lot of gay men just get trapped in the trappings, if you will. They get into routines that have passed through the collective consciousness of gay culture but aren't necessarily mandated by birth or required by law.

And I have organized Raleigh Dean's disarray of files.

I'm not sure he's noticed.

❖ ❖ ❖

It's unfortunate, I suppose, that I must use Karl's nocturnal emissions as an example. But what better way to illustrate the manifestations of our visitations! I'm talking about dreams and the comfort you must take in dreaming about the departed.

I remember as a child dreaming about my grandmother, Marguerite, my mother's mother whom I adored. She would stir my dreams frequently with her presence. These were not bad dreams, just testament to how much I missed her. I guess I was her favorite. After all, it was me and only me with whom she shared all the old stories about all my ancestors and what I assumed were the "olden days" but were more likely just a few generations before me. She seemed the happiest when she was telling her stories and remembering something blissful about an uncomplicated life somewhere in the French countryside. And she told me about cousins I would never meet, and uncles and aunts to whom she would send photos of me. And I became very attached to her. More attached, perhaps, than I was to my mother. Although I am, of course, just realizing this now. Her death was hard for me to understand. I couldn't reconcile myself to never seeing her again or hearing her soft voice, the chirp of her melodious storytelling, the smell of fresh-ground coffee roasting in her kitchen.

She never haunted me. She'd simply appear in my dreams and appear in them often. Years later a friend, Steven Taylor, told me that Marguerite had simply popped into my dreams to say hello and to tell me that she was fine.

"She's visiting you," he'd say.

"Visiting me?"

"Yeah. That's how dead people visit you. They show up in your dreams."

We were in high school then. I didn't question his wisdom, but I didn't exactly embrace it either. I thought it was sweet that he had conjured up this comforting image, but I did not do much with it—pocketed it, I guess, for future reference, stashed it away for more mature meditation.

But it turns out Steven Taylor was right.

As a dead person, I can tell you that, yes, we do visit, and we visit often. When you dream about us it is more than just a mere expression of your subconscious. Are not dreams, themselves, otherworldly? They do not exist entirely in your brain. No brain has that much capacity, enough to zip around the kaleidoscope of color and movement, across such an extraordinary passage of time, transition of places, to vault from memory to memory to fantasy and back. We, on the other side, must and do take some of the credit.

We visit.

We remind you.

We encourage you.

We instruct you.

As for Karl, well, surely he can ejaculate on his own, and surely he is a bit old for the average nocturnal emission. In fact, most nocturnal emissions are a function of puberty, nothing more than that. Few if any departed ones (the shooting stars excepted) are inclined to make their visit overly sexual. But with Karl, I thought I'd have some fun.

As someone who thinks orgasm a form of poetry, who believes it a god-given power, like eyesight, who, until very recently, kept a highly descriptive log of every load he shot ("I'll publish it someday"), Karl enjoys my visit. He doesn't know that I have, well, a hand in these mysterious eruptions. But it matters little, for a smile rests on his beautiful face for the remainder of his sleep and, indeed, surprises him in the mirror when he hobbles to the bathroom the following morning.

To me that's a blessing, really.

25

THE DRIVE TO RHODE ISLAND IS, IF NOTHING ELSE, excruciatingly boring. We left around four in the afternoon, expecting to hit Providence by five-thirty or six, depending on traffic. Down the Southeast Expressway, past the remnants of industrial efforts and city beaches, blue-collar neighborhoods pushed up against the highway. Yes, when we passed South Boston, Johnnie did an obligatory if not unconscious gesture to his Irish homeland and I smiled. The scenery, however dismal, is still scenery. That changes once you hit I-95 and travel south. It is just nothing. Especially this time of year, the winter, when everything is brown and scraggly and even the evergreens look tired and put out by the chill. You just drive and drive and the brownness gives you a vague, though unfair, concept of eternity. Whatever green is left is nothing more than an anemic distraction.

The gray-white clusterfuck of Providence hustled by us as we aimed for Warwick. Warwick, of all places. I had never heard of anything happening in Warwick, except, perhaps, a few failed financial institutions with links to state government. For such a small state, Rhode Island was as corrupt as any other. Darkness came quickly as we traveled the final leg of this journey, the night really seemed to swoop down over us, capture us as we exited the highway. The streets were instantly narrow, crowded by older buildings, roughed up by time and neglect. I removed the instructions Patrick O'Hare had provided me with. They were, essentially, the anatomy of a crime. He listed names, described peoples' faces (would I get close enough, I wondered, to recognize three birthmarks in the shape of an isosceles triangle?), and gave specific directions to an abandoned warehouse that hulked like a dying beast alongside a dark river.

Once at said warehouse, in our unmarked white van, we surveyed the area and pulled away. We parked several blocks from the building and watched. And waited. And nothing happened. Johnnie looked at me and rolled his eyes. I looked back and shrugged. Like, how the fuck should I know? I consulted my paperwork and looked at my watch. According to Patrick O'Hare we should have seen some activity about fifteen minutes prior. Ten minutes later, still nothing.

"Well?" Johnnie said.

"Well, nothing. I don't think these guys are worried about sticking to O'Hare's schedule."

Not a car in sight. Not the stealth movement of a body or shadows of crime anywhere.

Johnnie flipped on the radio. Deep Purple or Pink Floyd. Shame on me for not knowing the difference.

Then a car slid down the steep embankment, following the driveway to the edge of the warehouse.

Then a blue van.

There was movement, but all we could see were several pairs of legs scrambling through a doorway.

"Let's go," I said.

Johnnie strapped on his undercover camera—a fanny pack with $12,000 worth of metal and wires tucked inside—and we quietly slipped toward the back of the building. There were few windows. And those we could find were too high to be of any use. We crept around the entire perimeter and found another doorway, bashed in presumably by vandals, spray-painted with ganglike obscenities. The door hung there by a hinge like a piece of skin dangling from a neglected wound. We passed through it, tiptoeing in the direction of voices. They were farther away than they sounded. We walked what seemed like blocks through the tunnels of the old building, the creaking floors betraying our presence, the cold air biting at my ears and my fingers. Finally we reached the end of a hallway and, peering around a torn-out corner of wall, we found our men. There were four of them. Two short guys with bearded faces, one tall skinny dude, probably nineteen, and an older man who was unmistakably Gerard DeKashonni, owner of Rendezvous (no fucking shit!). I jabbed Johnnie's elbow. He responded with a terse, very terse warning in his eyes and pointed to the fanny pack, reminding me that every jab of my excitement only served to fuck up the steadiness of his shot. Well, yes, I acquiesced, how dumb of me. But Johnnie knew me well and knew that if it weren't for my enthusiasm (God only knows where I mustered it from), we would not be rolling on a spectacular moment of crime in action. In other words, Johnnie knew an Emmy when he saw one and could always count on me to land a trophy or two in his hands.

From around this dubious corner all we could see was the men engaged in fast-talking conversation. There were hands waving in the air, a few grunts of satisfaction, and, finally, the exchange of money.

That was it.

Money.

Gerard DeKashonni accepted several wads of bills and a few envelopes and disappeared into a far corner of the building.

The other men came our way.

Johnnie spun around quickly. "Fuck," he whispered. He looked at me desperately and I shook my head. No, I had not planned for this either. I gestured for him to follow me quickly and he did. We retreated down the dark hallway, hearing the shuffle of the men quickly approaching. I felt Johnnie's hand on my shoulder, pushing me onward. In one way, I guess I wanted to grab Johnnie by the hand and pull him to safety in some kind of romantic notion of heroism and unspoken love. Because we did love each other. You could tell. We deeply respected each other and the love was brotherly, I supposed, a love Johnnie would or could never admit to, but it was there. I felt nothing erotic toward the boy but would not have turned him away, either, if one day he came to me with a certain revelation about himself and the resulting sexual overture. Yes, I wanted to grab him by the hand and show the man who he could count on for heroics. Instead I led him into another hallway and pushed him toward an open room. We ducked inside while the three men continued on their way, down the first hallway. We heard them bang through the rusty door.

They were out. We were in. Instincts told me not to follow their path, but rather to reenter the room where money changed hands and find another exit, the exit presumably taken by Gerard DeKashonni. Johnnie was hesitant, but I was proud to see him lean on my intuition and follow. In moments we were through the room, creeping down another hallway, turning left then right, kicking broken glass, emerging from the building's shards, finally, at a door.

Once outside my eyes darted for the car and the van, saw neither. I peered around the corner, saw the van backing up the embankment, the car sitting there at the opening to the road. They pulled out in different directions.

"Who the fuck do we follow?" Johnnie asked.

I said nothing until we reached our car. Inside, I told

Johnnie to follow DeKashonni. It was more important to know where the money was heading than to follow the three others. Johnnie didn't offer an opinion, somewhat uncharacteristic of him—he seemed more tired than interested at that point—and simply backed the car out and aimed it tentatively toward the roadway, stalling there for a moment, like a small dog sniffing at some bushes.

"Uh, we're going to lose him," I prodded.

"I can see him," he said. "He's about two traffic lights ahead of us."

And that's just about the distance we kept for the entire dreadful ride back to Boston. I must say Johnnie was quite adept at trailing. Never once did I sense the driver ahead of us could suspect he was being followed. We listened to Alanis (every thought in my head is a song) Morissette and I was grateful that I did not have the bleak scenery rushing by me, but only black and blue patches of night.

DeKashonni got off the expressway in the South End. And I'm not sure why, because he led us on a chase through narrow streets and unremarkable neighborhoods only to snake his way back to the highway. We pursued him as he dipped into the orange tunnel beneath Chinatown, kept our distance as he emerged over the waterfront flanking Faneuil Hall and veered off toward Storrow Drive. It was only then, as we approached him a bit too closely, that I realized he was on the telephone. Perhaps he was following instructions, instructions that perhaps changed in the middle of the South End, rerouting him and his bounty.

After a few miles on Storrow, we landed in the heart of Kenmore Square—a crossroads of academia and addiction, where college students spent their parents' money on both textbooks and ecstasy, software and alcohol, and where sex, as it often does in the hands of prescient college kids, became a philosophy—an art, if you will, whose physical implications were merely incidental. Yeah, right.

DeKashonni darted left toward Boylston Street. We were on the verge of his neighborhood, a few blocks from Rendezvous, and I felt a quick pulse in my head as if maybe this night would score, after all. Maybe we'd get it all and be done with it. But, no, the club owner bypassed his establishment and continued instead to Park Drive where he started to slow. We kept our pace and watched as he cruised from one address to another, finally hitting the brakes and turning off into an alley. Obediently, Johnnie pulled to the side of the road, fastened himself into the fanny pack and hopped out. I followed. We ushered each other to the foot of the alleyway where we could see the man get out of his car and turn. And walk toward us. Shit.

We spun around and crept to the front of the building, calculating to ourselves just how far behind DeKashonni would be. I listened for his footsteps and didn't hear them. That was good. We had time to reassemble. We crouched down beside the stoop of the building and waited for the man to approach the door. He did. He knocked. A light went on. Immediately I could read the sign above the door frame: LANE & LANE INSURANCE. An inner door opened, exposing a wide lobby directly behind it. A normal office-looking place, secretarial, really. Chrome and glass, a steel staircase curving toward the back. DeKashonni was met by two men. White guys, probably in their late thirties. Stiff white shirts and suspenders. Alpha males working late, entitled to everything, even women outside of marriage. They smiled and shook hands. Right there in the open, DeKashonni handed the men the money. There was the wad of bills, followed by two envelopes, presumably more cash. I nudged Johnnie. "Are you getting all of this?" I whispered.

Another look of disdain. He loved me but disdained me all at once. That was very true. "Of course I'm getting this," he snapped back.

"Aim it at those guys, Johnnie. I know what DeKashonni looks like. But I want to get the other faces."

"No shit, Damon. You're not the only one with a working brain tonight."

Enough said. My reporter neurosis mixed with his photographer sensitivity was resulting in the classic clash of egos. We were well beyond that, so I shut up while Johnnie, trusted Johnnie with freckles on the back of his neck, aimed at the right people, and shot the right faces.

Then I said "good job" and told him he was done for the night.

His relief was not exactly inconspicuous.

26

N<small>OT EASY TO CONVINCE</small> J<small>OHNNIE</small> F<small>ANAHAN TO SPEND THE</small> evening at Rendezvous.

"You know what this means," I told him as he unpacked his gear in the shack of a room that was called a photographer's lounge.

He ignored me. The ride home from Rhode Island was admittedly tiring...more for him, I suppose, considering the focus he had to maintain to follow DeKashonni. I, on the other hand, had drifted off to fantasies near and far, fantasies of pissing in Gretchen's face as a prelude to my resignation, fantasies of walking along a beach at water's edge, silently rejoicing in my solitude—my disconnection—did I mention the beach belonged to a small island in the West Indies and that I had thoroughly assumed the lifestyle?— fantasies of fucking Garth Brooks. Don't ask. I never could figure that one out—he being the only celebrity I had ever considered fucking in my dreams. I had snapped out of my dreams, of course, during the brief stakeout at Lane & Lane—but other than that I had allowed by brain to wander through the serpentine channels of what-ifs and why-nots. I did not much think Johnnie Fanahan capable of such wild fantasy. Perhaps that is underestimating him, but I knew him as a very literal guy. There was baseball. Beer. Work, church, and the occasional vagina.

"Do you want to watch the undercover stuff?" he asked me, speaking up from his momentary exile.

"It can wait until tomorrow, Johnnie," I replied. "But speaking of tomorrow, it's Friday. That means Drag Night at Rendezvous."

He looked up at me, waiting, it seemed, for my point.

"We need to be there undercover," I said.

He laughed. "Come on..."

"What do you mean, Come on..."

"There's no way you're getting me to walk in there."

"Of course you will. We have to follow through with this."

He shook his head. "Look, Damon. I respect you. I accept who you are and what you do, but that doesn't mean I gotta go to a gay bar."

"Is that what this is about?" I asked.

"What did you think this was about?"

"Johnnie, we have to go in there with the undercover camera and see if we find anything."

He stuffed his battery pack into a locker. "What if someone sees me there?"

I laughed. "Please, plenty of straight people go to drag shows. It's entertainment, for chrissakes. It's a very mixed crowd."

"What are we looking for?"

"Those guys from the insurance company," I replied. "As far as I know the money is in their hands and somehow it has to get passed through the club."

He looked at me tentatively. "I don't know..."

"You have nothing to fear," I said, "but queers themselves."

He did not laugh.

But I did.

The following evening he sheepishly followed me into Rendezvous, breathing deeply, rapidly; I worried that he might hyperventilate.

We had screened the undercover tape earlier in the day (hiding it from Gretchen for fear she'd snatch it and air portions of it during the newscast—just because she could). We had studied the exchange of money in Warwick, and watched very closely the drop-off at Lane & Lane. The video was good. I told Johnnie so, dropping in as many encouraging words as I could to prepare him for the night he so badly dreaded.

"I can't believe how well you were able to capture their faces," I had told him. "I mean, I would recognize those guys if I saw them on the street tomorrow."

"Yeah, it's pretty good shit," he conceded.

Pretty good shit, indeed. I took a photographic memory shot of the guys from Lane & Lane, knowing they were the most recent link in the money chain, and it was their faces I looked for as we went creeping through the bars of Rendezvous.

"I don't see them," Johnnie said. He was anxious to leave and it was obvious.

"For chrissakes, have a beer," I told him.

"I don't drink while working."

"In the interest of the story, I think you should make an exception."

We stepped through a bar and heard the old-school chants of Donna Summer, toot-tooting her story of women for sale. I remembered those days. Those almost halcyon days of sexual awakening, discovery, harmony. The '70s for gays were like the '60s for straight people. It took us a while to catch up. It always does, which may explain why most gay people go through adolescence at twenty-four.

Johnnie relented and had a beer. Then another. I stopped him after that. "You do need to get this video, Johnnie. And I'd hate for you to lose your inhibitions and go home with Cha-Cha Marie."

"Cha-Cha who?"

"Marie. A drag queen."

He rolled his eyes.

When the show got under way we squeezed into the theater and found a small table several rows back from the stage. It was during the third performance when I first noticed Johnnie relax. An enormous black queen was screaming an Aretha ballad while twirling around on pink stilettos. She wore a big smudge of red lipstick. How could you not laugh at that? He leaned across the table and scream-whispered into my ear, "They get paid for this?"

I nodded. He shook his head, quite unable to reconcile the scene in front of him but void of judgment, it seemed, and that was the Johnnie that I really knew.

There was no sign of anyone. No sign of DeKashonni or the dudes from the insurance company.

Then the lines started forming at the stage. Men and women, fags and non-fags alike, waited for their moment of genuflection. The money started flying. The performers bowed slightly to their admirers and fetched their bills, never breaking for a moment from their performances. There was the obligatory Whitney, followed by Britney, Janet, and an Asian Dolly Parton—not a bad rendition, surprisingly. Smoke swirled above us, laughter erupted around us, the lines grew longer, and then, in the furthest reaches of my peripheral vision, I recognized someone standing there amid the pandemonium. He was a man I had seen only the night before accept money from Gerard DeKashonni. Standing next to him, of course, was the other guy from Lane & Lane. Two insurance agents at a drag show. They stuck out like two rabbis at a pig roast.

I nudged Johnnie, forgetting for a moment his aversion to being nudged. I scream-whispered to him, "Are you rolling?"

He nodded.

"They're over there, against the back wall," I told him.

My adrenaline rushed into the back of my neck and vicious endorphins went haywire in my brain. I wanted to dance. I wanted to celebrate the inevitable kill. This was the extent of my hunting experience: the urban landscape and its media prey. And it felt good. Real good.

"Do we have to move?" I asked Johnnie.

"Maybe," he said. "Let's see what they do." A discernable shift now, like a shadow passing over his face. This was no longer a drag show; this was a story.

We did not have to wait for long. Within minutes the Lane & Lane boys were pushing forward through the crowd, forsaking the safety of the rear wall for a closer look, it seemed. They moved steadily onward, keeping their eyes on the stage, not flinching for a moment, and then they got in line.

They fucking got in line!

They weren't wearing suits, but they might as well have been for their stiffness, their almost mechanical choreography. They advanced slowly in line, never saying a word to one another, barely acknowledging the crowd around them, staring, still, straight ahead at the performers, hypnotized, it seemed, by the spectacle in front of them. Their mission might as well have been powered by remote control. Then they were at the stage's edge. And it all seemed so perfectly rehearsed as they dug so calculatingly into their pockets, removing big wads of cash and handing them to the drag queens. Bills, bills, and more bills. Asian Dolly leaned over and the Lane & Lane boys stuffed money into her bra and spanked her big behind.

They spanked her ass!

The crowd went wild, hooting and cheering and whistling all sorts of sexy innuendoes.

The men waited there for two more performers, deposited the remains of the money with them, turned around, and retreated from the crowd.

I wanted to grab Johnnie, but I knew he was still shooting. I wanted to grab him and scream the biggest *gotcha* of my career. I knew better, but it was hard to contain myself. It was hard not to be intoxicated by that nectar of news-gathering that was so fucking addictive. I wanted to kick the fucking wall or swing from that bulbous mirror ball on the ceiling.

The men disappeared from the theater, slipped out in silhouette.

Gerard DeKashonni had not only laundered money through his club but through the cleavages of several drag queens.

What a fucking story.

GOD GETS FRUSTRATED. GOD DOESN'T GET MAD, PER SE, JUST moderately disheartened. You have to understand that the view from up here, like that from a spaceship, provides a mind-altering perspective.

Now, it's not like I have had the direct, one-on-one conversation with God. That hasn't happened yet. But God communicates to us en masse and we definitely hear what God has to say more clearly up here in the stark ringing of space. And we communicate with one another too, you should know. The stars that possess our souls pulsate as if in radiant Morse code. Where there are no words there are beats, vibrations. Think of whales swimming under the deep waters of heaven. The messages are graceful, abundant, and clear. The messages I have received from other souls up here suggest that God is fairly perplexed by Earth. And, sharing in this view from above, I must say that I am too.

The souls tell me that God looks down on Earth and wonders what all the fuss is about. From up here, Earth is but a blip in space, yet it has complicated itself with enough anxious energy to fill the entire universe. Bad energy. Dark energy. Confusion.

War, for example, is inexcusable. Most governments, for that matter, are inexcusable too. Anyone who presumes to rule the world, the nation, the land, or even the tiniest village has a huge, huge lesson to learn. People are not born to be rulers. At best, they are born to lead. And even then, it is in the eyes of God or the higher power to whom they answer.

Trust me on this: The Earth belongs to nobody and everybody. The common ground between the two parties is truly what God intended. When we see wars break out over land and territories we just want to gasp in our radiance and make it stop. People are fighting over turf they have no right, ultimately, to claim. God gave the land to his children. To *all* of them. God expected the children to be good neighbors and nothing else.

Humanity, alone, was supposed to rule the planet.

I know that in the context of the modern day these philosophies sound ridiculous. Like cosmic crap, righteous New Ageism. I realize this. What God wants, however, is for people to transcend time, forsake the modern day, and experience the innocence of the Earth's beginning. A planetary rebirth, if you will. It is only there and then that people will see the Earth for what it is; for what it was intended to be. Only then will the people of Earth see it in its naked truth, its primordial landscape, its unlimited potential, its open door to everyone.

No, there was no plumbing back then.

That came later.

And there were no boy bands.

Unfortunately, those came later too.

But there was sound and light and vision.

And there was the beauty of touch and smell.

God gave people an infinite canvas. God gave people trust and endurance, faith and fortitude. After that, anything could be possible. But after that, people became people and nations became nations and scriptures were written, civilizations instructed, borders drawn, laws amended, wars fought inside and out.

The stars can only weep sometimes.

Because from up here we can see how enormous a problem besets such a small place. We can see how the Earth is beyond helping itself.

Only the people themselves can turn back their centuries-old habits of dismantling God's gift. And so far, at this point, despite all their clever bumper stickers, people aren't so inclined.

28

JOHNNIE HAD SAID SOMETHING TO DONNA.

She came into my office the following Monday morning with a huge, ingratiating smile on her face. "Hey, Mr. Money-Laundering Undercover..."

I did not acknowledge her presence. Instead I kept my eyes on the screen, reading the e-mail that had accumulated over the weekend.

"Big story, huh?" she asked.

"Yeah," I said flatly, still not meeting her eyes. I was angered at Johnnie for running his mouth off about Rendezvous, for revealing anything about our investigation into Gerard DeKashonni. To me this was a hotter story than Gina Parr—hotter in the sense that I knew no one else was working the Rendezvous story, that I would have an exclusive. But for every person that knew about the investigation, there were probably six chances it would leak out and no longer be an exclusive. Six degrees of revelation, I would call it. Or six degrees of complication. Whatever it was, I was not comfortable with anyone knowing anything until we had nailed down more evidence. We had yet to see the actual object of the money laundering. No contraband: no story. We needed to see the weapons and I had called Patrick O'Hare first thing that morning to tell him.

"I don't know about that," he had said tentatively.

"I can't run a story about two goons stuffing wads of money into some drag queens' tits unless there's probable cause of a significant crime."

"Oh. When did the news business become so noble?" he quipped.

"I'm not doing this on behalf of the so-called news business, Pat. I am putting my name and my face on this thing and it better be credible."

"I'll talk to my people about it."

"Your people?" I asked.

He snorted. "Yeah, my people. You have a problem with that?"

"I can't tell whether you sound like Alec Baldwin or John Gotti," I told him. "But talk to whoever you have to—and get your butt down here to watch the video."

"Is there a problem?"

"No problem, man, but I need you to identify the plant. The undercover guy, so we know who's who."

"Did you get DeKashonni on tape?"

"Maybe."

"I can't see until I come down there?"

"You're catching on, my friend."

He hung up. It was moments later when Donna had breezed into the room. I still ignored her presence but for a few short answers.

I had an e-mail from wetpussy.com. I ignored that as well.

I had an e-mail from my sister Claire: "Did you know Dad needs surgery?"

Uh, no. I hadn't known that.

I could only guess it was his prostate that required the knife, but who knew?

"He said you guys almost got nailed in Rhode Island," Donna persisted.

Finally, I turned to her. "Nailed?"

"Caught. Johnnie said you two had to dodge some goons down there."

I laughed. "Yeah, I guess we did."

"When are you running the story?" she asked.

"I don't know."

"Boy, you're awfully cold this morning," she said as she leaned on another desk in the office. She sipped coffee. Her eyes looked hungover from a Sunday of drinking, watching football, maybe.

"Sorry, Donna. But I hate Mondays. I hate Mondays at work even more. And I really don't want word to get out about this Rendezvous story."

She wagged her head. "Come on, Damon. It's just me. I'm not going to go running my mouth to anyone."

"Even your cop friends?"

"Even my cop friends."

"Even your *Globe* friends."

"Especially my *Globe* friends. You know me better than that."

I nodded. "You're right. I do."

"Double standard," she said conclusively.

"What?"

"You don't mind getting tips from my cop friends. You don't mind when they leak *us* information, but you sure don't want to leak them any..."

"No," I told her. "That's always on a case-by-case basis. In this case I already know the feds are involved, so the local police really have no business with the case... Telling them would just somehow get it on the record and then, bang, the rest of the media knows about it."

She tossed her wispy gray bangs to the side, took another sip of coffee, and headed for the door. "I gotcha, Damon. Enough said. Hope your Monday gets better. At least you didn't lock yourself out."

"Yeah," I said when she was already gone. "That would have sucked."

❖ ❖ ❖

I called my sister Claire, later that day. She worked for a travel agency that was on the verge of going out of business, so I pretended to be a client seeking advice on an around-the-world cruise.

"First class," I told her. "First class all the way."

"Inside or outside cabin?" she asked.

"Outside, of course. A beautiful suite with sweeping views, in fact."

"Okay, sir."

"Can you arrange for a nightly blow job?"

"I'll see what I can do."

"Preferably from a Norwegian crew member. High-ranking, if possible."

"Captain's table?"

"Yes, you could have me spread out on the Captain's table and have the Norwegian crew feast on me like a buffet."

"Is there anything else I can do for you?"

"Tell me about Dad's surgery. It is the prostate, is it not?"

"It's not. It's the bottom deck."

"The bottom deck?"

"The rear of the ship."

"He's having surgery on his bum?"

"Exactly."

I shivered for a moment. The repertoire no longer amused me. "Don't tell me he has cancer there too."

"Possibly," she said.

"What, they have to go in and do a biopsy?"

"Yes," she replied.

"Please e-mail me more specifics," I told her.

"Will do," she said. "And thank you for calling Now Voyager Travel."

I kid you not, Now Voyager Travel. The owner had to be a homo, don't you think?

Work was pretty much all I ever talked to Claire about. My job, her job, have a nice day. And she was the sibling to whom I felt closest. I never spent all that much time lamenting about the lack of affection in the Fitzgerald home, or the sterile gestures, the barriers to expression, feeling, love. No, I never even spent that much time thinking about it, deferring to my father's favorite sentiment: "It is what it is." As I grew older I'd often snap back: "And it *isn't what it isn't*." Or if I were feeling particularly petulant, my comeback would be: "And it ain't what it ain't," to which my mother would tersely chant, "English, Damon, English, for heaven's sake."

I considered my prostate for a good hour or so later that afternoon. Wondered exactly what it was and what it did. I'm pretty sure I knew where it was because the nature of a prostate exam was fairly well-known, plus I had always heard there was actually an anatomical reason why a finger up the butt felt good, or why a sensation in that wonderstrip between the balls and anus was always welcome.

Did I mention that Patrick O'Hare never showed up to view the tape that afternoon? Well, fuck him. Did I mention that there would be no story if Patrick O'Hare failed to see this thing through? I was not hanging my neck out for any slimebags in the nightclub business—I think I had made myself very clear on that. As I said, fuck him. And fuck everybody else who had expectations of me, including Fryer Rant and Todd Murphy, who confronted me on my way out that evening standing between the door and me like two defensive linemen. They wore big, disingenuous smiles and folded their arms across their chests. Todd (Mr. Special-Projects Stud) was wearing a plaid flannel shirt, I think, and jeans tight enough to bust a testicle, and Fryer (Mr. I-Kissed-All-The-Right-Asses-To-Get-Into-Management) wore paisley (paisley!) suspenders that stretched down the slope of his bulbous torso to a pair of wide-ribbed corduroys. They had a reminder for me.

"Sweeps start in less than two weeks."

"I know," I told them.

"We put a calendar together today. Thought you'd want to have a look," Fryer said.

"Well, actually guys, I'm sure it can wait till tomorrow. I'm on my way out..."

Todd leaned against the wall, resting on one foot. The basket of his crotch protruded forward. If his jeans had been any tighter, I could have counted the veins in his penis, which would not have pleased me or enhanced my appetite for dinner. "Your fake-diploma story is running first. We have it down for the second night of the book."

I did not respond.

" 'Statehouse Kickbacks' will run the following Monday," Fryer added.

"Those are both ready," I assured him.

"And Gina Parr will run the third week of February," Todd said.

I squinted at him, feigning interest and concern. "Hmm," I began. "I'm not sure Gina Parr will be ready to run at all in February."

Todd lodged his eyes into one of those *You've got to be kidding* glares and I simply shrugged, which consequently made him stiffen. "Not at all?" he asked.

"It's a murder case," I explained. "I'm at the mercy of law enforcement, the courts, a few really bad attorneys."

"It has to run in February," Fryer said.

"Has to?" I asked.

"Has to," he repeated. "The promotions department has

already bought billboard space and radio time and we've already scripted the first campaign."

"Oh," I said. "I would advise against that. First of all, this story could take many turns between now and then. And, secondly, I'd hate to tip off the competition."

Todd shook his head. "You're missing the point, Damon. We need something to promote. We *need* to know what we're going to promote and what slot it's going to fill."

"I think you guys *need* a new approach."

"Damon, we don't want an argument."

I smiled. "Well, you won't get one if you get out of the way and let me leave."

"What has gotten into you, Damon?" the black man, crudely outlined in suspenders, asked me.

"Nothing has gotten into me, guys. I'm just trying to be responsible to my stories."

"But we have this argument with you every time sweeps roll around," Todd said.

"Because I'm always trying to be responsible to my stories. Nothing has changed. If you want someone who is more promotion-driven, you ought to talk to Geraldo."

"Very funny," Fryer said. "I think you need to go home with the calendar, study it hard, and maybe we can have a refreshed talk in the morning."

A "refreshed talk"? Give me a fucking refreshed break.

Fryer slipped into the newsroom and reappeared moments later with the calendar. Todd gave me a heterosexual, good ol' boy pat on the back that made we want to spit and led me to the door. "Damon, you are one of our best reporters," he said. "We wouldn't do anything intentionally to upset you. You know that, right?"

I looked at him squarely but did not answer.

"You're one of the best reporters in town, for chrissakes. Work with us and we'll work with you. I smell an Emmy," he said.

I smell shit on your brain, I thought, as I turned for a quick, sly smile of closure and flung open the door.

Throwing my car into first gear, then second, and then peeling out of the parking lot, I resolved to write my astonishing debut novel, rewrite it, submit it, sell it, and pose for the jacket cover by the third week of February.

Three weeks.

The way I saw it I had a better chance of astonishing the literary world than figuring out what the fuck happened to Gina Parr.

HEARTBREAK IS NOT THE ANATOMICAL EQUIVALENT OF hyperbole. *I realized that seven years ago when my dearest friend told me about her cancer.*

I watched her die.

Her death mesmerized me because it really seemed as though I could see her letting go, her life evaporating like gentle waves of steam over a teeming stew. Was that not her life? The stew? Was that not her soul? The steam? And yet she talked me through her death much the way you talk someone through instructions to set the VCR or driving directions to the company picnic.

The heart really crushes. The chest feels stepped upon. Sometimes it's hard to breathe because the pain and the sadness all but suffocate you.

Her name was Jessica. She was forty-two when she finally smiled at the beauty of it all and laughed at the irony of everything and said goodbye. Her death does not make me think as much about her as it does about us. How's that for a selfish revelation?

I had two other sisters. But Jessica was my favorite.

Finally. I finally had a first page.

I didn't know where it came from and I didn't care. I sat there and stared at it for the longest time, maybe even an hour. I worried about rushing things, rushing the story like rushing relationships that begin so passionately and fizzle out just as swiftly. I studied the lines, then the whole page, as a composition, really, for its appearance, more than anything else. I wrote a page. And it stared back at me quite satisfied itself, it seemed, with my moment of triumph. And nowhere in the text—once I returned to the context, to the words and their meanings—did I see even the faintest hint of News You Can Use.

Thank God.

Two weeks later I had little more than that first page. Honestly, I had nothing more. I had been swept up in sweeps, the damn pressure and hype and spastic stress of it all got its claws in me and carried me off like a vulture parting with its prey. The story about statehouse kickbacks ran and the overnight ratings weren't bad. The fake-diploma story followed two days later and it too fared well in the overnights. And now, of course, I was empty-handed, with no stories to hide behind, trying desperately to stay under the radar. Maybe if I didn't think about Gina Parr, no one else would think about her either. If I removed Gina Parr from the general discourse, who would notice?

Gretchen noticed.

"We need an update on Gina Parr. Nobody else is running anything on it so we can really own the story."

We were in the break room. I was drinking one of those neon-colored sports drinks and she, of course, was drinking coffee. Black.

"Maybe nobody else is running anything on it because

there's nothing to run," I told her.

She grimaced. She really did. It was then that I realized certain faces were made for grimaces. Hers was one of them. It looked so perfect parked there under her crinkled eyebrows and twitchy nose. "Damon, you need to give us something."

Truth was, I had something. Or at least I was getting somewhere. Somewhat unceremoniously, as if he were calling me to chat about good places to stick your parents when they get old and cranky, Raleigh Dean rang me up a few days before and said he was ready to talk about more evidence.

"More evidence?" I asked. "Against whom?"

"Not against my client."

"More evidence that someone else did it?"

"Enough to prove reasonable doubt."

"Well?"

He snorted. "Well nothing, my friend. This is not a conversation we're going to have over the phone."

I anticipated the hungry news machine. "Anything you can sit down and say in front of the camera?"

"Absolutely not."

"How did I know that?"

"Because you're pretty *and* smart."

He said he wouldn't come by the station, that I would have to meet him at Kelly's Toe.

"Later in the week," I told him. "I have very little time."

"This is turning into one amazing case of murder," he said.

"Well-teased," I offered.

"You better not put me off for long, Damon. We think we'll get a trial date soon."

I was surprised. "For Cruz? You're kidding. These cases usually take a year before they get to trial."

"And it may," the public defender said. "But methinks the D.A. wants to dispose of this one quickly before it gets messy."

"I'm intrigued," I told him.

"Thought you would be."

"Truth is, Raleigh, a lot intrigues me. Don't get too excited."

And that was it. A professionally flirtatious conversation and, days later, I had not yet had a chance to follow up. Gretchen would say I had "dropped the ball," but I wouldn't give her the chance. First, there was no ball to be dropped. Second, if there were a ball to be dropped, it would have been dropped long ago. And life is not an endless supply of balls, is it?

"I have to take a leak," I told Gretchen.

"Donna says you have a story about a money-laundering scheme."

What?

I flinched. Had Donna cunted on me? Had she actually appropriated the knife from the aspiring *All About Eve* anchorwomen and plunged it into my back? "I don't know what you're talking about."

Gretchen folded her arms across her chest and assumed a self-satisfied posture. "Turns out Donna has had a few stories fall through. She says she can take the Gina Parr story off your hands so you can devote more time to this money-laundering thing."

I smiled. "Donna must be mistaken. The money-laundering thing is a figment of some informant's imagination. Can't be trusted. So don't count on it."

"I have to count on something from you. Donna says the Cruz case is going to trial quickly and by then it's an old story."

I laughed. "You mean that whole guilty or innocent thing is just a bore, right?"

She walked away. I lowered my head and muttered a tirade of obscenities under my breath. I heard the *click-clack* of her heels stop. She turned around. "Don't fuck with me, Damon. Before you know it I'll be running this place. So if I were you, I'd stay on my good side."

"Didn't know you had one, Gretchen."

"I'm serious, Damon. If you want to keep the Gina Parr story, you bring me something concrete within a week."

What the fuck?

I did not want to keep the Gina Parr story. I should have been celebrating the opportunity to shed it like the decaying hide that it was. But I was not going to hand this story to Donna Donovan. I might have, under different circumstances. But not after getting cunted. I never acquiesced to a cunting.

I called Raleigh Dean immediately and arranged to meet him at Kelly's Toe. Coyly, he accepted my invitation with a caveat. "Some things have come up," he said. "Can we do it over the weekend?"

"No," I replied. I did not trust Donna Donovan's hunger for my story. "If not tonight, then tomorrow."

"Let me get back to you."

"No," I insisted, trying to camouflage my desperation in the garb of urgency. "I need to know now. Can we do this tomorrow?"

"Fine," he said. I could tell he was grinning like a Cheshire cat when he hung up the phone.

How to confront Donna Donovan?

How to outcunt the cunt?

Was it possible? Did it matter? I told Johnnie about it. He told me to "let it go."

I hated that. I hated when people told me to "let it go." How could they possibly know how impossible it would be for me to let something go unless they too were holding on to it? *Let Go Not, Lest Ye Be Let Go.*

"Let it go?" I asked. "Are you fucking her finally?"

"No, asshole, I'm not."

"Then why can't you see what a nasty thing she did?"

He shrugged. Somewhere on the downside of the shrug I realized Johnnie Fanahan had no spine. That was too bad. I really had wanted him to be more a friend, a brother even. But he was like all the rest of the TV people. Shallow, insincere, disingenuous.

"Maybe," he said, "she really wants to help you. I know the two of you have some connection between your stories. You know, the banking thing. The loan scams. Maybe she thinks there's only enough there for one story and she wants to free you up to do the Rendezvous piece."

I laughed. "The one that you went and blabbed to her about?"

"Yes. That one."

We were standing in the parking lot at the end of the work day. The night was chilly. Our words turned into clouds of steam that disappeared into the air. The lampposts overhead shed halos of frigid sweat.

"Thanks, Johnnie. If you had kept your mouth shut, this wouldn't be an issue."

"Maybe you should talk to her," he said, as he nodded and stepped away.

I stood there in the lot, alone, under the domes of light and shook my head. Does everyone leave work at night wishing to never return? Does everyone wish to sample life in a parallel universe?

Hard to know.

Before I could even remove my keys from my coat pocket, a voice from the corner of the lot distracted me.

It was Sam Young.

He waved. "Hey, Damon," he called to me again.

Jesus.

I tried to back away, look the other way, in fact, as if I thought the voice had come from another direction and that I could not have possibly seen him. But he was on top of me within seconds. He shook my shoulders and turned me around. "I have to talk to you," he said.

SPACE IS THE ONLY PLACE FOR SOULS. IT MAKES SENSE. ONLY an infinite space could accommodate all the souls the Earth has to offer. If and when space does become too crowded, a likelihood I sincerely doubt, well, then, I have it on good source that another Big Bang will simply produce another universe full of galaxies ready for the overflow of stars.

Up here you feel a real sense of forever. Not immortality which teases and frustrates man's imagination. But a true sense of boundlessness as if life does not have the beginning or end that is your earthbound frame of reference. Your existence here—your pure energy and light—does not come with margins. What I am trying to say is that your soul has no linear sense of time the way your consciousness on Earth calculates your life.

I stole Karl's underwear today. It was for his own good. He had taken a vacation to Key West (must even your vacation be a cliché, Karl?) and had browsed the homoerotic emporiums for the perfect souvenir. He emerged with one gold sequined thong, which I watched him try on in the privacy of his hotel room. I laughed a meteor shower of hysterics when I saw in his eyes my own disappointment and then ultimately his admission that the silly penis sack and ass floss had been an embarrassing mistake. And yet he pranced. Beautiful Karl indulged himself in a moment of posing and strutting and then flicked the thong from his body like a slingshot, laughing at himself, laughing at anyone who would make this same mistake and not, in fact, realize it in the nick of time.

And now, days later, as he packed his things for the trip back to Boston, I made sure to scoop up the thong with heaven's mysterious vacuum and drop it far out at sea somewhere between the British and U.S. Virgins.

The other stars admonished me, reminding me that gold sequins were environmentally unsafe for the delicate species of the ocean. Sometimes you just have to tell the other stars to piss off. I was fairly certain that sequins were not biodegradable, but I was also fairly certain that sixty sequins and one elastic band would not an environmental disaster make.

I'm hoping, in fact, someone will catch a shark and think it ate a fag.

31

SAM YOUNG CONVINCED ME TO GO FOR A RIDE. HE HAD found me there, that night in the parking lot, in a particularly vulnerable moment. Maybe not vulnerable, but certainly ready and eager to walk away from that television station and never look back. Perhaps Sam Young would murder me and I would achieve my objective. My car would be found the following morning; there would be no trace of me. There would be only those shadow moments, those still, empty places of where I should have been—my office, my condo, my car—and vague imprints of what I should have been doing.

At the time, of course, I had no idea just how prescient that morbid fantasy would be.

But that's not what Sam Young had in mind.

He wanted to suck my dick. "I promise you it'll be the best blow job you've ever had."

"How could you possibly know what you're competing against? I've had many blow jobs."

"But not one from me."

"Sam," I said. "I don't think this is appropriate. I realize you've suffered a tremendous shock, a real horrifying grief. But I don't think this is the way to get through it. Besides, I don't trick."

"No?"

"No. Never have." He seemed disappointed, the way he lowered his face, pulled by a pout. "No," I continued, "I'm just a plain, old-fashioned, run-of-the-mill, everyday kind of homo."

He snickered. "I'm sorry. This must seem odd to you," he said.

"Not really," I told him. "I've been propositioned before."

He smiled coyly. "But never by a ghost..."

"A ghost?"

We were driving up Memorial Drive toward Harvard. We had decided to duck into Campus, a collegiate gay bar in the heart of Cambridge. "Yes," he replied. "A ghost. I swear Gina is telling me to suck your dick."

"Gina?"

"I'm almost sure it's her."

I shook my head and sighed deeply. "Look, if you really can channel Gina, why don't you just ask her who murdered her?"

He paused for a moment. In that silence I figured I had exposed his act for what it was: a scam. To actually think you can get a penis in your mouth by invoking the presence of ghosts!

He turned to me now but did not confess. "It isn't that simple," he said. "Gina never believed I could channel. That's why I can't really channel her. I have found that the only people who you can bring back from the afterlife are people who believed in you while they lived among you. She didn't."

"Well then, I guess she couldn't be telling you to suck my dick."

"Maybe. Maybe not," he said.

He parallel-parked. Hit the curb four times.

"I don't suppose you can channel a valet?" I asked him.

160

He didn't laugh. "I don't expect you to trust me so fast."

"That's good."

I said nothing else until we were in the bar.

Youthful faces clamored for attention. House music banged around us. Crispy computer riffs and other unintelligible sounds mingled for a most unpleasant atmosphere. Most of the men were dressed like stagehands, all black, only their white faces showing. There were few women tonight, evidently not Estrogen Night at Campus. Sam pulled me closer. "I haven't satisfied the homo part of my bisexuality lately," he confided.

"Well, it would appear you came to the right place."

"Do people know who you are?" he asked.

Before I could answer, a group of fetching college boys, about four of them, drifted toward us in an amoebic mass of darling dimples and smiles, sparkling eyes. "Are you Damon Fitzgerald?" one of them asked.

"Yes," I replied.

"Oh, wow," another spoke up, "we watch you on TV all the time."

"Thank you," I said.

"You're our favorite reporter," the first one told me.

The smiles had not subsided. I felt like I was auditioning the boys for *Teeth: The Musical*.

"Thanks," I repeated. "Have a great evening." And they drifted away.

Sam looked at me curiously. "I can't tell if you like that or you hate that."

"Depends on the day."

"Did I mention I have a very big cock?"

We were whisper-yelling above the music. "Yes, in fact, you told me that when we first met."

"Doesn't do much for you, huh?"

"It depends on who's attached to the cock, Sam," I explained. "And besides, I'm celibate."

"Like a priest?"

"Yes," I replied. "Except for the child-molesting."

I felt my pager vibrate at my hip and thought, *Thank God, let this be my escape.* Here I was escaping from life at Channel 11 only to be rescued, in the end, by Channel 11. That's the thing about TV news; once it's in your blood you either have to stick with it or get a transfusion.

Call the Station, Damon. Urgent.

32

I CALLED THE STATION. NED, THE ASSIGNMENT EDITOR, apologized for bothering me. "But the guy sounded kind of whacked out," he explained. "Says he's an attorney."

I rolled my eyes. I figured it was Raleigh Dean but there were, of course, any number of whack-job attorneys who might want to hunt me down. The attorney, perhaps, for one of the fake professors....or for one of the legislators who wants to sue me for defaming him in the kickback scandal. With every sweeps came the threat of lawsuits. Boo. Like a ghost, they'd scare everyone except me. Because only I knew, apparently, that I had done my homework, that I had done diligence and would gladly take the stand to defend my work. No, lawyers didn't scare me. At best, they amused me. The starchier their collars the sorrier I felt for them. They were alpha males and type A females and they all looked like they could use a good, plunging fuck up the ass.

"Raleigh Dean?" I asked.

"Yes," Ned replied. Ned talked like a Ned would talk.

Flatly, without a bounce of inflection. "Says he has to hear from you tonight. Very important."

"Thanks."

"Do you need his number?"

"Yes."

Ned gave me the number, but before I dialed I went to find Sam Young. I had stepped outside to call the station and now, upon reentering the club and searching for Sam, I, indeed, looked like a man combing through a pile of boys for the treasure of all treasures.

"Something came up," I told the most unlikely treasure in the place.

"Your dick?" Sam said fiendishly.

"You've got a real problem," I told him earnestly. "And I gotta go."

I took a cab back to the Channel 11 office and called Raleigh Dean on my way. He asked me to meet him at Kelly's Toe and I refused. "Look," I explained, "I've already been to one bar tonight. If this is so important, meet me at the station."

Reluctantly, he agreed.

The driver smelled of salami and beer. It was a bit unsettling to be driven by a cabbie who was so obviously in need of a designated driver (and mouthwash).

The night crew looked surprised to see me back at the station. I crossed the newsroom swiftly, to crisply avoid conversation. I threw the lights on in my office and the room stared back at me with a fluorescent groan which made me feel all the more pathetic for being there so late. Raleigh Dean arrived about twenty minutes later, escorted into my office by a curious security guard whom I simply dismissed with a wave.

"Well?" I said. "Have a seat and tell me what the fuck is so urgent."

"You're not angry, are you?"

"No," I told the disheveled man. "I'm not angry. Just tired. Would like to put myself to sleep right about now."

He tsked. "You may not be able to sleep tonight after you hear the latest."

Apparently he did not understand my reference to sleep was more about euthanasia than a good night's rest. "What's the latest?" I asked, half interested, half regretting he had come.

"This is all off the record," he stated.

"You've got to be kidding, Raleigh. I can't do much with off-the-record crap. You gotta give me something I can use."

"Sorry."

"What the hell good is this conversation, then?"

He smiled. Gray teeth emerged in a half-moon grin. "You'll certainly have the right questions to ask when we're done here tonight. You're absolutely right about New England Savings, by the way."

I nodded, knew this was leading somewhere. I leaned back in my chair and put my feet up on my desk. He hulked down into a chair, kept his coat on, and waved his stubby hands when he spoke.

"Am I?"

"Gina's firm was the one working on those real estate loans. That box of files found in her apartment contains the goods, Damon."

"And?"

"And no one, *no one* was allowed to take files home from the firm."

"You know this, how?"

"I've checked. I've sent someone into that firm posing as a client and asking questions about confidentiality."

"That's a lot of work, Raleigh, just to verify a box of files." I knew there was more but I enjoyed this rare opportunity to cross-examine an attorney, even a bad one.

"Like I said," he continued. "No one is allowed to take

files home from the firm. And there they were in Gina's apartment. Does that mean anything to you?"

"Not yet." I offered him coffee. He declined.

"Well, what do you think she was doing with those files at home?"

"Hiding them?" I asked.

"No," he replied. "The box was not hidden. It was found in the middle of her damn bedroom."

"Oh." I decided to show my cards, if only for a flash. "Well, I have wondered if Gina was in on the banking scandal. Like, maybe she was doing the loan approvals for the bank and getting a kickback herself."

"Wonder no more..."

"She *was*?"

"No, she wasn't," he said.

"Then what, Raleigh, for chrissakes? I don't have all night for this off-the-record chat."

"Gina didn't have anything to do with the loans. But she knew about them. She somehow found out the firm was overseeing bad loans and she started her own quiet investigation."

"And you know this, how?"

He smiled again. "This is the good part. Remember that journal her family handed over to the cops? Well, I've had a chance, through discovery, to examine it, and it just about tells the whole story."

I sat up. "What's in that journal?"

He folded his arms across his chest, satisfied by my sudden attention. "Like I said," he snorted, "she discovered the bad loans and started digging deeper. She wrote about it in her journal. She changed a bunch of names and places, but it's all there. It's not all that cryptic, Damon."

"I need to see it."

"You can't. It's not public record. It's all being entered as evidence. That's the only reason I got to see it, of course."

"So, she kept notes about this scam in her journal?"

"Yes. And she was reviewing the files to see who in the firm was getting a kickback. The loans would be pushed through, the firm would sign off on them. Several officers of the bank would get a kickback and so would two senior partners at Gina's firm."

"How many loans do you figure?"

"Enough to bring down the bank," he replied. "You can't keep giving out loans that you know are going to default and expect to stay in business."

I shook my head. "But I suppose that didn't matter to the assholes involved, because they were getting their cash all along the way. The bank would fail, but they would still be rich."

"Exactly, Damon. No wonder you win awards."

"We have to be talking millions of dollars."

"At least." Raleigh Dean's smile was beginning to repulse me, kind of like the faint circle of shit at the end of a used condom.

"So, this exonerates your client, how?"

He waved his hands again, as if the answer was obvious. "He had no motive whatsoever, and I have established that others, in fact, had a very compelling motive. Reasonable doubt."

"Let's hope the jury will buy it."

Raleigh stood up. "That's where you come in, Damon. You need to ask the district attorney about the connection between New England Savings and Berger, Berger, Cooke, & Langham. You need to aim your camera, zoom in, for chrissakes, at his pathetic face as he admits that he has more evidence implicating other suspects in this murder than he does implicating my client."

"Maybe someone at the bank or at the firm hired your client to murder Gina Parr," I said defiantly.

"What? Are you joking? Cruz is not a hit man. He's no Harvard grad, but he's not a hit man. I'm telling you he's an

167

opportunist who got caught at the wrong place at the wrong time, Damon. You've got a hell of a story here if you have the balls to tell it. Her fucking apartment was open for three days after she was murdered! Cruz merely ducked his head in there, saw the goods, and stole them. She was already dead, Damon. You've got to believe me."

My tired eyes scanned the room. What was left here for me but this? What had I expected? To graduate from journalism the way I had graduated from college, that this was just another definitive phase for me, a four-year commitment from which I could move on and start a new life? This *was* the new life and it pretty much sucked. "I'll do the best I can."

Raleigh made for the door. "Look, Damon. I trust you. You don't have the goods but you do have the goods. You know how to ask a good question. I know you do. I think you need to ask the D.A. about evidence."

"He won't discuss evidence pretrial."

"Ask if there is any physical evidence linking my client to the scene."

"All that shit he stole from that apartment."

"Ask him for more," he begged me. "Because there is no more, Damon. No forensic evidence whatsoever. No physical evidence that my client was anywhere near Gina Parr's body. Dead or alive."

He ducked out of my office, said he knew the way to the door.

33

I'VE TRIED THUS FAR TO DESCRIBE THE HEAVENS. LET ME NOW attempt to describe hell, or the lack thereof.

My soul sought this curiously upon arrival. Not, of course, for residency reasons, but simply to unlock the mystery of religion. To know, for sure, if evil is punished, if good and bad souls part ways and heaven remains intact. You come this far: You really want to know.

My soul searched far and wide; I sent out vibes and got back cosmic giggles. The older souls flashed their twinkling smiles at me and guided me further on in my quest, understanding, it seems, because they too had taken this journey, had had these questions.

And then it all made sense.

Throughout God's vast horizons is a phenomenon scientists only recently discovered. It was God's secret, actually, until the latter part of the twentieth century when advances in space exploration yielded yet another universal truth: the existence of black holes. What the scientists did not realize is that this truth, itself not good or bad, was perched quite stolidly at the gates of hell. These were, after all, scientists, not philosophers, not necessarily religious men, and that is fine, for it is not for mankind to know all the secrets of the universe. In fact, the other souls around me have mixed feeling about my reporting all this information. They don't understand that some of the journalism came with me into this afterlife.

I can tell you what hell is not better, perhaps, than I can tell you what it is. I have not been there. I have seen it from afar. This much I know: It is not below the Earth, or inside the Earth, or deep within its crust. It is not Satan's blazing basement. All souls go to the heavens, but not all stay here. The evil souls are simply the stars that collapse into black holes. They do. They lose their light and spin tornado-like into the oblivion of black holes.

What about all the images of fire and brimstone we think of when we think of the place called hell?

Fire and brimstone is the passageway through which bad souls journey on their way to the dark eternity. Like everything else in life and death, it is the journey, not the destination. The entryways to black holes are characterized by physical violence and hot, swirling gases. Huge bubbles of intense radiation. There is no escape, no backing out. I can't say from personal experience, but this must be torture. The cosmic pitchfork, if you will. And what's worse: The black hole inhales the soul in such a way as to graphically inform the soul of its unforgiven, godforsaken destiny all along the way. It's like falling off a building and remaining conscious all the way down to the pavement.

As such, the star and the soul, which have only just come together at the very birth of death, are separated. What is the bad soul, what is evil, is lost to the vast stomach of the black hole, an inverted volcano that incinerates and compacts an infinite amount of universal garbage. What might have been redeemed, what could have been restored, all the potential for good unrealized hovers forever, frozen in time, in a pile-up of dark energy. And there it stays—among the others just like it—in an eternal traffic jam, knowing forever it should have taken a different road.

No wonder the Catholic Church is so afraid of hell.

But fear not, less than perfect souls.

Only the very worst of you, the most unforgiven, will meet this fate.

Hitler did.

Serial rapists and murders do.

The person who designed the Gremlin should, but won't.

But Pol Pot did.

And I expect that many Bible-thumpers will be disappointed by this: Homosexuals do not. Unless they are serial murderers, rapists, or really bad at decorating.

Okay, so this is not a full list, or in the case of bad decorators, not entirely serious. But I have better things to do here in heaven than stand like a ticket agent at the boarding gates to hell.

Just remember this: *Star* spelled backward is *rats*.

And, thus, the true opposite of a star shall reside in its rightful rat hole.

34

MY FATHER DID NOT SEEM TO HAVE A STRONG OPINION ONE way or another about death. I was back in Connecticut for the day this time, not the weekend. I made the visit based on information from my sister Claire; neither Marilyn nor John had come out of the colorectal closet with any details of their own.

"I heard you were sick again, Dad," I said to my father when his eyes widened with the surprise of my arrival.

"I told your mother not to say anything."

"She didn't. I heard from Claire."

"Where do you think Claire heard it from?"

"Mother."

"Exactly," he said with a malicious smile. "And she only told her because they were having a fight and Mother used this as leverage."

I nodded. "Yes, of course. But how are you feeling?"

"I'm fine. I have some polyps in my rectum. But other than that I'm just a regular old guy with prostate cancer."

I frowned. "Sorry, Dad, you have to go through all this crap."

172

He shook his head. "If it wasn't this, it'd be something else, right?"

"I suppose."

My mother entered my father's study, where we were sitting. She carried a small tray of cookies and a pot of tea. "If I had known you were coming, I would have prepared something."

"I didn't come here for a snack, Mom. I came to see what is going on with Dad."

She smiled thinly. "But I don't want you to leave without a meal."

"I'm not hungry for a meal."

"How long are you staying?" the woman asked.

"Not long. A couple of hours. I'd like as many details as possible about Dad's asshole."

She dropped the lid of the sugar bowl and it clattered on the floor. "Damon! Must you be so graphic?"

I smiled. My father tried to conceal one of his own. "No, Mother," I replied. "I suppose that wasn't necessary."

She turned to leave the room. "If you need anything, either of you boys, just yell."

I stood to stop her. "Don't you want to stay and chat for a few...?"

She shook her head. "No, this is between you two men as far as I'm concerned."

I narrowed my eyes and waited for her to acknowledge my unease. "No, it isn't," I said finally. "It's not between just the two of us."

She wiped her hands on her apron, as if paying homage to the legions of put-upon housewives before her. "I have things to do. Like I said, if I knew you were coming, I would have planned differently."

She left, her skirt billowing obediently around her.

"She can be a real piece of work," I told my father.

"Oh, give her a break," he said. "She's under a lot of stress right now."

His eyes seemed more gray than blue to me today. His lips were pale and chapped. His expression worried me; it was vacant. There was no character, good or bad, radiating from him. Gone even was the smug, haughty New England chill from his face. And yet it was not replaced by warmth or particular kindness. His faced just stared back at me with nothing to say.

"How do you feel?"

"I'm fine," he said. "Tired sometimes. Would like to head back to Palm Beach, maybe play some golf. But I don't think this is the right time."

"You're not up to it?"

"I guess not. Would you be?"

"I hate golf," I said, hoping for a laugh.

He did not deliver one. "You'll golf someday," he said. "Everybody does."

"That Tiger Woods sure is something," I said solicitously.

"Hmm," was his only response.

"How are your doctors?" I asked.

"Fine."

"Do you trust them?"

"What if I don't?"

"You find other doctors."

He sat up and sipped some tea. He wore a red cardigan and a white turtleneck underneath and I almost instantly wanted to cry. If not for his pain, then in some narcissistic sort of way, for mine. That not only would I lose him, but that someday that would be me in the cardigan sweater, the white turtleneck. I would live in an empty house. I'd be too tired for emotions. I would see everything and feel nothing.

"There are not a lot of variables when it comes to prostate cancer," he told me. "It's pretty much routine. As for the other thing," he added, avoiding the true articulation of his rectal concerns, "that too has little gray area. There are polyps. They have to come out. Hopefully that's the end of the story."

"Okay..." I said and sighed quietly to myself.

I surveyed the room and found, as always, the same framed pictures of my past staring back at me. Family pictures where we grouped for the camera, dressed for the camera, and smiled for the camera too. There were no serious poses allowed. No closed mouths. All openmouthed smiles for all the world to see our many teeth. On another shelf, our lineup of graduation pictures, a procession of memories that at the time seemed golden, but really, when you consider it, are not completely worth remembering.

On top of the piano in another room were pictures of the boys together, the girls together. Marilyn had a system. An obsessive-compulsive approach to organizing the inventory of her memories. My father now sleeping, I wandered onward through the house and studied the Individual Wall of Fame. Pictures of my siblings and me in individual moments and poses, to somehow celebrate that while the intentions of my parents were always the same, we, of course, ended up quite different. There I was on a horse. His name was Sergeant. He had a beautiful chestnut hide and a tremendously strong body...muscular even. I had trained with him for about six years and won a few ribbons. But then, at some point during my junior or senior year in high school I lost interest in anything other than drinking and hanging out with jocks whose hormones seemed to tempt me with a smell of their own. The jocks were sweaty and loud, and since I was not a bad athlete I could camouflage myself among them and not be discovered as the fucking queer I was surely becoming.

One of them, a baseball player named Kevin Cameron, let me jerk him off. It was, at the time, the single most important event of my life. He had refused to reciprocate at first (as if he were only doing me a *favor* by letting me stroke his dick), but then, about three weeks later, after a school dance and the obligatory drinking in the woods, he gave me a blow job. I came so hard, so strong, I thought the fucking explosion from my cock would never stop. He swallowed some, let the rest drip on his face. I didn't see him as a baseball player then, or as a high school jock, but as another *boy,* a *man,* a guy with hairiness and young muscles, with promise in his eyes, if not for me then for himself; either way the promise that he radiated stayed with me, I think, guided me in a way toward a self-acceptance I might never have known. At least not at that age, perhaps not for years. I always wondered what happened to Kevin Cameron. I grieved the possibility that he might be, probably was, married in the suburbs with two or three children. Or maybe he had kept me as a reference point too, and had gone on to great things homosexual.

I woke my father up before I left, wished him well, told him I loved him. From the vacancy of his face came a subtle sign of gratitude tempered only by a wrinkle of concern.

The trip home had been, after all, informative.

35

CONFRONTING DONNA DONOVAN WAS NOTHING LIKE confronting my parents. It was very direct and full of emotion.

"What the fuck, Donna? You went behind my back and tried to take the Gina Parr story out from under me?"

She sniffled. "I'm sorry. I thought I was doing you a favor, Damon."

"Bullshit."

We were having lunch on Boylston Street. The winter sun glared through the windows, making it difficult to face each other without squinting.

"Your heart hasn't been in that story from the beginning," she said. "You and I both know that."

Her nostrils flared. I had never noticed that before. But they did. Her straight gray hair made her look severe today, not distinguished. "That's not the point, Donna. The story is mine. I offered to work together with you wherever our stories intersect, but I never offered to give you the thing outright."

She tossed a fork through the already tossed salad. "I don't know," she chanted. "Maybe I don't think there is enough here for two stories."

"Of course there is," I said. "We've got a major financial institution that collapses...and a dead lawyer from a law firm that happens to be doing loans for that bank. Hello? That's enough for ten stories."

She shrugged. "You make the call, Damon. If you think there's enough material, so be it..."

"Oh, you only know the half of it, Donna. Only the half of it."

"Really," she said with a hungry grin. "Do tell..."

I leaned forward. "Well, here's my point, Donna. Here's the very heart of our lunchtime chat... Yes, I happen to know a lot more now about the Gina Parr murder. But you are the last person on Earth I'd tell considering you can't keep your damn mouth shut."

Her head bobbed up from the salad, amazed. "Huh?"

"You went ahead and told Gretchen about the money-laundering scheme after I most expressly told you not to. You not only told her about it, you used it as leverage to get the Gina Parr story. That is *really* fucked up."

"You sound like you don't trust me."

"Very perceptive, Donna. If nothing else comes out of this lunch, you should know that, no, in fact, I don't trust you. I like you. I like your drive and determination. But don't ever expect me to trust you in the newsroom."

She dropped her fork. "Fine, then. Are you through?"

I shook my head as I swallowed my final morsel of food. "No," I replied. "I was just wondering: Is this how reporters regard each other at the *Globe*? Or were you thinking that this kind of backstabbing is simply more acceptable in television because it's lower on the food chain."

She didn't answer right away. We listened to a city bus screech by. A blast of wind hit the window pane. Donna removed her napkin from her lap and dabbed the sides of her mouth. She sniffled again. "I'm sorry, Damon," she said. "Truly I am. I promise I'll make it up to you."

"You'll give me the banking story?" I joked.

"No," she said with a guilty laugh. "But I'll make it up to you. Just understand where I'm coming from. My review comes up right after sweeps and I know that corporate wants to make cuts everywhere in news. Unless I shine, and I mean really *shine*, I could be through."

"Doubt that."

Her eyes started to fill. "You don't understand, Damon. You've got youth and looks, not to mention seniority, on your side. What the hell am I going to do if I get my ass fired? Go back to the police department?"

I tilted my head so my eyes could sneak up below hers, until she could see I was unconvinced. "No one is firing anyone, Donna. You're just paranoid because it's ratings."

She drummed the table lightly, nervously. "Maybe you didn't hear me, Damon. My contract is up for renewal right after sweeps. Perfect time for them to cut me loose."

I gestured the waiter for the check. "You can't live like that, Donna. It'll destroy you, if not the relationships around you."

Later that day I called Raleigh Dean and told him I needed to see some evidence.

"You don't believe what I told you?" he asked.

"Perhaps you don't understand this journalism thing all that well. It's not about what I *believe*," I said. "It's about what I can verify. I need you to send me copies of Gina's journal and copies of whatever files from her firm indicate she knew something was wrong. Can you do that?"

"Absolutely not," he huffed. "Maybe you don't understand this law thing all that well, Damon. Surely you've covered the courts before. I can't hand you any of that information. It's evidence. I'd be thrown out of the Bar."

"I do understand this law thing, and I have covered the courts before. And I know you can make copies appear in my mailbox...out of thin air, so to speak."

"No," he insisted. "No way."

"The copies could've reached me from anyone, anywhere..."

"No, Damon. We might as well end this conversation now."

I laughed. "Then what, Raleigh, was the point of sharing all that astounding information with me?"

He sighed heavily. "Jesus Christ, Damon, now you can go to the district attorney and ask the right questions."

"So you said," I told him bitterly. "But if you expect me to go to the D.A. without seeing the goods, you're out of your mind. I can't ask him about something I've *heard*. He'll throw me out of his office window."

Silence. A few moments of nothing passed and then Raleigh Dean spoke very slowly. "Look, I'm going to make this easy on you, Damon. Hard on me, but easy on you. I'm going to file a motion to dismiss for prosecutorial misconduct. I'm going to allege that the state tried to subvert the evidence by not readily handing over the journal and that box of files. It's a stretch, but I'm going to attach the pertinent journal entries and legal files to the motion as exhibits, and then, guess what? They'll be public record."

Suddenly, Raleigh Dean was talking like a lawyer. Like a lawyer who knew what he was doing. His words, I imagined, changed his exterior. Like an iron to the wrinkles, a cleansing facial to the skin.

"Beautiful," I said.

"But keep this conversation off the record. You did not hear about the motion from me."

"Whatever..."

"Look, Damon, I've never done this kind of thing with a reporter," he said.

"Yes, I can tell."

He took no umbrage with my honesty. In fact, he laughed. "You are one cocky son of a bitch, Fitzgerald. This is very risky for my client and me. I have to trust you one hundred percent."

"Yes, of course you do."

There was a pause, a hesitancy from his end.

"And you can," I added.

"Fine, then," he said. "I'll have the motion and the exhibits ready in a few days. As soon as I file it, I'll drop you a copy."

"Sounds good..."

"At your home, Damon."

"My home?"

"Yes," the public defender said. "You can't pick it up at my office. Too many people may be watching me."

"You sound paranoid, Raleigh."

"Think about everything I told you, Damon. If that fucking law firm is involved, I promise you they'll do anything to keep it quiet."

"Why don't you just drop it off here at the station?"

"No," he said. "If they're watching me, that's just as bad as you coming here. No one can know that I'm having any further contact with you."

"Then just call me when you file the damn motion and I'll be at the courthouse waiting."

"Uh, no, Damon. That'll look pretty obvious. Don't you think? I'm not going to give the state any reason to accuse me of misconduct."

"Fine. I understand. I'll give you my address. Nobody knows where I live and you can come by there without raising suspicion."

"Exactly," he said, waiting for the address.

As paranoid as the man sounded, I had to admire him for remaining so committed to his client's innocence, for arriving at a verdict in his mind and digging his heels in so firmly. I also realized that he truly believed his new version of the crime, believed it to a fault, believed it because it may have, in fact, made perfect sense.

36

Two nights later Raleigh Dean was at my door. He stood there hangar-shaped, waiting awkwardly for me to welcome him across the threshold.

"Come in. Have a seat," I offered, gesturing toward the living room.

"Nice place," he said. "Swanky."

"Uh, yeah, I guess."

"I don't have much time," he said.

"No problem. Can I get you anything? Something to drink?"

He rumpled himself onto the sofa and waved his hand. "No thanks." He methodically removed files from his briefcase and dropped them on the table, each drop punctuating his cantankerous demeanor, his unadorned sense of himself, of his case, and ultimately those around him. "Swanky" would be one of the few adjectives he would use that evening. Raleigh Dean did very little talking, in fact.

"I filed the motions," he said. "With all the exhibits you could possibly want. It's all public record. But I've saved you a trip to the courthouse."

And that was it. Barely another word from him. Instead he allowed me to comb through the documents, all the while watching for the exclamation points to jump out of my eyes. And they did. They genuinely did.

Some excerpts from Gina Parr's journal (as best as I can remember them):

Ass-Stain is fucking his secretary while his wife is out of state caring for her dying mother. I write about him not because he is more of an Ass-Stain than any of the other Masters of the Universe (thank you, Tom Wolfe) at the firm. I write about him because he is one of the two who are in on IT. He is a greedy man—greedy for sex, greedy for money. It will be his downfall. His arrogance is only exceeded by his stupidity. Does he think he can continue to do this shit and not get caught??????

Dickless wanted me to stay late to work on SAVINGS. When I resisted I think he suspected something. Does he really think I can't decipher his notes? In fact I even asked him why we're charging SAVINGS three times the normal fee for loan work... All he could come up with was "premium client status," whatever the fuck that means. Puh-leez, these guys are the biggest fucking idiots on the block. It's amazing they haven't gotten themselves into trouble before. Lorna Doone, the coffee bitch, is said to give fellatio to the senior partners. All they have to do is ask for "extra creamer." Is that not positively disgusting?

Ass-Stain just bought a new plane. That's right, as in AIRplane. The pretentious piece of shit doesn't know how to fly, doesn't want to learn, says he will keep a fucking pilot on retainer to jet him around. He better hope this whole thing doesn't come crashing down. It will make a nosedive from 22,000 feet sound like a joyride. I know scammers come in all colors, but there is something about a white male, who has had all the privilege and advantage of the world, resorting to this kind of scam. Arrogance and stupidity is a deadly combination, and with apologies to my dear, dear dad, I must say the combination is particularly infectious among white males.

Okay.

There was no need to read on about Berger, Berger, Cooke, & Langham. Gina Parr had made her point. To a most unintended audience.

I combed through the New England Savings files. These were copies of the files found in her apartment, presumably copies she had made from the originals; her handwriting was all over them.

Gina Parr had done her research.

She had scribbled notes, planted question marks, tossed in a few exclamation points. I could see where the math just didn't add up. For every invoice sent to New England Savings regarding work on a loan deal, Gina had stapled copies of several invoices the firm had sent to other lending institutions. By far the charges to New England Savings were larger than the standard charge to any other. In some cases double, in most cases triple, in at least one case New England Savings was charged eleven times more than the average institution. The scheme was pretty easy to figure out. The overcharge was the kickback. Plain and simple. Routine, everyday, fairly pedestrian corruption.

"What does 'P.D.' mean?" I asked Raleigh Dean.

"P.D.?"

"Yeah. It looks like she scribbled 'P.D.' at the bottom of all of these invoices..."

"Oh that," the attorney said. "Just her shorthand for 'private deal,' I'm guessing."

"Can we identify which two attorneys were involved in this scam?"

"We don't have to," he said flatly.

"No, of course you don't," I conceded. "But it would make it a stronger case to go to the district attorney with."

"I'm sure it would, Damon. But this is enough to lead the D.A. in the right direction. I don't have to do all his investigating for him too. Besides," he added with a snort, "I think it will be a better story if the district attorney has to answer to the media about this, as well. You don't have to wait for it to go to court."

"Why don't you just come right out and say you're using me, Raleigh?"

"I'm using you, Damon," he said, rising to his feet. He put his hands on his rolling hips. "Happy now?"

I turned again to the documents. My eyes scanned the pages, connected the numbers and names and dates and deciphered Gina's notes. Like a handwriting analyst, I studied her calligraphy to unearth the character within her characters, the sensibilities of her strokes. This was an eager, ambitious young woman. A driven overachiever who was planning, no doubt, to go to the authorities with her painstaking research had she lived to do so.

37

Jessica Sloane asked for a promise.

"Take care of my children," she told me.

request confused me. I mean, she had a lovely hus-
real rock of goodness and strength and we all knew
would take on the painfully unwanted job of raising
dren alone tremendously.

at about Lane?" I asked her.

laughed softly, wearily. "Lane will be fine," she said.
want a woman's influence too. You be that. You're
vorite aunt."

then one tear slid down my cheek and there was no
it from her. I had fought it back, really steeled myself,
but there it was inching toward my lip, exposing my fear and
my sadness to a face full of nothing but trust. "Okay," I
whimpered.

"He may marry again, one day," she continued. "I know
he'll choose a good woman. But they still have our blood. I
want them to know that. I want them to have a part of me in
you..."

I all but choked on the lump in my throat. I swallowed hard and smiled, feigning good cheer, nodding emphatically that, yes, of course, I will stand in.
"Selfish of me?" she asked.
I grabbed her hand. "Of course not."

I had no idea why I was writing about women. I didn't really understand women all that much except that I did know when I saw qualities in them that I didn't like about myself. Those qualities—enabling, people-pleasing, codependent crap—informed me that I had a lot of bad habits to break and that I was, perhaps, more of a girlie fag than I had ever admitted. Other qualities—like moody, clingy, needy, bitchy, menstrual Gretchen—just confused me, so I stayed away from those kinds of women. And then there were types like Donna. Driven and determined, ballsy and precise—traits I admired. So what if she had tried to fuck me over? I had to respect her hunger. But I also suspected that Donna Donovan had a drinking problem which could only make for an unpredictable relationship, a stop-and-start kind of alliance, never really knowing how far in the bottle she had been and what would happen with the emptiness that was guaranteed to follow. I wanted to study her, but I wanted to let her be. I had learned a long time ago not to do other people's thinking for them. Waste of time. Until you write an astonishing debut novel. Then you have to do everyone's thinking. You have to write like actors method act. You have to dive into character and figure people out like Jessica Sloane.

Jessica Sloane had very graciously told me to fuck off for a while. To let her be. To come back some other day. She was giving no more. Revealing not another thread of her story or grain of her personality. In the absence of Jessica, I wandered through a desert muse, keenly aware I was not wanted there, that I was needed in a tangible place, that my actions were waited for, that somehow my wrist twisted the hand that held the key that unlocked certain truths more important than fiction. For the first time in my life I think I felt a sense of duty, a calling, an obligation—and it amused me some; I found it lithe and curious but at the same time compelling, maybe even dreadful.

My next move was important. My next move was decisive.

That's how it came to me. That's how I realized it was time to sit down with Roberto Cruz and ask some questions.

Raleigh Dean protested so physically over the phone I could all but hear his blood pressure rise, his mouth frothy with sputterings of indignation. "You need to go to the district attorney, Damon. Tell him what you know and get this over with."

I had to laugh. "Not only are you trying to use me. You are trying to do my job too."

"What in hell does that mean?"

"I don't tell you how to defend Roberto Cruz. I wouldn't presume to tell you how to be a lawyer. I don't need you telling me how to be a journalist."

"I'm just telling you what has to be done."

"And I'm just telling you that I don't work for you, Raleigh. I have a job to do, and I will decide when it's time to go to Neckingham. Right now I want to do a jailhouse interview with your client. And I want to do it soon. Set it up."

"If he's willing..."

I gave him a syllable of a laugh. "Well, I'm not going to tell you how to do your job, Raleigh. I think I've made that clear. But I'm sure you can convince him to be willing."

And I was not wrong. That's how decisive, how compelling my revelation had been. It had not only revealed, it had delivered. Three days later I sat opposite a soft-skinned Hispanic man, his legs chained together, his hands folded in his lap—Roberto Cruz, boyish and scary. His eyes were dark-er than I had remembered them, almost black, and his lips had a sharp curl which looked so sinister I wanted to lean forward and instruct him on a smile if only to improve his presentation for the upcoming trial. I resisted that urge, however, and fumbled nervously with my notes while Johnnie adjusted his camera.

This was not my first jailhouse interview. This was not the first time I had sat down to chat with an accused murderer. Still, the mystery around the prisoner crept under my skin and tingled in my veins. I felt my face flush with anticipation. Cruz had straight black hair to his shoulders. Cleaned up, he might have been handsome. His skin was cocoa and smooth, save for a shadow of a beard at the contour of his jawline. He titled his head to one side, to such a precise position I was sure he would leave it there, taking me in at an angle for the entire interview. But I was wrong. As soon as Johnnie said "we're rolling," Cruz straightened up, took a deep swallow revealed in the bulge of his Adam's apple, and unlocked his folded hands. He now put his arms just under his chest and sat back with attitude, daring me, it seemed, to begin.

"Hey, Roberto, how're you doing?" I asked.

"Fine, man. Yourself?"

"Real good," I said. "Thanks for agreeing to meet with me."

"Whatever."

"The case is called the *Commonwealth of Massachusetts versus Roberto Cruz*. What do you want the people of Massachusetts to know about you?"

"I don't really want them to know anything about me," he said. "You know?"

"But you want them to know you're not a murderer."

"I'm *not* a murderer," he repeated. "I didn't kill nobody."

"Yes...but did you know Gina Parr personally."

He fumbled with his hands, as if he wished he had had a cigarette or something there to either draw out or punctuate his thoughts. "Never met her. Never even seen her till I seen her picture, you know, in the paper."

"Okay, you never met her, Mr. Cruz. You'd never seen her. But suppose someone paid you to kill her..."

He protested with his feet. He lunged his chained ankles forward and they dropped with a heavy clang. He had not become combative, I could tell—just frustrated that he had found himself in scenarios imagined by strangers and at the rawest mercy of those very same strangers.

"Look, man, I don't kill people. It ain't my thing, you know? Nobody hired me to kill nobody. I don't even know that many people in this freakin' city, man."

Of course not. Only then did I hear the Bronx in his voice. Yes, a New Yorker who had migrated north to Massachusetts and had found a life of crime here as appealing as a life of crime in the Big Apple. "So, you don't kill people. You just steal from them."

Raleigh Dean coughed hard, hoarsely. A warning? I wondered. An editorial intervention, perhaps? He had been sitting in the corner of the room the entire time. He had insisted on supervising this interview and I can't say I was surprised; never had I conducted a jailhouse interview without the presence of an attorney. There's no law like that, but there might as well be one.

I glared at Raleigh and moved my head back evenly to face Roberto Cruz. "Well? What's with all her stuff found in your apartment?"

"I snatched her things. Okay? You leave your friggin' door open, it's about the same thing as saying 'Come on in and rob me,' you know?"

"So all you did was take her things?"

"That's all. I was thinking, man, how stupid is this, somebody leaves their door wide open and jewelry out all over the place and, like, fuck, you know, it's like you're gonna get some kind of bad punishment for *not* taking the shit. Like you're supposed to take it." He laughed. "Like it would be some kind of crime not to take it, you know?"

"You took her keys?"

He said nothing.

"Mr. Cruz?"

"Yeah, I took her keys. So what? They was sitting on top of the TV and I had to move the TV so I put the keys in my pocket."

"You didn't mean to steal her keys."

He smiled. "That's not what I'm sayin', man. I *did* mean to steal her keys. But only 'cause they were sittin' on top of the damn TV. It wasn't like I went in there searching for keys. I didn't go looking through the place for keys. They were sitting on top of the TV and I was, like, hey, this is a nice extra, you know. But then I go and look for her Beamer and there's no car like that in the garage. Well, there were two other Beamers, and I tried the keys on those but they didn't work, so I figured maybe her car was somewhere else, or maybe she had gone out and left the door open by mistake."

"But you figured the keys belonged to a *she*?"

"Huh?"

"You said 'her car.' And you said, 'maybe she had gone out'..."

He shook his head, returning it to that tilted position, that imposing angle. "Don't start this with me. Don't be putting words in my mouth. I said 'she' 'cause I know the jewelry was women's shit, and I could tell it was a woman's place...okay?"

I conceded with a nod.

"That's going to be all," Raleigh Dean said from the corner.

I looked at him as if I hadn't heard him, thinking I could stall him for at least an explanation. "So, what do you want the people of Massachusetts to know about the man who stole Gina Parr's car keys, TV, and jewelry?"

"I said that's it, Damon," Raleigh persisted.

I turned to him. "This is TV, for chrissakes! Your client is not exactly articulating a very good case for himself."

"That's why we love the law that keeps him off the witness stand," Raleigh snapped.

I couldn't believe he would carry on like that in front of his client, but when I looked again to Roberto Cruz I could tell he was not a man who really lost time worrying about his impression on others; one of those fuck-the-world snarls had landed permanently on his face much the way they had landed on the faces of countless defendants before him. Not even educated enough to deflect the look of guilt.

"Raleigh, let him answer."

"Yeah, man," Cruz said, spinning his body toward his attorney. "Let me answer so I can get my fifteen minutes of fame."

Un-fucking-believable. Warhol's projection of his own embarrassing desire had found its way so universally, so democratically, into the general discourse of life, both good and evil, civil and criminal.

"Well?" I asked the accused.

"Well, I want these people to know I didn't do it. I had no reason to kill nobody. And, no, nobody hired me to kill nobody. And I even seen she had a nice place with nice things so maybe she was a nice person and, like, I'm sorry she's dead. But I ain't got nothing to do with it. Why don't you find out if she had a boyfriend? 'Cause it looked like maybe there was a fight there, you know. I mean, I didn't go lookin' in the apartment, man, 'cause then I woulda seen the dead chick, but I did see the punch in the wall, I mean, you couldn't miss the punch in the wall."

"Punch in the wall?" I asked.

Raleigh Dean leaned forward and bore his eyes into the back of the suspect's head. "You didn't tell me about a punch in the wall, Roberto."

The suspect shrugged. "No, I didn't," he said defensively,

argumentatively. "But all this talking about her place made me remember I seen it. It's not like it's a big deal, okay? I mean, it coulda been there for months. How do I know? I just remember seeing it 'cause I bent over for the TV, and then when I lifted the thing up I saw this big hole in the wall."

"Behind the TV?" I asked.

He shook his head, disgusted. "No, man! On the wall. Nowhere near the TV. Just on the wall. I didn't see it until I lifted the TV and looked around to make sure nobody's seeing me, okay?"

Raleigh nodded and waved a hand toward the door, indicating it was time for me to take the exit seriously. I thanked Roberto Cruz. He shrugged and said "whatever" and asked me when he was going to be on TV.

"I'm not exactly sure. I'll let your attorney know."

Roberto Cruz could not have known what a huge favor he had done me. Not only had he offered a fairly provocative interview, not only had he revealed a new piece of information—the hole in the wall—but he had furnished me with an answer for everyone at Channel 11.

I had my story for February sweeps.

It would not be "Anatomy of a Crime: The Murder of Gina Parr." But it would be an exclusive jailhouse interview with her suspected killer. The interview would give Gretchen something *exclusive* to promote besides the steam from her cunt, and it would give me more time, buy me more time to investigate the stuff that really mattered.

WE DROVE OVER TO THE SPRING HILL SECTION OF THE CITY, to the apartment building where Gina Parr lived and died.

"You're crazy, Damon," Johnnie told me as he maneuvered our vehicle through the twists and bends and forks of the cobblestone streets. "It's not a crime scene anymore. It's probably been rented out again already. You know the rental market."

I could have been annoyed by Johnnie Fanahan's doubt. Instead I luxuriated in his Southie voice, the way he said words like *mahhket*. I found it not only endearing but somehow anchoring, reminding me I had a place and a life and a home. Not bad things to think about every now and then.

The superintendent of Gina Parr's building was less than thrilled when we came knocking on his door. Buzzing, actually. We buzzed from the lobby first; he let us in and then met us at his doorway.

"No it hasn't been re-rented," the man said. He didn't want to smile. His lips parted for speech and returned to a flat line of indifference. He was an older man with young-boy skin. Real white, translucent skin, with a faint blush of red across his cheeks. He had a broad forehead that supported a sweep of white hair. The jacket he wore, a waist-length windbreaker, seemed insufficient for the February chill.

"Has it been renovated?" I asked.

He squinted at me. "Doesn't need renovation," he said.

"Hmm, perhaps not, but I suppose the place has been, well, painted, cleaned up a bit."

"Oh, you mean the blood?" he asked. "Of course. You'd never know someone was murdered there—unless you knew about it first, which is why nobody is in such a hurry to rent the place."

"Can we see it?"

He shrugged. "I don't see why not."

"Can we bring our camera?"

He shook his head. "You want to get my ass fired?"

"No," I assured him. "But I am working on a very important story, and it would be so much more complete if we could videotape the scene of the crime."

"I'm sorry," he said. "I can't let you do that. I'll take you up there, you can look around, but if that's not good enough for you, then I think you better move on."

Well, okay then. We would take what we could get. We followed him to the tiny elevator. We squeezed in, just enough room for the three of us. The gate zipped closed and we started to climb the stories of the building, clanking and scraping our way up this vertical tunnel.

The man opened the door to Gina's apartment. "And you know this door was ajar for a few days after the mur-der?" I asked him.

"Yes."

"Did it never occur to you that something was wrong up here?"

"I'm the super of the building, buddy, not the social director. I don't even think I noticed."

"But there's a security door downstairs," I said. "We had to buzz to get in. So how did someone get in here if Ms. Parr didn't let the person in?"

"What? You a detective now?" He shook his head and offered a snarl of disgust. "It doesn't take a high IQ to know that people come and go from the downstairs door... The door opens....and sometimes other visitors get through without having to buzz."

The man did not allow us to see the bedroom or the kitchen. "You can look from here," he told us in the front room, apparently the living room. "Too ghoulish for you to be walking around this place looking for a story, if you know what I mean..."

I knew what he meant and knew that he was enormously ignorant of the fact that this is what reporters do; we walk around places looking for a story. "Well," I said, turning to Johnnie, "I don't see any hole in the wall."

"Me neither," my partner replied.

"Oh, I fixed that," the man said. "I patched it up and repainted it."

"Can you tell us where it was?"

He shrugged. "Yeah, I guess. It was right beside that archway there."

He pointed to the doorless doorway that led from the living room into a secondary foyer, the threshold, I assumed, between the kitchen and the bedrooms.

"Had you noticed the hole before Ms. Parr's murder? Was it something she told you about and had asked to have repaired?" I asked.

He shook his head. "No. And believe me I would have noticed it. I was up here fixing Gina's toilet about a week before it happened, you know, the murder, and I would have noticed it. I mean, it was a pretty big hole. It was hard to miss."

He walked over to the perimeter of the archway and pointed to a spot high up, higher up than I had imagined, maybe a foot from the ceiling.

"That's where it was," he said.

"Are you sure?" I asked. "That seems kind of high to throw a punch."

He offered yet another impatient look, with almost pitying condescension in his eyes, and said, "I know exactly where it was because I had to get a ladder. I'm not exactly tall enough to play for the Celtics. I couldn't repair the hole without a ladder, okay?"

I smiled thinly. "Yes, great, that's fine. I don't suppose you have a tape measure..."

"I'm the super of this building. Of course I have a tape measure. You boys wait here. Don't go snooping around. I'll be back."

Johnnie and I stood there looking at each other coolly, wondering who would make the first move. Kids at the forbidden cookie jar. Teens at the forbidden liquor cabinet. Virgins at the forbidden genitalia of a first date.

"Well?" Johnnie said with his hands in the air.

"Well, follow me," I said cockily. He fell in behind me as I crossed the empty living room. The vacancy of the apartment brought the chill from the outdoors in, made our footsteps echo against the floor all the more crisply. We peered into the kitchen. It had a vague smell of garlic, or maybe that was just my imagination, an olfactory assumption messing with my guilt receptor, warding off the vampire I had become with this job. Then we turned to the two bedrooms. It was impossible to tell which was her bedroom and which was, say, the guest room or study. Both rooms said little to us. We saw no more than the floor plan, no better than had we been studying a one-dimensional blueprint on waxy paper.

We returned to the living room just in time to hear the

banging and clanging of the elevator reach the floor again.
The man came into the apartment and tossed me the tape
measure. I walked to the archway, extended the tape.

"Here?" I asked.

The man shook his head.

"Here?"

Still not right.

"Here?"

"An inch higher," he said.

"There?"

"Yes."

Seven and a half feet.

I wrote that down: 7' 6".

Then I raised my arm and put my fist to the wall.

"Don't you dare," the super warned me. "I just fixed the
damn thing."

"I'm not going to punch the wall, sir."

I measured the distance from my fist to the floor. Six
feet, ten inches. I could not reach the site of impact. Which
meant if the murderer and the hole-puncher were one and
the same, then the suspect would have to be taller than me.

I was six feet even.

So much for Roberto Cruz's theory. He had blamed the
murder on Gina's boyfriend. But I knew for sure that Sam
Young was not nearly as tall as I. In fact, I found it rather
shocking that such a short guy could brag about such a
large penis. Even though I knew better I had always
assumed big lanky men to have big lanky dicks, and small,
compact men to have short, small, compact penises (nothing lost in girth, of course, only length).

Downstairs we thanked the man for giving us access to
Gina Parr's apartment. We asked him if he would reconsid-
er letting us videotape upstairs. He declined again. "Maybe
you should call the building owner if you want to do something like that. I can give you the number."

"I didn't get your name, sir."

"You don't need my name. I'm the super."

❖ ❖ ❖

I had no intention of calling the building owner. Video of an empty apartment was not that important to the telling of the story. But I wondered intensely about how tall Roberto Cruz stood. His height would make all the difference if it could be proven that the murderer and the wall-puncher were the same individual. I would raise the question. That would be yet another point of intrigue of my story. Another way to make Gretchen and Todd and Fryer salivate, wet their pants, even, over the completion of my piece. It would not matter if I could or could not prove Roberto Cruz a murderer; raising questions, raising doubt was the easiest journalistic shortcut I knew of. The producers, in fact, would not have it any other way.

Raise questions.

Raise doubt.

Raise fear.

"It could happen to you."

"Or, worse yet, your CHILDREN!"

I put a call in to Raleigh Dean from the car. His catatonic secretary said he was not available. I left a message for Raleigh to measure Cruz.

"That's an odd request," the woman said dryly.

"Well, yes, I suppose it is," I conceded. "If it's too odd for Attorney Dean to figure out, have him call me. If not, tell him to get back to me with an answer."

I tried to remember Cruz's stature from his court appearance. I tried to remember his physique from my visit earlier that day at the jailhouse. He was small-framed but muscular. Wiry, but not tall. Not lanky. Small and tough. I would wait for an accurate measure. In the meantime I would gloat all over Channel 11 with news of my impending story. I would gather Gretchen, Todd, and Fryer and spill all the guts of it to them at once. I would wait to see who would come first.

39

Hi, this is Danielle Corcoran. I'm a student at Emerson and I'd like to know if you have any need for an intern. I'm available two days a week. If you'd like to talk some more, just give me a call.

Damon, it's Pat O'Hare. Look, if you don't want to follow through with the Rendezvous story, just let me know. I can go to someone else in the media. No hard feelings. Just call me, because things are happening and I need to know if you're in or out.

Damon, it's me, Claire. Dad has a polyp-free colon now. He's doing well. That's the word from Mother.

Hello. This is your mother. Your father's biopsies came back today. His polyps were noncancerous. I repeat, noncancerous. That is the news from here. We won't be offended not to hear from you, Damon. We know it's that busy ratings period for you. Good luck from both of us.

Well...the easiest call to return was the call to Danielle Corcoran. "No, thank you," I told her. "I don't have any personal need for an intern. But let me give you the name of Donna Donovan. She might welcome the help."

Truth was I had had my share of interns. Most of them had been bright, eager students from Emerson and B.U. who had surprised me with their diligence. Some of them really "got it" and were able to roll up the sleeves and cut through the bullshit and get their hands dirty gathering news. Others, however, were fucking nightmare Kens and Barbies who wanted nothing more than voice and makeup training for their quest for the anchor chair. Few of them believed they would actually have to *work* insane hours in small markets before they could get even close to saying, "Good evening. Our top story..." They simply arrived and waited for someone to hand them a blow dryer. They were the interns from hell who came and actually created more of a workload, not less. Danielle did not sound like one of them, but I was not taking any chances. It would not be fair to her anyway, what with my attitude, what would she learn? How to hate everything about broadcasting?

I called Claire and thanked her for the news.

I called my mother's bluff and did not call home.

I agreed to meet Pat O'Hare later that evening.

First I broke the news to Lloyd Lasser and his team of middle mismanagers.

"That's great!" Gretchen shrieked. The others nodded vigorously in agreement. "Can you have it ready by next week?"

"I can have it ready tomorrow."

"Let's hold it until next week," Gretchen said. "This way we get more promo time."

"Definitely more promo time," Todd agreed. "We can promo the shit out of it this weekend."

Lloyd turned to me and smiled. "Way to go, Fitz," he said.

I shrugged off the compliment. "Well, I had really hoped

to get to the bottom of the case, you realize. I had hoped to shine the light on other suspects..."

"You can still do that," Fryer assured me.

"Not by the end of sweeps," I told the room.

Gretchen leaned forward. "Don't worry about that, Damon. We've got a sexy story here. A great exclusive. You can work on your deeper investigation for the May sweeps."

May sweeps? I should have known. Of course I should have known. Television news was nothing more than months of filler between months of calculated ratings stunts. "Yes," I told my audience, "I suppose I can really deliver by May."

"The case won't go to trial for a year or so," Todd said. "Damon's got plenty of time to deliver the goods."

They all nodded. A room full of gleaming, hungry eyes nodded. I had put the monster to bed. The four-headed beast (Gretchen, Todd, Fryer, and Lloyd: the Mount Rushmore of TV Travesties) had retreated to the cave; it would hibernate there for a while. Within a week or two I would rouse them from their numbing slumber with news about Rendezvous. That story would hit air during the home stretch, I figured, the last week of sweeps when all but the dust mites of broadcasting were swept out to the feeding trough, when all that was fit for human consumption had been all but consumed.

40

"You will remember
But I will die a slow death
It's only an overture
To something that was best
And don't condescend to me
Take your leave of me now
Disappear into the air
I wish you gone
And I don't care"
—Stevie Nicks, *"Planets of the Universe"*

FRANK COULD HAVE KILLED ME BUT DIDN'T. HE HAD THE
means: After all, he still had a key to the apartment; I hadn't
changed the locks (more so because of my laziness and my
aversion to melodrama than for any sense of wishful, hopeful
possibilities—leaving the door open for a reconciliation, so to
speak). It would have said too much to change the locks. It
said nothing to leave them as they were.

He had the opportunity. Since he had the means, he could

take just about any opportunity to gain entrance to the apartment and choke me out of a sound sleep.

But motive? What would his motive be? Anger? I don't think Frank was all that angry about the breakup. In fact, I suspect he was only too happy to have the freedom to fuck virgin assholes with impunity, to spread his wings, sexually speaking, to spread the legs of barely-legal hotties without guilt. I had not traded in Frank for another lover—I had chosen celibacy instead—so he could not have killed me in a jealous rage. Frank did not kill me. Which is why I find it so aggravating that Detective Raul Sanderplaatz of the Massachuetts State Police still has him listed as a suspect. What the fuck is that? From here in the afterlife I am clearly dialed in to the frequencies of the detective's investigation and I cannot believe how much feet-dragging is tolerated in the pursuit of justice. Maybe my murder did not have the urgency of the Gina Parr case. After all, I was a journalist, not an up-and-coming lawyer. And I was a faggot. Gina Parr made for a more sympathetic victim. But here in the afterlife, we do not judge. We observe and we contemplate, but we do not judge. I'm still learning the ropes, I guess. Still learning to let go of the baggage packed during a lifetime of mortality. That baggage is not welcome in heaven. You should start unpacking it now.

Frank, as it turns out, had an alibi. He was in Montreal with three eighteen-year-olds. Credit card receipts from that weekend indicate he had checked into a hotel, bought rounds and rounds of drinks at one of Montreal's hottest male strip clubs, and stopped often at the drug store, presumably to fill up on lube and restock his condom supply. Let's face it: A lot of fucking went on that weekend, as Frank desperately tried to recapture his youth somewhere deep inside the rectums of circuit-party bottoms. Three of them! An orgy of tastes and choices! Again, no judgment. Just stating the facts: Frank had an alibi. I'm not bitter.

There's no bitterness in heaven, I'm told. My star has yet to burn out the last contaminant of mortality, but the other souls assure me here that it's only a matter of time. Which would explain my mixed feelings, I suppose. Why I can report what I observe and, unlike a solid journalist, have my observations laden with the weight of carry-on luggage.

That's what I'm down to now. Carry-on luggage. The rest of my baggage has burned up in the atmosphere.

The other souls promise me true objectivity here. I will observe and only observe and that detachment will be both a gift and a blessing and it will, ultimately, usher in the purest form of serenity. This is another one of the reasons they call it heaven.

Have you ever been in somebody's presence and felt utterly weightless and joyful? Have you ever felt intoxicated by that person's goodness, warmth, and light? It's an euphoria that only occasionally visits us on Earth, but it's an euphoria that awaits us all in the heavens. Because that is what it's like to be in the presence of other stars. Their souls radiate goodness, warmth, and light. And while scientists think it's very cold up here, it's not. The dark places and spaces are colder than you can imagine. But star to star, soul to soul, there is only warmth. And the only intensity is the extent of the brilliance.

41

I HAD REALLY HOPED TO AVOID ANOTHER ROAD TRIP. BUT ALL
Patrick O'Hare was willing to do was hand me a map and tell
me to go.

I sighed long and hard and he knew I was not pleased. "I
promise you," he stated, "you do this and you will have
everything you need to break the story of the decade."

I sighed long and hard again, not inhaling and exhaling my
reluctance to go, this time, but rather my surrender to the way
things were in the business of investigative reporting. All the
deals we made, the sacrifices we endured simply to "break" a
story. It felt so backroom, muckraking, cliché even. I'm sure
Woodward and Bernstein never felt this way, which is why I
was almost sure I had chosen the wrong profession.

The map did not direct us, once again, to Rhode Island.
This time we followed a route to Fall River. I had never spent
much time in Fall River. Had been there once to cover a major
drug bust, and maybe once before that to look at a series of
arsons. Sitting to the southeast of Boston, this was the quintessential old industrial town. There was metal everywhere.

Ships and bridges, hulks of trade and commerce getting things done, moving things from ship to ship, ship to train to truck. The city was an assembly line, with monster warehouses standing guard like broad-shouldered and stoic shift supervisors in charge of the entire operation. We stopped at Canal Street and waited. When we spotted the designated truck we fell into place slowly behind it. Johnnie kept his distance and we followed along Canal Street waiting for the truck to veer off behind one of the warehouses. I counted four warehouses (at least two of them abandoned, the flesh long decomposed, only bones left, huge skeletons) and the truck disappeared. We followed the truck behind a fifth warehouse and watched it pull into a loading dock. Night was falling and dusk, as always, was tricky. A perpetual adjustment of rods and cones, which did not provide for good surveillance.

Quietly, Johnnie slipped out of the car and grabbed his gear from the cargo space. As he did so I climbed over to the driver's seat and he took my place and started to roll tape. Two men jumped from the truck and disappeared into the mouth of the warehouse. I did not recognize either of them. Patrick O'Hare had refused to come by my office to identify the foursome caught on tape in Warwick; I had implored him to do so but he felt that his presence in the station so close to the airing of this story would raise too many suspicions. Guys like Patrick O'Hare overestimate their importance, assuming everyone is interested in them and what they're doing every minute of their lives. Not so, but it was tough to convince Patrick and so I just threw my hands up that evening as we negotiated this stakeout over beer at a small, dark pub on the fringe of Government Center.

I had seen him only a few weeks before, but I was almost sure he looked slimmer to me. More attractive? God, I hoped not. But there he was with his fetching smile, ready to hand me what would arguably become the best story of February sweeps. We chatted cordially for a few minutes before he pulled the map from his inner breast pocket. His move seemed rehearsed, but I indulged him his sleuthful fantasies and then he outlined the plan. Two men would pull up to the warehouse. They would be met by DeKashonni and another at the loading dock. All four would load up several crates of contraband. The truck would leave immediately and head for a waiting cargo ship. The undercover agent would be the man with DeKashonni.

"But it would be really helpful if you could identify him in the video we shot in Rhode Island," I told O'Hare. "That way we would know for sure. No chance of screwing up and losing the whole story."

My appeal was unheeded. "Sorry, Damon. You have nothing to worry about. The agent is the only other man with a moustache besides DeKashonni."

And, now, here in Fall River, his setup, while not exactly to my specifications, proved precise and accurate to the very choreography of what we observed.

The truckers emerged from the warehouse and waited on the loading dock. Moments later DeKashonni appeared, pushing a crate the size of a coffin. Then came another man, presumably the undercover agent, bearing a moustache as promised, pushing a crate identical to the one handled by DeKashonni. The truckers took custody of the crates. By that I mean they handled them from that point on. They pushed them from the loading dock into the waiting truck while DeKashonni and the agent reentered the warehouse for the rest of the goods.

"Are you getting all this?" I asked Johnnie.

He steadied his camera on his shoulder and looked my way disgusted. "No, Damon, I'm shooting the fucking trees."

"Sorry."

Two more crates came out, and then two after that. I was almost sure O'Hare had said we would see four crates, not six, but, hell, who really knew the intimate details of these underworld exchanges. One thing that was clear: DeKashonni had taken the money and had delivered. Here he was presenting the truckers with six crates of contraband.

"Wish we could see what's inside," I told Johnnie.

"I'm betting it ain't Beanie Babies."

"Unless of course they're smuggling drugs inside of Beanie Babies," I said. "That wouldn't surprise me."

He relaxed his camera for a moment. "We're talking guns here, not drugs, right?"

"That's right."

"Good," he said. "I'm not wasting my time and energy on another drug bust."

As if Johnnie Fanahan had seen it all. As if he now could pick and choose his criminology. I laughed to myself.

The truck pulled away and we watched DeKashonni and his companion follow it in a separate car that had been parked at the bottom of the loading dock.

I drove.

"I'm still rolling," Johnnie warned me. "Don't take any sharp turns. And keep your distance."

Reporters rarely drove, and when we did it was not well. That's not to say we are bad drivers, rather we do not know the art of accommodating photography in motion. I had, more than once, swerved around a corner too fast only to send Johnnie and his cumbersome camera slamming against the passenger window. My stops and starts only made his shooting jerky and his stomach convulse. I tried, now, to ease gently on the gas, to accommodate his work in progress and, at the same time, to keep pace with the caravan of contraband. What a curious parade we had become. I had to pee. I squirmed in the seat a bit calculating how many hours it had been since I last emptied my bladder. Four. Hmm...what to do?

"I don't suppose this would be a good time to pull over so I can take a leak," I said to Johnnie.

He snorted. "Yeah, right."

"Well, I can only hold it so long."

"There's a cup in the backseat."

"I'll hold it, thank you very much."

"Just drive, Damon."

We followed the car and the truck into what seemed like fingers of a port, long narrow roadways separated by stripes of canals. I looked ahead and saw only water and realized we had followed the vehicles into a dead end without leaving ourselves a way out, save for a big, fat U-turn, which would have all the stealth of, say, a creeping white Bronco on a Los Angeles freeway.

"Cut the lights, Damon," Johnnie told me.

I not only cut the lights, I stopped the car.

We waited. About fifteen or twenty minutes passed—it was now genuinely dark and the criminals would be said to be conducting this matter under the cover of night—and then we watched the side of a ship open; a wide gangway, at least two car-widths wide, came down and plunked into place on the dock. From the bowels of the ship came a square of light, just enough light to see what was coming or going, what would happen next. The two men from the truck appeared and quickly maneuvered themselves to the rear where they hoisted up the accordion-like door—it made a strong zipping sound as it rippled back into the ceiling of the truck. Then DeKashonni and the agent scrambled from their car and helped the two men move the crates off the bed of the truck. Three men from the ship crossed the gangway and met the foursome on the dock. Someone patted DeKashonni on the back. It was another man with a moustache. Shit, now I was confused. Not really confused, just anxious much the way I could get anxious covering a trial, worried I would not be able to keep track of everyone's name and who was sitting in the witness stand for what reason.

A huge white light scarred the sky like a devilish flash of

lightning. Then a blue light, a whirling blue light. Then one of the men from the truck spun around and yelled, "Oh fuck!"

A distant churning rolled toward us like an underwater earthquake. I worried the roadway would collapse into the sea. And then I saw the source of the noise as a chopper swung into view, its searchlights soaking the scene below, revealing the petrified, stunned faces of the men who were standing there now between the ship and the truck. They froze, all of them. I saw the agent, the one who had gone undercover, withdraw his gun from inside his jacket.

The chopper was still whirring as it settled to a landing on another ship, a quiet dark vessel to the left of us, on the opposite side of this finger. Meanwhile a dozen or so agents swarmed the scene, all with rifles drawn, all moving with the precision of military ballet as they approached the suspects.

When the chopper cut its engine I could hear an agent yelling, "Nobody move. Not one inch. Nobody move. All right...all of you facedown on the ground. Facedown!"

And we watched. And Johnnie rolled. Eventually, the men were handcuffed. The undercover guy now eagerly approached the crates, busting one open and then another. Two other agents assisted him as he removed guns and ammunition and laid out the array like bar graphs of evidence.

"Unfuckingbelievable," I chanted.

"No shit," Johnnie whispered.

We leapt from the car and approached the scene. We were stopped by two agents before the insider, the undercover guy, waved us forward. He let Johnnie shoot close-ups of the weapons and better shots of the criminal ship. When the men were walked, one-by-one, to the waiting cruisers, Johnnie was there in their faces and I was right beside him shouting the obligatory questions:

"Where were these weapons going?"

"Where did they come from?"

"Mr. DeKashonni, how long was Rendezvous operating as a front for illegal arms sales?"

"Mr. DeKashonni, is it true that you laundered money through the drag queens in your club?"

Of course, no one would answer my questions. They rarely did in circumstances like these. But it didn't much matter; it was another one of those unwritten rules of broadcasting that you use your microphone like a powerful erection and ejaculate your questions right into the faces of the suspects, if for no other reason than to reinforce to the viewers that you, in fact, were there.

When all the suspects had been pushed into cruisers (I always loved the cupping of the head, the duck-and-push of the criminals; it was tender and masculine all at once, homoerotic only in the sense that it reminded me of a hand gently pushing a willing skull down, down, down into the lap of fellatio), the supervising agent came over and told us we should be on our way. "We need to clear the scene so we can gather evidence."

"Who can make a statement?"

"A statement?"

"Yeah, is there someone on the scene who can make a statement about the seizure here, the arrests."

"That'll have to come out of Boston. You can call our PIO in the morning."

I shrugged and thanked him. No big deal. I could wait until the morning. After all, I stood there devouring the utter absence of competition, knowing no one had come even close. Tomorrow would be fine.

Johnnie sang his Emmy song for most of the ride back to Boston.

Even though the radio offered tunes of its own, classic rock like the Rolling Stones, the Doobie Brothers, and Fleetwood Mac, Johnnie blended his music with theirs, out-singing their chorus with the chorus I had taken quiet pride in waiting for.

"We're going to win an Emmy, we're going to win an Emmy. Me and the big ol' femmy! We're going to win..."

42

Love to love you, baby
Oooh, love to love you, baby
Aaah, love to love you, baby

THE MOANS AND GROANS OF DONNA SUMMER BROUGHT ME
back to the reckless days of my sexual awakening when my
penis served me like a compass, blazing my way toward sexual pleasure and logging each discovery in a pocket almanac of
dreamy conquests. Yeah, but hearing the music now in my car
on the way home from Channel 11 made me feel old. Older
than fun, older than daring, and older than any inclination
toward recklessness. I wondered if I had sublimated my sexual
recklessness with professional recklessness, but, no, I debated,
I, of all people, was the conscience of the newsroom. Several of
my bosses told me that and they didn't mean it in a good way,
though that's how I always received such a remark. In a good
way; it was good to be the conscience of the newsroom. It was
good to be known for integrity and truth. But it was also good
to fuck and be fucked and I was beginning to wonder if this

216

celibacy thing really was such a good idea in the first place. I had poked into the station for a few minutes before getting in my car and driving home. I had lingered in the hallways outside the tape library hoping to see Ernesto, thinking maybe I could consider him as my next object of desire, debating whether desire was sufficient or whether there was something in that crotch, in the groove of his ass, that would prove, ultimately, quenching and satisfying, resolute even. How would I know if I didn't look? Or ask?

But I couldn't ask.

And so I drove home listening to the radio, listening to my soul, my psyche, and my libido battling for dominance, and dodging the drivers that gave Boston the dubious distinction as worst city for motorists. So, it was no surprise to me when someone pulled out of a side street and spun onto Memorial Drive, nearly swiping me off the road. I caught up with the asshole and flipped the fuck finger, but the night was so soaked in darkness that I'm sure he didn't see me; I could barely make out the person behind the wheel, the kind of car, and I didn't really have a chance to take notice because the next thing I knew I was dodging him again. This time he swerved into my lane, forcing me to slam on my brakes. Then he stopped and spun his car around, headed the wrong way, his headlights overpowering mine, blinding me out. I heard him accelerate, his engine roar wild. And I thought this whole thing was crazy. For an instant and only an instant I judged the event to be surreal. Somehow I felt compelled to understand the physics that came flying at me at highway speed. Head-on. And then I felt lifted off the ground, the scraping and pounding of metal against metal against pavement against curb.

By the time I opened my eyes a paramedic was hovering overhead and the lunatic in the oncoming car was long gone.

I spent the night at Mass General Hospital. I was not fluent in the color-coding of the staff, but someone in green scrubs told me I had suffered a concussion.

"And multiple contusions to your head," she said.

"Multiple? Hmm. That's not good."

She smiled. "You only took four stitches."

"Stitches?"

"Yes," she said. "You'll probably be discharged in a few hours. For right now, we're going to let you eat a normal breakfast."

"Pizza? That's my normal breakfast."

She responded with a hearty laugh as she left the room. My breakfast arrived about twenty minutes later. I had never tasted anything so vile. The eggs smelled like a dirty sponge and tasted just as bad. Even the toast, my God, the toast was awful. How do you screw up toast? Flat and flavorless, not even the little cube of jam could redeem its malevolence.

Then I had a visitor.

"You made the front page, darling!" It was Karl. "I don't know whether to be excited or scared to death. Are you okay?"

"Yes," I told him. "I'm fine."

He tossed *The Boston Globe* at me. Thankfully, I was not the headline.

But I was right below the fold: TV REPORTER FOUND UNCONSCIOUS IN CAR.

The article said very little. There were no witnesses. My car had been spotted by a passing driver who happened upon the scene within a few minutes of the incident. The suspect and his vehicle had not been found. Police called it a hit and run. They would not comment on whether this was a premeditated crime.

Of course it was.

Lots of people held grudges against me. It was an occupational hazard that I was, at the same, quite aware of and terribly complacent about.

Had word leaked back to Boston in only a matter of hours

about the bust in Fall River? Had DeKashonni already sent out a thug to hunt me down?

Did one of those phony-diploma professors want to teach me a lesson in mortality?

Was it not within the realm of the possibilities that I had pissed off a few too many politicos at the statehouse with the recent kickback exposé?

Fuck them all. My car was a mess, I just knew it. I had multiple contusions. Not just contusions, *multiple* fucking contusions. And four stitches.

"Oooh, baby. You got yourself a cut," Karl whimpered.

"Is it real bad?"

He shook his head, then landed on the mattress beside me. "No, pumpkin. It actually makes you look butch."

I patted his hand. "Thanks, baby. That's good to know."

"What the hell happened?"

"I don't know," I said. "Some maniac tried to run me off the road."

"He *did* run you off the road."

"Thank God I drive a Volvo."

"The cage?"

"The cage."

"I'm scared for you, Damon," my dearest friend said.

"Don't be. This shit happens. And, if nothing else, it shows the world how stupid people can be."

"How do you mean?"

"I mean sometimes people who are the most angry act the most stupid. Whoever did this to me had to know it would make the news. If he didn't know, he's the dumbest fuck to come down the pike."

A doctor entered the room. "Will you excuse us?" he asked Karl, who simply rolled his eyes and swaggered into the hallway.

"Am I going to live?" I asked the physician.

"I'm Dr. Garcia. You lost consciousness for a few minutes

from what we can tell. But all your signs are normal this morning. How do you feel?"

"Tired. A little sore."

"Do you want to go home?"

"You mean I have a choice?" I asked. "The insurance company isn't waiting down the hall with a calculator?"

He smiled. "Not today. We're allowed to keep you here if there's nobody to look after you at home."

"I need someone to look after me?"

"Just for a day or two. We don't want you to be left alone."

"I'll take care of him," Karl said stridently, pulling the curtain from around the bed. "I couldn't help but overhear."

"What he means," I said to the doctor, "is that he couldn't help but listen in."

"If you're comfortable with the arrangement, we can't keep you here."

"What arrangement?" Karl asked. "Damon is my lover. Of course I'll take care of him. Doesn't this hospital have any sensitivity to same-sex couples? Our needs are no different..."

"Karl, shut up," I interrupted. "We'll be fine," I assured the doctor.

He smiled thinly, politely. "Well, I want you to see your primary care doctor next week to get the stitches out. We'll send him a report. You must make a follow-up appointment."

I promised that I would and he left Karl and me to ourselves. "What the fuck was all that about?" I asked my friend.

"Just trying to make a point..."

"If I had any strength, I'd whack you upside the head."

The phone rang.

Karl answered it for me. "It's work," he said. "Do you want to talk to them?"

I shrugged. "Yeah, give it here."

It was Lloyd Lasser. "You okay, Fitzie?"

"Fine."

"Call us when you get home, okay?"

"I'll be leaving within a few hours. I've got a friend here. We can swing by the station if you want to see me."

"No. Absolutely not. You go home and rest. But keep in touch. We've already had a visit from Boston PD. They're asking a lot of questions."

"It was just a car accident, for chrissakes," I said.

"C'mon, Damon. You know that's not true. It was no accident. Someone wants to fuck with you just like they tried to fuck with Donna."

"Donna? What happened to Donna?"

A skittish pause, and then, "Nothing," he said. "She's fine. But her car was found torched this morning."

"Shit...I'm coming in," I told my boss.

"No. You're not," he insisted.

I thought for a moment, really considered the news. "Look, Lloyd, this is some serious shit, this is the Gina Parr thing...and the New England Savings story... Something's going on."

"Yes, Damon, we realize that. But don't come in. That's a fucking order. If anything, I'll come to you. Call me when you get home."

43

OKAY, SO I NEVER KEPT THE CLEANEST HOME. NO GOOD
Housekeeping Seal for me. Dishes in the sink, ring around
the toilet, dust on the Emmy. Consequently, it was hard for
me to convince even my dearest friend that, no, I had not
left my apartment looking like the landfill that we found
when we swung open the door upon returning from the
hospital.

"The place has been ransacked," I said with a genuine
gasp.

Karl smiled. "Nice try, Damon."

I was silent, absorbing the scene of chaos before me.
Bookshelves were toppled over, cabinets emptied, pictures
smashed. It was as if a god-size fist had smacked my home
in the face, leaving bruises, contusions even, a dire need for
stitches.

"God, Damon. You earn enough money. Can't you
afford a cleaning lady?"

"You don't think *I* knocked those bookcases over..."

He pulled me further inside. "I know you can be a little

clumsy after a six-pack."

"Yikes," I said.

"Well, you're in no condition to clean," Karl said. "I'll do it."

The cops came about an hour later. They took a report: I chanted answers flatly, concentrating only somewhat on their questions, more so on the internal investigation I had commenced in my head. Had Raleigh Dean been followed here that night?

I had tried meticulously to conceal my address, my phone number from the public. Though I dismissed the idea of celebrity, there were, in fact, nutcases who would stalk the likes of local TV people. I had been threatened several times in my career, but never stalked. I had had countless doors slammed in my face (you learn not to take these things personally) but I had never had the sanctuary of my home invaded.

The police officers did a cursory tour of the apartment. I prayed that my cock magazines were in their rightful hiding places (even when you live alone you hide things, if not to conceal them from the unsuspecting guest, then to keep those guilty, nasty pleasures from reminding you you're human); I wondered if they would notice the *Ryan Idol: Idol Eyes* between the lips of the VCR. The whole city knew I was gay, but they didn't necessarily know how I spent my most intimate moments of solitude. The officers came back to the living room poker-faced. If they had seen cock, it had not fazed them. If they had recognized Ryan Idol, well, then maybe they wanted to stick around for a glass of wine.

Apparently not. They made for the door. One stopped before stepping out and said, "There's no sign of forced entry. Someone was able to get in here without much trouble."

Frank?

No way. Frank was too neat and anal to have created a mess such as this. If Frank had ransacked the apartment, he would have stayed long enough to clean it up.

I called Lloyd and told him he'd better stop by.

Karl boiled some water, said I should have some tea.

He called Louise, who panicked and said she'd be right over.

"I don't need a live studio audience right now," I told Karl.

"Shut up and drink your tea."

I sipped the hot liquid and had to admit it felt soothing as it went down. My body was warmed, the stress, somehow, leaving through the same pores it had entered.

Lloyd showed up. He brought Gretchen.

"I've never seen your place, Damon," she said.

And that is no accident, was all I could think.

"Have you talked to the police?" she asked.

"Yeah. They were here."

Karl had cleared a few places to sit in the living room. He had used his rippling muscles to lift toppled furniture, to clear a few pathways. I watched him hurdle the heaps of clutter left behind, a drawer here, a drawer there, a haphazard maze of criminal intent—and I realized then that I had fallen in love with him. I did not try to understand it, nor did I try to fight it; I simply made a mental note that I had fallen in love with Karl and that I would probably never tell him. What good would it do?

We all need at least one friend to be in love with outside the bounds of a love affair. If for no other reason, to remind us of the beauty of real love when the love affairs of our lives destroy us.

I needed a drink.

Lloyd wanted to talk about pulling me off the Gina Parr story.

"Dropping it altogether," he said. "Not reassigning it."

I shook my head. "No."

"This isn't really a suggestion," Gretchen said.

"Nor was my 'no,'" I told her.

They sat on the sofa. I parked myself on an ottoman across from them.

Gretchen's lipstick was too red, her mascara too dark. She looked haunted and I had to look away not for fear but for lack of trust. She, as a decision maker, did not comfort me.

"Look, Damon," Lloyd said. "We want the best stories in the city, but we don't want you to get killed getting them."

"Uh-huh," I chanted flatly.

"And the people at corporate are getting nervous," Lloyd added.

"So this is what this is about?" I asked. "You're afraid I'll get killed and my family will sue?"

He hesitated. He cleared his throat. "Corporate says we have to consider our insurance exposure."

"I think we're too close on these stories to turn back now, Lloyd. We're too close and this isn't about getting a hard-on for a story. This is a story that *has* to be told."

Gretchen began to fidget.

I continued. "Ironic, I can see, Gretchen. You get a hard-on bigger than any guy I know for all the wrong reasons about a story. But now when there's a legitimate reason to shoot our load, you want to castrate the thing..."

"Your penile analogies are not necessary and they're inappropriate," Gretchen warned.

"Puh-leez," I begged. "You're in my home. In my home I make all the analogies I want. Penis, penis, penis."

"That's enough, Damon," Lloyd said. "You've obviously been through a lot. You need to rest. It was wrong of us to come over now. We won't make any decisions without talking with you further."

"I appreciate that," I told him and only him. I avoided Gretchen's eyes. "And Lloyd, I have an amazing story that's going to knock you out."

"Really? Do tell," he said. "Between dodging Christine, the attack automobile, and interviewing thugs in jail, what else do you have up your sleeve?"

I entertained them with my version of the Rendezvous story.

"They're laundering money in their cleavage?" Lloyd asked.

"I love it! I love it! I absolutely love it!" Gretchen cried. "Can we air it tomorrow?"

I looked at her. Lloyd looked at her. Even Karl looked at her like she was out of her fucking mind. "What?" she asked the room. "I can see it already: 'Drag Queen Deceit! Risky Rendezvous, a Channel 11 Exclusive.' "

"Well," Lloyd began, running his fingers through his half-bowl of hair, the horseshoe of curls that ringed his head, "I'm thinking we better just wait before we put Damon on the air so fast. I mean, look at those stitches."

"What about them?" Gretchen asked. "I say we shoot a promo with him tonight and get a good close-up of the wound."

I watched Gretchen's foot as it maniacally tapped the floor.

I told my bosses that I really needed to get some rest, that I'd be happy to meet with them tomorrow and put together a story as soon as the day after that. "I intend to get something on the air before the end of sweeps, folks. You can either have the interview with Roberto Cruz, or you can have the Rendezvous thing."

"We'll let you know," Gretchen.

"I'm tired," I announced to everyone but no one in particular.

Karl was the only one who really *heard* the desperation

in my voice and, while I was drifting off into the fluffy land of painkillers, he ushered my guests to the door.

The next thing I knew Karl was lifting me in a fireman's carry and taking me down the hall to my bedroom. He laid me there and put his hand on my chest. "I'll stay with you a while," he whispered.

"Thanks."

"Louise will be here soon. Maybe we'll do shifts."

"I love Louise," I warbled.

"I know you do."

44

HERE'S THE THING ABOUT PAINKILLERS: IF YOU'RE ALREADY feeling unmotivated prior to taking them, you're sure as hell not going to have a zap of ambition once they're in your bloodstream. I stayed home for three days. I had never taken three sick days in a row in my life. I had never taken more than three sick days in three years, but the dubious combination of journalistic fatigue and Percocet left me fogged in like Logan Airport on a warm winter morning. I settled into the comfortable swing of convalescence. My caregivers, Karl and Louise, took shifts, indeed. I padded down the hallways of my apartment in thick athletic socks. Karl made me constant cups of tea. Louise cooked me meals. We watched TV Land for reruns of *The Mary Tyler Moore Show* and Lifetime for a good laugh at the sentimentality of housewife entertainment. We critiqued CNN, CNBC, MSNBC, and FOX. We hated FOX.

I had created the perfect snow globe for my life. Inside this bubble my dearest friends called on me, everything seemed soft and velvet (maybe that was the Percocet, on second thought), and while the world swirled outside my window I paid it no mind. I had retreated. I had burrowed. The outline of me was fetal and I was protected as if in a womb.

Of course the family called. They asked about my condition and if there was anything any of them could do, and all but Claire sounded distinctly relieved when I said: "No, I'll be fine."

The ultimate act of class came from Natalie Jacobson, the darling of Boston's news brigade, the star of WCVB, who sent an abundant bouquet of flowers with a short note of encouragement. The crime against me had made a curiously uncomfortable slice of news on other channels for a night or two. It was interesting to hear the competition talk about me. WHDH, Boston's answer to the *National Enquirer,* was the only news station to refer to me as the "openly gay reporter," as if somehow my homosexuality had something to do with my fate, as if I had been driving in the Openly Gay lane of Memorial Drive.

You can imagine that I came back to work to find my voice-mail all but shut down by the onslaught of well-wishers and other messages of missed calls. Among them: one from Raleigh Dean.

"Roberto Cruz is five-eight. His reach is six-four at best."

Okay...if we could prove that Gina's murderer and the wall puncher were one and the same, then such proof would most certainly exonerate Roberto Cruz. But that was not my first order of business. I quietly congratulated Cruz on his height and its possible implications, but my first call went not to Raleigh Dean but to the office of Richard Neckingham.

The D.A. was not in (rarely was) but I left a message.

People dropped into my office that first day back as if they had come to wake a body, checking me out with curious eyes and solicitous smiles. There I was, on display. My stitches, my bandages; I was not quite a corpse but the closest living thing to the death and destruction these people normally disseminate in the daily fare of news. I even had visitors from Sales and Accounting, people whose names still elude me because we work in vastly different worlds, just checking in on the resident crime victim.

Johnnie observed this all patiently, knowing it would be a while before we would get back to work. That time in the void, however, did not last all day. In the early afternoon Gretchen busted into the office with tremendous fanfare, all giddy to see me, to stake her claim to the crime victim, to boss me around lest I should assume my victimhood granted me boss-free status.

"Okay," she gushed. "When can we have the Rendezvous piece? I ran it past Promotions and they are so psyched about it..."

"I suppose we can turn it by next week."

"Next week?" she asked in that managerial way of choosing not to hear the very truth and reality of what a subordinate has said.

"Yeah. Next week."

"You mean you weren't working on the thing during your sick days at home?"

"I was not," I told her. "Get real."

She laughed and snickered and laughed again. "I'm just *kidding*!"

No she wasn't.

Neckingham called back late in the day. My office was full with yet another round of well-wishers. I indicated to them that this was an important call, that symbolically speaking, all good caskets must come to a close. They filed out.

"Need to speak to you, Rich..."

"About?"

"Gina Parr."

He laughed. "You're incredible, Fitz. You practically get yourself killed and all you want to do is talk about Gina Parr."

"Yes. That's about it."

"You know we're investigating what happened on Memorial Drive."

"Yes. I know."

"My investigators will want to talk to you."

"I've already talked to the cops."

"I want *my* investigators to talk to you. You'll get a call or a visit from CPAC."

"Fine. I'll be happy to talk to them if you'll be happy to talk to me. Tomorrow, maybe?"

"I'll have a secretary confirm it," he said. "What's this all about?" he asked.

"I told you...Gina Parr."

"But the case won't go to trial for nearly a year."

"Your case won't go to trial for a year, Rich. But I have questions that won't wait a year."

"You know I'm not going to try this case in the news."

"If I had a dime for every time you've said that..."

"You'd pay off the debt for the Big Dig?"

"Hell, no," I told him. "I'd retire to Tahiti."

"Someone will call tomorrow to confirm," he said. "And, Damon, I hope you're doing okay."

"I'm fine," I assured him before putting the phone down to suck up even more voice-mail from the masses.

So, where the hell was Donna Donovan?

"I have no clue," Johnnie said. "I haven't seen her."

"Her car gets torched and she stays out longer than a guy with stitches?"

"No one told you to come back."

He was right. No one had. I had mixed feelings about that but I did not indulge them. Instead I asked to see all the video-tape from that night in Fall River and followed Johnnie into the charcoal darkness of an edit suite. I slid the door closed, sealing ourselves in with our little secret. The booth was cold and the hum of the machines was soothing. He rolled tape.

It was fucking great.

If I hadn't felt such an odd obligation to the Gina Parr story I would have right there and then dropped it to focus exclusively on Gerard DeKashonni and Rendezvous. But there was an obligation. Go figure. Some would call it journalistic responsibility, some might call it a personal fascination, or God forbid, *closure,* but there it rested on the shelf of my consciousness calling me like a half-read book or an unfinished manuscript. Unfinished manuscript? The astonishing debut novel? Not another syllable of text. Three days with nothing but time and shifting blurs of Karl and Louise and the delicious meals they cooked, and I had not written a damn thing. Perhaps I thought that at this point it should have written itself. After all, had I not been thrust into enough of a drama? Must I still create another?

45

Thursday, February 17

Things to do:
Interview Neckingham re: Gina Parr.
Confront Lane & Lane re: Rendezvous.
Call FBI re: statement.
Buy Celtics tickets for Claire.
Fuck Ernesto, the tape librarian.

While I was reticent to make too much out of my near-death experience it did cause me to rethink celibacy. When I should have been hearing flashbacks of scraping metal against metal and the pounding of pavement, I, instead, kept hearing that old "you could be hit by a bus tomorrow" refrain. That bus, that screeching, polluting city bus could, in fact, be the one thing that stood between me and Ernesto, the tape librarian. I was not in love with Ernesto. I wasn't even sure I liked him. But I wanted to get to know him and I wanted to get to know him fast so I could fuck his bubble of a butt before the bus came rumbling toward me. How many casual, whimsical fucks, I wondered, could be blamed on the mere threat of a mass transit accident?

I called for Claire's Celtics tickets on the way to Neckingham's office. Neckingham looked surprised at first to see me, as if he had forgotten about our appointment or forgotten which story required this visit and which mask, consequently, he would need to slip on in order to accommodate my questions.

"Gina Parr," I reminded him.

He cleared his throat and said "right" with a quick, sympathetic smile. "And when we're done, if I could have one of the CPAC guys talk to you about the other night...," he said.

"Sure," I said. "Not much to tell. I blacked out pretty quick."

"That's what we've heard. But CPAC still wants to talk to you."

CPAC: Crime Prevention and Control. A team of brawny, elite state troopers, most of whom sported big hands, tree-trunk thighs, and imposing bulges in their trousers—they were the ones who investigated and interrogated on behalf of the D.A.'s office, carrying with them dire severity in their eyes, their speech, the way they shook your hand. They were, ultimately, the perfect marriage of sexual fantasy and military state.

Neckingham and I sat ourselves across the conference table from one another while Johnnie set up his gear. I hated these moments of dead space before an interview because inevitably the issues would come up before the camera rolled and it would be almost impossible to replicate the candor of the dialogue. Better to chat about the weather, the stock market, the fastest way to breed ferrets, anything to avoid shooting the interview's load prematurely.

We talked about the weather, about the D.A.'s midwinter travel plans to sunny Florida.

"I hate Florida," I told him.

"Do you?"

"Too flat and swampy."

"We like the beach," he said. "My wife and I..."

"My parents do Florida. For the golfing. I hate golf."

Neckingham straightened his tie. "Then I don't suppose I can get you to golf in a celebrity fund-raiser?"

"No," I said kindly. "You can't."

"Rolling," Johnnie cued me and my questions began.

The questions at first were generic. "Anything new on the Gina Parr case?"

"No."

"Trial date?"

"Not yet."

"I understand the defense has filed a motion to dismiss."

"Standard. We were prepared for that."

"Have you looked into the connection between Berger, Berger, Cooke, & Langham and the failure of New England Savings?"

"I thought this interview was about Gina Parr," the district attorney said firmly.

"It is," I assured him. "Gina Parr worked for Berger, Berger, Cooke, & Langham, and the firm is implicated in the failure of New England Savings."

Neckingham took me at an angle now. His eyes made a diagonal for mine. "And you know this how?"

"Sources," I said.

He laughed. It was not a laugh of comic relief; it was a defensive chuckle. I knew it well. "Care to elaborate?" he asked.

"All I can tell you, Rich, is that another reporter at Channel 11 has been investigating the New England Savings story and has come up with very reliable information linking Gina's firm..."

"And you think that has something to do with her murder?"

"I think someone needs to explain why files of loan documents were found in the dead woman's apartment."

He sat back, straightened out the angle of his chin. His jaw tightened subtly. "She was a lawyer who worked on bank loans. Makes perfect sense to me," he said.

"Really? Has anybody inventoried that evidence? Has anybody seen the way Gina had marked up the paperwork, red-flagging the problems? Has anyone read her journal?"

"We've gone through that evidence several times, Damon. There's no smoking gun."

"How can you say that?" I persisted. "There's clear evidence that Gina Parr knew the firm was doing something illegal, that she might be preparing to blow the whistle. It's all there!"

The D.A. shook his head. "I see Raleigh Dean has planted some colorful fantasies in your head, Damon."

"Do the senior partners at Berger, Berger, Cooke, & Langham have alibis for the night of Gina Parr's murder?"

"What?"

"You heard me, Rich. Were they ever considered suspects?"

He sputtered a moment. "That is one of the most reputable law firms in the city, if not the state. Do you know what you're asking?"

"I'm asking if the senior partners had alibis..."

He leaned forward until his torso was almost parallel to the table. He stretched out an arm and pointed a finger at me, more or less in my face. "I don't like where this interview is going, Damon. Not at all."

I leaned forward to meet his aggression unfettered. "I think these are reasonable questions."

"You mean to tell me," he continued, "that you'd risk destroying the reputation of that entire law firm just to make your investigation sound more intriguing. I can't believe you'd do that."

"Of course not," I told him. "That's not my objective. For all I know Gina was in on the scam at first and is as guilty as the rest of them, Rich. Maybe she was murdered by someone at the bank, I don't know. I'll get to them too. I just wanted to clear the firm, first."

"The senior partners were on vacation at the time of Gina Parr's murder if you must know. Two were in Florida. Two were in St. Maarten. But be careful how you go about clearing the firm, Damon. This is a warning."

I sat there rather amazed. Was the district attorney actually swooping his protective arm around the firm right there on camera?

"But, Rich," I said, "surely you have seen evidence that there may be criminal wrongdoing by the firm in its dealings with the bank. I know that's not your jurisdiction or your case to investigate, but surely that evidence has been a by-product of this murder investigation."

He tried to interrupt me. Unsuccessfully. "And knowing that Rich," I continued, "knowing the truth about Berger and Berger doesn't that change your fervent defense of the firm. Doesn't it say they don't deserve such a spotless reputation?"

"You're right, Damon. The banking scandal is not my case. The murder is. And nothing you have told me has even come close to raising questions about the firm's involvement in this murder. So if I were you, I would just drop it. You might find yourself on the end of a lawsuit, Damon. If you try to taint that law firm, they will turn around and look for blood."

"My sentiments exactly, Rich. Gina's blood."

"I'm not kidding," he said, huffing. "You're being entirely irresponsible, Damon. You're better than that. You are and you know it. We have our suspect in the Gina Parr case. Sorry it's not sexy enough for television viewers, but Roberto Cruz is our suspect and he will go to trial. Stop the camera. This interview is over."

237

"But..."

"No buts, Damon. Shut the camera off."

Johnnie complied.

He carried his gear from the room.

Neckingham rose to his feet. "I'm sickened you would pull this stunt, Damon. Take me seriously. That firm is above reproach. Always has been, always will be. They're the foundation of the legal community here. I thought you were more experienced, more seasoned than to fall for such obvious misdirection, by a public defender of all people."

"Are you done chastising me?"

He spit out a remark that was inaudible and left the room.

For the first time in a long time I could honestly say that I earned my pay. The day was far from over. Next, Johnnie and I pulled into the alley beside Lane & Lane and waited for the ambush. We were there for almost an hour when the two men we spotted at Rendezvous emerged from the office building. We bounced from the car and chased them down.

"Can either of you tell me what you were doing at Rendezvous last week?"

"Who are you?" one snapped back.

They both kept moving. We followed.

"I'm Damon Fitzgerald from Channel 11 News and we have videotape of the two of you taking money from Gerard DeKashonni."

They both spun around. The taller one, the one with the perfect goatee and almond eyes, lunged for the camera. "No comment," he said. "Get that thing out of my face. Get that fucking thing out of my face."

I persisted. "We have video of you taking the same envelope of money that DeKashonni received from arms smugglers... What would an insurance company have to do with that kind of payment?"

Again, a lunge for the camera. The shorter man tried to

knock the microphone from my hand. His face had turned purple; a family of serpent veins squirmed in his neck. "Hey, man," he said, "we'll sue you and own your fucking station unless you turn that fucking camera off."

"On what grounds?" I asked. "You'll sue on what grounds?"

They made a dash for their car and I pursued them.

Johnnie followed, huffing and puffing for breath.

"Was that the first time you laundered money at Rendezvous? Or were you simply giving the drag queens a very generous tip?"

They slammed themselves into the car and peeled out of the alley, swerving at us. They came well short of striking us but I suppose the swerve made them feel that they had had the last word, that they had not been completely emasculated or overpowered.

Truly, they had to be shitting their pants.

❖ ❖ ❖

As for my interview with the FBI, it was mechanical at best. Government employees rarely gave good sound bites and Donald Watson was no exception. He did give me the facts I needed, though, to put the Rendezvous story to bed. He named those arrested and provided their mug shots, spoke a bit about the investigation that led to the sting, and shared his onion- and garlic-laden lunch with me by means of acute halitosis.

I asked about the involvement of Lane & Lane. Watson said he could not confirm or deny an investigation into the insurance company or the two men we saw stuff cash into cleavage.

"That's very interesting," he said, though, when I told him about the videotape from Rendezvous. "Something we will definitely want to take a look at."

"Subpoena it," I said. I wasn't trying to be a prick. It was station policy: no handouts to the authorities. It was a good policy. This way we could maintain our independence from law enforcement agencies and maintain some shred of objectivity.

"We will," Watson assured me. It was only then, when he assured me with a subtle wink, that I caught on to the flirtation, the suggestive inflection in his voice. I made a quick sweep of his physique from head to toe, lingered on his crotch for an undetectable micromoment of extra assessment, and graduated to his face with the conclusion that, his stiffness and polyester notwithstanding, here was a man with whom I would not mind taking a steam bath.

Enough said.

We shook hands. I asked for his card. He gave it to me. I slipped it in my back pocket and imagined it going directly for my asshole from there. Why the hell not?

46

DONNA DONOVAN REAPPEARED THE NEXT DAY.

"Hmm, nothing like coming back to work on a Friday," I said after she rolled herself in her chair into my office.

"Nice to see you too, Damon," she said. "As a matter of fact I've been working from home all week."

"Good," I told her. "I want the banking story and the Roberto Cruz interview to run in tandem on Monday night. We can work together on it over the weekend."

"Does management know?"

"They will today."

"I thought they were going to drop the Gina Parr story...I mean, after what happened to you, and all..."

"Yes, but between the two of us we have a fucking huge story, and I've seen files from Berger and Berger that are going to make this thing explode."

She nodded. Then flipped her bangs from her forehead. Her eyes looked bluer than usual, steelier, I guess. "Great," she said. "I'm yours for the weekend."

"Sorry to hear about your car," I told her.

She laughed sadly. "Yeah, me too."

"Any ideas who did it?"

"Probably someone from the bank," she said. "I'm all for getting the story on quickly. Once it airs, they'd be stupid to try anything else."

"Agreed," I said. "What are you doing for wheels now?"

"A cop friend has a pickup he's lending me."

"Good."

"Are you recovered from your accident?" she asked.

"It was no accident," I told her.

I smelled fresh coffee, knew Johnnie could not be far behind.

"No, of course not," she said. "The bankers and the lawyers know we're putting them together. They're scared shitless."

"You might say that."

Johnnie stepped in, gave us a nod of the head, and made way in the doorway for Lloyd Lasser, who rarely strayed this far from his corner office across the newsroom.

"Busy?" he asked us.

"No," I told him. "We just got in, planning our pitch."

"Pitch?" he asked with a dodge of doubt in his eyes.

"Yeah," I said. "Donna and I think the Gina Parr and New England Savings stories are ready to run in tandem. We want to pitch it to you and the managers...when you all have the chance."

"I see," he said without a nudge of commitment in his voice. "But now, Damon, I need you to come with me. We have some unexpected visitors in the GM's office."

I looked at Donna and offered a passive shrug of ignorance. How was I to know why I was being summoned? It didn't happen often. I didn't think I was getting fired.

Lloyd escorted me out of the office and whispered, "These lawyers showed up on our doorstep this morning demanding a meeting with Gary and me."

"Lawyers?"

"They say they're from the firm where Gina Parr worked," Lloyd whispered.

"You're kidding!"

"I'm not."

We reached Gary Sullivan's door and were greeted there by his secretary, who asked us to wait a moment while she delicately informed her boss of our arrival. I wondered why everything seemed so fragile there. The people in the executive offices seemed to be eggshelling their footsteps, their every move, in fact.

Sullivan came out of his office and shook my hand. "Damon, we've got a very angry law firm on our back."

Lloyd cleared his throat but apparently could not locate his spine, because he just stood there clearing his overcleared throat and saying nothing.

"What do they want?" I asked the general manager.

"They're threatening to sue us if we so much as suggest a link between the firm and that girl's murder..."

"Well, that's quite valiant of them, Gary, but we have information, good information that a link does, in fact, exist."

Gary was a tall guy. A real tower of a fellow with friendly eyes and floppy hands. I imagined him to be happy but clumsy. "I'm not telling you not to do the story, Damon," he said. "I think you know that. I've never tied your hands, but I do want you and Lloyd to come in and hear what these guys have to say. I'm just going to sit back and listen."

"Fine," I told Sullivan. "Thank you."

The two sitting men stood when we entered the inner chamber of Sullivan's office. They were both large men in height and girth. Neither one was Ross Littleton, the man I had interviewed at the firm's office immediately after the murder. With a round of introductions and handshakes I learned that the balding man was Donald Berger and the other man was Reginald Cooke. Berger was probably early fifties. He spoke with a nasal voice and showed off rocks of gold as cuff links. His partner, Cooke, was younger, maybe mid forties. He spoke little, preferring, it seemed, to condescend with his eyes not with his speech. He had a chiseled jawline and cheekbones and seemed well aware of these attributes, and I say that only because he kept turning his face in certain ways, feigning interest in what was being said, positioning his profile at perfect angles. He wore no wedding ring. I wondered instantly if the man was a homo, but dismissed the notion when I caught a whiff of Grey Flannel wafting from his body. I hated Grey Flannel. I thought it made men smell like wet felt. Didn't really care if the man was a homo or not. I had no intentions of dating felt.

We sat.

"We have a real problem," Donald Berger sniffled at us. "We want this station to be on notice that our firm is ready and fully prepared to file a defamation suit should our name be linked in any questionable way to the murder of our former employee Gina Parr."

I leaned forward. "With all due respect," I began, "you just gave us what sounded like a prepared statement but told us a whole lot of nothing."

Cooke cleared his throat. Berger bristled. "Let me make myself clear, young man. You're barking up the wrong tree and you had better be very careful about using our name in the context of Ms. Parr's murder."

"Are you threatening me, Mr. Berger?"

"The only thing I am threatening is a lawsuit."

"Hmm," I continued. "I cannot imagine why you would think we would be investigating your firm's involvement in the murder..."

That was a lie. I could clearly imagine that Richard Neckingham, district attorney, had tipped them off. Why he had tipped them off, I could not be sure. But I was damned sure that Neckingham was behind this pathetic visit. No one else knew we were making the link between the collapse of New England Savings and the murder of Gina Parr. The D.A. had reacted so viscerally to our questions and, now, the very morning after my meeting with Neckingham these two fuck-wads show up at Channel 11. No coincidence.

"Let's just say we have sources who tell us that you're trying to implicate us in this most unfortunate tragedy," Berger said.

"Perhaps your source didn't tell you that we have some very provocative information to suggest that your firm would have something to gain with the murder of Gina Parr."

Berger nearly jumped out of the chair. I saw him hold himself back, restraining himself with hands clasped around the armrests. "What? That is absolutely sickening!" He turned to my general manager. "Mr. Sullivan, if this is the kind of journalism you encourage at this station, you might as well hand over the keys right now, because we will own every square foot of this building when we're through with you."

Gary flopped his hands on the desk and wobbled his big face. "I don't know about that, Mr. Berger. You'd have to win control of a media conglomerate in order to claim as much as a square foot of this building. But we'll get to that later. I want you to know that Damon is one of our best reporters and he knows quite well the rules of the game here. We are not going to air anything defamatory, anything irresponsible, anything, in fact, that will land us opposite you or anyone else in court."

"May I ask some questions?" I piped in.

"Of course," Sullivan said.

"Mr. Berger, Mr. Cooke, can either one of you explain why Gina Parr would have a box full of New England Savings loan files in her bedroom?"

"She took her work home with her," Berger said.

"But she did tax law, I thought," I retorted.

"She dabbled in various areas of the firm."

"Yes," I conceded. "But wasn't it strictly against firm policy to bring confidential files home?"

"No," Berger replied. "That's misinformation."

"Maybe so," I said. "But we've also had a look at Ms. Parr's private journal. In it, she refers to wrongdoing at the firm that aided in the collapse of New England Savings. It is she, not us, who implicates your firm."

"We would have no comment on that," Cooke said with a puff of his chest.

But he was wrong. There would be a comment and it would come from Donald Berger.

"Perhaps her private journal was more an attempt at fiction than anything else," Berger said.

"How do you mean?"

"I mean she had a vivid imagination and she probably was making a stab at writing a book... You know, one that takes place at a law firm."

Cooke smiled. He seemed satisfied with that conclusion.

"Well, actually, Mr. Berger, it would have made for very compelling fiction. Very plausible, when you consider how Gina inventoried pages and pages of loans made by New England Savings and compared them to loans made by other client banks. We've seen the huge discrepancies."

Berger started to speak, but Cooke put his hand out, shieldlike. "Don't say another word, Donald," the younger attorney insisted. "We're not going down that road. All those documents have been entered into evidence and if they had rendered us suspect, we would have been hauled into court by now."

"Besides," Berger added, ignoring the advice of the other attorney (the irony was not lost on me), "this was a tremendous tragedy for us. It rocked us at every level, gentlemen. That woman brought so much to the firm. We had high hopes for her."

"But what if she found out the firm was doing something wrong?" I asked. "What if she was preparing to go to the authorities?"

"We're not going down that road, Mr. Fitzgerald," Cooke repeated. "You're basing your assertions on evidence you don't understand."

"I see," I said plaintively.

"Again, gentlemen," Berger said, rising to his feet, "let me be very clear. You have no story here. Ms. Parr's death is an unimaginable tragedy. And it will not be used to harm my firm. We will pursue any avenues available to us to defend ourselves from defamation."

"We think we understand you," Sullivan said from his desk. He didn't rise to escort his visitors to the door. He left that gesture to Lloyd and me.

"I hope we haven't scared you," Cooke whispered to me as we crossed the reception area.

I laughed. "Attorneys don't scare me," I said.

"Well, we figured you might be a little skittish after that car accident of yours."

"No sir," I said. "You mustn't leave here thinking you've scared anyone."

In the parking lot we shook hands. Berger leaned forward and said, "If there's anything we can do to help you tell the *real* story, let us know. We don't want to stand in your way."

"And you won't," I assured him.

Then he stopped. His whole frame seemed to halt like a dark slamming door. "Look, Mr. Fitzgerald," he growled. "Don't fuck with us. You're a cocky little shit, but you're not cocky enough to mess with the big boys. You've crossed the line, young man. You have offended and insulted and affronted us by your wild accusations. You should know that I personally identified Ms. Parr's body at the crime scene. It was a gruesome task. The most horrifying thing I've had to do in my life, but I thought of her as a daughter. I was at the scene as soon as I got the call."

"Come on, Don, let's go," his partner insisted.

Berger exhaled a few residual, wild breaths in my face. They were not unlike the wild exhales of a man who had taken the witness stand, who had emoted testimony with passion and fervor. The drama notwithstanding, I knew I had him.

47

I HAD DONALD BERGER BECAUSE DONALD BERGER WAS A
liar. Lies, however little, gathered like thunderheads to form
huge, dark clouds of suspicion. Donald Berger had lied and
had cast himself in a most dubious light. Donald Berger had
not identified the body of Gina Parr. He said he had, but he
had not. I remember how painful it was for Sam Young to
remember that dreadful task. Sam Young had identified the
body of Gina Parr. He had told me so, and minutes after
Berger and Cooke left the building I called the district attorney's office to confirm that. Neckingham, of course, was not
available, but I spoke to one of his assistants, who checked
and said, yes, Sam Young, had identified the body, that, yes,
Sam Young is the only one on record offering a positive ID.

"Thanks," I told the assistant. "And tell your boss I appreciate the visit."

"The visit?"

"Yeah, the visit from a certain Boston law firm. It appears
Mr. Neckingham referred the firm to us for, shall we say, a
consultation."

"I'll pass the word on."

"And tell Neckingham he should call me. I have some information he can't afford to be without."

"Uh-huh," the assistant said and hung up.

Could I prove that Donald Berger had murdered Gina Parr? Absolutely not. But his lies and his motives could, in fact, cast reasonable doubt on the guilt of Roberto Cruz. I dialed Raleigh Dean, told him what I knew, told him I'd be preparing the report over the weekend.

"Neckingham tipped them off," Raleigh said. "I don't know why he'd go to such lengths to protect the bastards unless he really thinks they're innocent."

"It's a very tight group, that old boys' club," I said. "Who the fuck knows? Maybe Neckingham had been counting on the firm for some kind of political endorsement, or more likely, campaign contributions. It's no secret he was planning to seek higher office."

"When will the story air?"

"Monday and Tuesday nights, I think."

"I'll be watching as asses fry," the public defender said.

A few hours later I learned the stories would not air Monday and Tuesday. Donna and I were called into a meeting with management. We were given the green light for the team report. "You two had better be careful," Lloyd warned us. "We're doing this against my better judgment. You'll both be driving station vehicles for the next few days and you will keep us informed at all times of your whereabouts."

I laughed. Not outwardly, but I laughed to myself at the posturing. This meeting was held for no other reason than to satisfy the insurance company. Lloyd had to be heard on record telling us to be careful. He had to be surrounded by Gretchen, Todd, and Fryer and their nodding heads and their somber eyes, his three witnesses, accomplices even, in this masquerade of concern.

"But here's the caveat," Gretchen announced. Of course

she would be the one with the caveat. Good cop, bad cop, so damn transparent. Lloyd played the dad, Gretchen the designated cunt. "We want the Rendezvous story for Monday night. So we'll be able to promote the hell out of it this weekend. And then the team report will run on Wednesday and Thursday. Donna will kick it off Wednesday at five with her investigation of the bank's collapse. Then Damon will come on at six with his exclusive interview of Roberto Cruz. Okay? And then we'll pose the question: What do these two stories have in common? And on Thursday we'll hit 'em big with the connection between the bank and Gina Parr."

I said nothing. Neither did Donna. Apparently, our input was not needed or wanted.

"Can you pull this off?" Fryer asked.

"If we couldn't pull it off, we wouldn't be having this discussion," I replied.

"Yes," Lloyd said. "That's true enough. I want all scripts run by Legal and I want all edited packages screened by every manager in this room."

Donna and I nodded obligingly.

It would be a busy weekend, but it would be worth it. My brain was now rewired to the task. Again, the sweet addictive nectar of a story had dribbled across my lips. Once I got this much of a taste, all the bitterness went away, all the hesitation and reservation just washed away in the potent gargle of hot pursuit. Now, it was almost as if I had never had a quiver of reticence. I was reminded somehow of waves...of small waves that hit the shore and as they begin their rightful retreat succumb to the subsequent crash of a much larger wave. The small waves lose themselves to the bigger ones. They are overpowered by an energy, a force much greater than themselves.

48

MOST OF YOU HAVE PROBABLY HEARD THE EXPRESSION "A star is born."

But, no, this is not about Judy Garland or Barbra Streisand, though you might argue that no gay life is complete without them (my gay life, you should know, was entirely Judy- and Barbra-free).

This is about the birth of stars.

Your death = your birth.

Your death is the birth-wail of a new star. You really need to understand this because, ultimately, it will show you the reunions that await you.

Just as there are generations of life, there are generations of stars. Perhaps that is the reason that scientists talk about "young stars" and "parent stars"; they are talking about the mystery of heaven without realizing the light they are shining on the truth.

Astronomers say a star is born when huge interstellar clouds collapse under their own gravity. When scientists see new stars forming, they almost always see powerful streams of plasma. Those streams can extend for up to ten light-years from the parent star. So it really matters little when those before you have passed; you will be reconnected to them in heaven.

Your family of stars comes together one death at a time.

So, yes, you are reunited with your loved ones in heaven. Not so much physically as spiritually and soulfully. The parent star guides you from afar and you feel this electric reconnection to the souls of those you've loved. In this cosmic electricity all kinds of communication is possible. Mostly it is gentle interstellar murmurs of love and appreciation and, ultimately, gratitude.

When a child dies before a parent, as I have, we are called orphan stars. Orphan stars simply reconnect to other loved ones (grandparents, aunts, uncles, generous teachers) until the parent star appears from another reach of the universe. That reunion is something to behold. Some say it is the very phenomena those on Earth call a "shooting star." I do not know, as I am still an orphan.

Personally, my experience suggests that a "shooting star" is, more appropriately, the heavenly equivalent of orgasm. And I by no means intend to be glib by that remark. But, every so often, you feel the energy of your star thrust powerfully through a shining space, a long shimmering tunnel, and it's the closest thing to orgasm I have experienced up here. And appropriately so. After all, one of the things we love about life, those of us who can admit such things, is the pleasure of sex. When we die we mourn the loss of such a magnificent sensation that is orgasm. I can tell you this: Orgasm is only a preview of the things to come (please!) in heaven. Why do you think they call it heaven?

An orgasm, as I've come to understand, is a transport of sorts to a higher level of consciousness. Most on Earth only enjoy the ride, the transport, if you will, without stopping for a moment at this higher level of consciousness to look around. That's why the sensation of orgasm remains a mystery to most, a presumption to many, and, unfortunately, just a payoff to those who miss the point entirely. Orgasm as transport: to the sensations of another world. I'd leave it at that but I fear you might expect heaven to be one huge orgy of shooting stars. It is not. I only mean to say that heaven would never deprive you of the most heavenly feeling of life. If anything, it improves upon it.

So when you're here you know love in so many ways. You reconnect. You leap and shimmer and soar and, occasionally, you explode.

And then you die.

Yes, all stars die.

This is, after all, just another cycle of life. And the generations follow.

However, you should know that the life expectancy, the longevity of your star, is infinitely longer and larger than you could ever imagine on Earth. Besides, do you know what a dying star truly is? It's a supernova: extremely bright, lasting. Supernovas can be seen blazing from six billion light-years away. That's a very long time to enjoy the extinguishment of your star.

After that, I do not know.

I don't really know what happens when your star dies. Is the afterlife of a star actually a heaven to the heavens?

I'm not there yet. I cannot say.

LOGGING TAPE SUCKS. I HAD ALWAYS HATED LOGGING TAPE, but that is precisely how I spent the weekend, holed up in an airless viewing booth watching hours of tape, transcribing interviews verbatim, taking notes. That's what glamorous television reporters do with every story. They revisit every interview and transcribe every word of every sound bite worth pulling for the story. I sat there in my attention-deficit-disordered state, my eyes glazing over, my brain fogging in, and I determined to call that Danielle Corcoran, the wannabe intern, and give her a chance. If I could get an intern in there to log all my tape and call back all the assholes who clog my voice-mail with bad tips and worse excuses for stories, I might consider not quitting my job and joining the circus.

Donna sat in the viewing booth next to me. She had already written most of her story (I had, as you may recall, reviewed it for her), but now she gave her sound bites a second spin in the cassette deck, searching for more material with which she could expand the piece now that it was a Team Report. Don't even get me started; suffice it to say the working title bestowed by Gretchen upon our team report was something like: "Banking, Betrayal, and Death."

Ick.

My first order of business was to get the Rendezvous piece written (it would air Monday night before the icky team report), so it was those tapes I logged first. There wasn't a whole lot of sound-bite material, but it took me hours to get through all the undercover surveillance video we shot. There was the Rhode Island sting, the drag-show video, the Fall River footage, and the confrontation with Lane & Lane. When I arrived at the drag-show video I called Donna into my booth and we both roared at the pure campiness of the scheme. My source at the FBI had stated quite clearly that the performers would not be implicated in the crime as they were innocent conduits; "unwitting participants" they were called. The drag queens been forced to hand over all tips after their performances and only drew a small percentage of the bounty. Most of them were stunned to see how much money had been stuffed into their cleavage. In fact I interviewed Jasmine Jism and she still seemed flustered by the whole ordeal.

"Like, honey," she said, "I'm telling you none of us suspected a thing. We figured some rich daddies had finally discovered our show and were simply showing their appreciation." She said "appreciation" as it was meant to be said, benevolently. "But," she continued with a crackle in her voice, "the girls and I were getting mighty peeved handing over all that cash to DeKashonni. I mean, sweet thing, we were ready to unionize when we realized how much money Rendezvous was raking in and how little of it we were taking home. You know what I'm saying, sugar?"

I told her I did.

"Are you going to use her in your story?" Donna asked.

"Oh yeah. That's the color this story needs," I replied. "You can only do so much with grainy undercover video..."

Donna nodded and returned to her booth.

We stopped for lunch at the same eatery where I had chastised Donna for her futile attempt at backstabbing. "Do you forgive me now that we're officially a *team*?" she asked.

I munched into my turkey club. "No," I replied after a swallow. "But I do believe you'll never do it again. I have that much respect for you."

"You can be a smug little shit, Damon Fitzgerald."

I nodded. "Yes, I know. Makes you think I should work for FOX."

Her eyes gleamed at me as if she loved me or hated me. I couldn't tell. Her eyes simply came to a frozen glare while her mouth gave way to a smile. "We're going to rock this town," she said reflectively, coolly, savoring, it seemed, every morsel of our inevitable triumph. "You just wait until we break these stories. Every other reporter in town will be chasing our tail."

And she was right. Dead on, right.

Tuesday morning proved her right. Both the *Herald* and the *Globe* ran headlines echoing my Rendezvous story. Both newspapers gave brief but definitive credit to the investigation conducted by Channel 11.

Johnnie gave me the obligatory high five. Todd and Fryer came in to congratulate me and tell me how we had outperformed all other newscasts in the overnight ratings. Gretchen had multiple news-gasms.

Donna rolled into my office with a gleaming "way to go" smile.

Karl called to tell me he understood my pain.

"What pain?" I asked.

"The pain of having to betray your own people for the sake of a story."

"You've got to be kidding."

"Yes," he said. "I'm kidding."

"You had me worried there for a minute. Because I did have some mixed feelings about doing the story."

"I know you must have," he said. "But you handled it like a pro. I want to take you out for dinner tonight."

"Why?"

"To show you off," he replied.

"What the fuck?"

"I'm so proud to know you, Damon."

I laughed. "Okay, fine then. I'm proud to know you too."

"I'm serious!" he cried.

"So am I, Karl. You're the lover I never had."

His voice cracked. "I'm going to call Louise. Let's make it a celebration."

"Are you sure you don't want to wait until later in the week?" I asked. "It just gets better if I do say so myself. I've got a two-part investigation that will be wrapped up by Thursday."

He scoffed. "This is just you putting me off, Damon. Let's do it tonight."

And so we did.

Louise met us on Newbury Street for dinner and we indulged in three appetizers, three entrées, three chocolate soufflés for dessert. We drank two bottles of wine between us and then finished the night with three Irish coffees, accent on the Irish, thank you very much.

Feeling no pain, we kissed and hugged and swaggered down Newbury Street laughing about everything.

"Why doesn't your penis freeze like an icicle in the cold weather?" Karl asked.

I rolled my eyes and nudged him. "Let us not forget your penis is not even real."

"I'm ready to get laid again," Louise announced.

"Any candidates?" I asked.

"Three guys at work. I'm going to pull a name out of a hat."

"You don't have a preference?" I asked.

"Not really. It's only sex," she said. "It ain't love."

"That's sad," Karl told her, then he busted out laughing and we joined him for a drunken rendition of the Tina Turner classic "What's Love Got To Do With It?"

Then we kissed and hugged again and drifted our separate ways.

Not one of us realized, had any inkling, that less than three hours later I'd be dead.

50

It happened around midnight, I believe. I was in bed, sleeping, having just watched Jon Stewart on *The Daily Show*, eschewing the real news for Comedy Central. The room was dark, save for a field of opaque light cast over my bed by the TV I had failed to turn off. I woke to a slap on the face.

Weird. Very weird.

When I finally realized I had an intruder leaning over me, all I could think of was, what a weird way to wake up your victim...series of slaps on the face. Mad slaps. Like, how dare you sleep?

I bolted up in bed, pushed against the intruder. But that's precisely what the guy was waiting for, for me to lift my head so he could cover it with a sheet and slip a cord around my neck. And pull.

First I thought this must be a joke. Because the first tug of the cord was tentative, mocking even. And then after enough of a pause for me to hope this would stop, I felt a hand grip my throat, dislodging my Adam's apple, it seemed.

The cord.

The hand.

Tighter.

Pressuring me to gasp for air, to float away into breathlessness with mild, tender attempts at survival, and then surrender, peaceful, knowing surrender.

That's all I really remember about my murder. It's been a while now; it's hard to recollect all the details. Except, of course, the smell. I will never forget the smell of my murder. Not a foul odor, really. Not offensive at all. Just distinctive. It was the smell of something that smelled like nothing else. Wet wool. I can only guess my murderer was wearing a sweater and had just come in from the rain.

51

Approximate time of death: 12:50 A.M.

Cause of death: strangulation (pending autopsy).

Kin notified: yes.

The medical examiner filled out a stack of forms and placed them among the pile of paperwork on his desk, a pile that, no doubt, represented other dead bodies, other causes of death.

I did not see my life flash before my eyes. This surprised me. I did feel myself letting go and dreamily drifting toward a light, but the light was unadulterated; it was brilliant and white and unwrinkled by the facts of my life.

And so I died, passed over, crossed over, bought the farm, kicked the bucket, croaked, expired, journeyed to the other side, and it was well covered by the Boston media. By noontime Wednesday my death was reported on every Boston news channel. The *Globe* and the *Herald* both had reporters assigned to the story. My family had been notified early that morning. Marilyn inhaled a whoop of surprise that nearly knocked her out. My father tried to comfort her but, instead, sank into her arms and broke down in tears.

At Channel 11, there were a few scenes unfolding. First, there were those who wanted to grieve, colleagues of mine who wrung their hands in anger, bereft by my demise. And then there were those whose silent vibes encoded a sense of inevitability. *It was bound to happen,* they whispered to themselves.

Lloyd Lasser called my family to express in a most sincere and humble way his devastation. Gretchen arranged for flowers and cried openly in front of the news staff. Her eyes wandered, though, never fully absent from the other news of the day.

Todd and Fryer were left to decide how to handle the story of my murder.

They, smartly, decided to report the facts. I had been murdered. There were no witnesses. No signs of forced entry. No suspects at this time.

They approached Donna Donovan and told her that she would need to package our team report solely. "But Damon and I spent the whole weekend packaging it together," she said with a grieving sniffle. "Do you really want me to undo all of that?"

Todd nodded. "Yeah. We think Damon would want the show to go on, so to speak."

Fryer indicated his concurrence with a mournful nod. The mournful nods were becoming overplayed, a quiet cliché of a gesture.

Besides, how the hell did Todd and Fryer know what I would have wanted? Maybe I would have wanted the world to stop and acknowledge the gravity, the tragedy of my death. Maybe I would have wanted the news operation to so visibly break from the norm as to inform the audience just how special, really special I was. Well, no. The truth was I just wanted the freaking show to go on. They were right. A man who knows little narcissism in life rarely calls for it in death.

It wasn't long—maybe a few hours—before Detective Raul Sanderplaatz of the Massachusetts State Police made the rounds of the newsroom. He talked to the entire staff but was most interested, of course, in talking to Donna Donovan, who revealed what she could about my recent investigations.

They knew each other from her days in the department.

"Do you think any of these people would have been mad enough about the stories to kill him?" he asked.

She shrugged. A single tear rolled down her cheek. "I don't know. I don't know any of the people. Maybe one of them wanted revenge...but that's all it would be at this point, revenge. You know, those stories—the fake diplomas, the state-house investigation—already ran. It wasn't like killing Damon could have stopped them from airing." She stopped for a moment and sniffled. She shook her head, dismayed, and then, "*However,* I would think the people at Gina Parr's law firm would want Damon dead. I mean, there was more at stake. That story hasn't run yet. Killing Damon might have prevented our investigation from airing tonight, I suppose. Everyone knew the team report would be starting tonight."

"Oh?"

"Yes, Raul. The station's been promoting the investigation for the past three days. Everybody knows we've uncovered some provocative information."

"Everybody?"

"Yeah, everybody. Trust me, Raul, the people at Berger and Berger were watching us closely. Go talk to my boss about a certain surprise visit on Friday."

"Okay," the detective said tentatively.

Donna turned to her keyboard, indicating to Sanderplaatz that she had nothing more to say. He asked anyway. "Anything else?"

"No," she said. "I don't think so."

Sanderplaatz walked into Lloyd Lasser's office and closed the door. "I need a few minutes," he said. "I realize this isn't a good time, but I need you to tell me about the lawyers who came to see you on Friday."

Lloyd related all the details to the detective in a plain, even manner. There was no inflection in his voice, little emotion in his eyes. It was then that I realized from my hovering vantage point that Lloyd must have felt that he had let me down somehow, and I resolved to communicate to him in some way that he had not.

Soon, Sanderplaatz had a short list of people who might want me dead.

Frank was at the top.

Then came all the lawyers at Berger, Berger, Cooke, & Langham.

A few names from the statehouse followed.

Then the names of each phony professor I'd exposed.

Then came a visit from Sam Young.

Sam Young eyed the detective up and down and lingered for a noticeable moment on the detective's ample crotch. He had rushed over to the police department only to find that the detective had left hours ago to visit Channel 11. He waited for the detective to return.

"I warned Damon that he would die," Sam explained after he talked his way into the inner sanctum of Sanderplaatz's office. "I don't think he really heard me."

"And you claim to be psychic?" the detective asked with a fleck of impatience in his voice.

"Exactly," Sam said confidently.

"Are your psychic abilities any more specific? I suppose any number of astute people might have warned Damon Fitzgerald that his work could get him in trouble."

"I'm sorry, detective. I didn't know Damon long enough to get anything more specific."

"I see..."

"I know you people don't think all that highly of psychics..."

The detective snorted. "We don't think about them all that much, to be honest." He leaned forward. "But we might be skeptical of the fiancé of a dead woman who suddenly knows something about a second murder."

Sam stood up in protest. "How dare you, detective? I've done nothing less than cooperate fully with you in the investigation of Gina's death."

"Yes, you have, Mr. Young. But forgive me if this all feels too much like a coincidence."

Sam was still standing. His hands on his hips now. "Well, you can't convict on coincidence."

The detective eyed him warily. "Who's talking conviction?"

Sam shook his head but said nothing. The detective extended a handshake indicating it was time for Sam to go. Sam left, and as he did I had to wonder if the psychic bisexual had not been merely covering his tracks. Perhaps he killed me because I rejected his advances.

Stranger things have happened.

✧ ✧ ✧

The anchor team at Channel 11 assumed the most aggrieved posture they could muster, affecting the darkest tone they could utter, and kicked off the evening news with news of my death.

"It's a tragic day here at Channel 11..." the newscast began.

52

I<small>T MADE FOR A BEAUTIFUL SEGUE</small>. F<small>IRST THE ANCHORS SADLY</small> reported my death, and then with a Gretchen-induced flourish they introduced the "final story Damon Fitzgerald would file in his tragically short lifetime."

Hmm.

Actually, it was part one of the two-part investigation into New England Savings and its link to the Gina Parr murder. And while the anchors had introduced it as my final farewell, the story had been repackaged by Donna Donovan, who, in this first segment, stayed mostly on course with the New England Savings information but referenced me amply as her coinvestigator.

"And tomorrow," she chanted squarely into the lens of the studio camera, "the murder of a young Boston lawyer. I'll take you deep inside the case and show you why Gina Parr may have cashed in too soon at the bank."

Ugh.

I'm almost sure Gretchen had fed her that line, because I could see the unearthed grimace behind Donna's poker face.

✧ ✧ ✧

How fucking ironic that what would have been my most compelling story of February sweeps should run, as it did, on the evening of my wake.

How fucking ironic that I should barely get any credit.

How soon they forget.

Donna referenced me once in part two, and then within moments it was: Damon who?

Suddenly, it was Donna who had meticulously linked the evidence at the crime scene and the death of Gina Parr to the collapse of New England Savings. Suddenly it was my video-tape and Donna's voice.

Okay, the other souls tell me, take a deep harmonic breath, exhale it into the seas, create a tide of forgiveness, and move on.

The first few days of death are difficult, let me tell you. You ultimately have to let go of all you have come to know as habitual. You have to let go of old emotions and expectations. You have to surrender your modus operandi, in general, and that is quite tough. Actually, it is harder to let go of your horrible habits than it is to let go of your wonderful relatives.

Because you find yourself reunited with the energy of those loved ones who have passed before you, it is with full faith and a lightness in your heart that you fully expect to be reunited with the ones you've left behind. You don't feel the separation and the sorrow that your survivors are enduring. But you do have a hell (not black-hole hell, just rhetorical hell) of a time unbecoming the *person* you were. Your person must separate from your soul, and while the transport to heaven is brilliant, heady, and as thrilling as the rush of a theme-park ride, you can't ride the transport accompanied by your person. Persons of any height not allowed.

The things that people love about you truly reside in your soul, so don't worry about leaving any of that behind. The trick is to get on the ride having shed the baggage. No carry-ons allowed. I think I have referenced this before. But you know travelers: They never quite listen to the rules and fully expect that there will be exceptions anyway.

Sorry. No exceptions.

So there I was, waked at a Farmington, Connecticut, funeral home, my person and my soul struggling with the all-too-familiar separation anxiety, my ego bruised by the slight of an industry where yesterday's news is about as useful to the populace as a placebo is to the addict. People came and wept.

It was touching, really.

Donna Donovan showed up and I wanted to slap her.

Johnnie came and said how much he'd miss me. His eyes were moist.

Lloyd came with Gretchen, Todd, and Fryer. They all looked miserably incapable of translating this moment beyond, say, a thirty-second voice-over with, perhaps, a sound bite from a close friend or relative. Consequently, they paid their respects and were quick to leave because they had been there at least an hour and, in the context of television news, that was an eternity. And an eternity is absolutely unheard of.

The next day, I must say, brought a lovely gesture. Lloyd asked Johnnie to edit together a minute's worth of video (a full minute!) of my most memorable work. The anchors paid tribute to me using that video on the evening newscast.

I passed over Karl's house where he watched the tribute in tears. I blew a kiss into his ear and watched, tickled and fascinated, as he brushed the unknown object away with a semiconscious hand.

This was the part of the transport that I loved. The moving in and out of people's lives and dropping little hints, or sending little morsels of truth, or blowing supernatural kisses. There is no high quite like it.

❖ ❖ ❖

Within a week, Richard Neckingham held a news conference announcing he would widen the probe into the murder of Gina Parr. He did not mention Channel 11 specifically, but he did reference certain "media reports indicating other avenues that may need to be explored."

I deemed that triumph enough.

Donna's, er, my, er, our story had shaken the city of Boston like an earthquake. The fault lines ran deep and wide through the legal community and the media. Donna had had the fine journalistic sense to quote me insofar as what I told her about the unannounced visit by Berger and Cooke. She put it out there: that these men had claimed to be first on the scene, that, more important, they had claimed to have identified Gina's body when, in fact, they had already gone public with a different story—the one that had them playing golf in Boca Raton at the time of the murder.

That would raise enough suspicion to knock Boston, a city not normally prone to tremors, off the Richter scale.

Why would the lawyers have lied about ID'ing the body? What were they trying to hide?

You can't salivate in heaven. But your star can twist and shout in celebration. Mine did.

As much as I resented Donna usurping my story and leaving me no more than a dust particle on the lens of truth, as much as I felt upstaged and undermined and stabbed in the backside (she and Johnnie actually high-fived each other, elated over the prospects of winning an Emmy, my freaking posthumous Emmy!), I had to give the steely woman credit. She had put out a fine piece. She had produced a well-researched, well-balanced story of "Banking, Betrayal, and Dead Bodies." It was not lost on me that my own death had been built into the plurality of the title. And that made me think about Sam Young's premonition. And it made me think that Sam Young had made me an offer much more promising than a blow job.

53

THE PHONE RANG IN SAM YOUNG'S APARTMENT. HE answered it. There was no one there.

But I was there. Just checking to see if we had a connection.

I called again.

"Hello?" he asked.

I hung up again.

This was a bit creepy but, at the same time, a real kick. Prank phone calls: the work of the spirit world. Who knew?

I tried one more time.

His voice trembled with impatience. "Yes?"

"Hi."

"Can I help you?" he asked.

"Yes."

"Is this Damon Fitzgerald?"

"It is."

"Well, hello Damon. Now do you believe me?"

"Obviously, I do."

Sam scratched his head and yawned. I might have woken him up. He had the distinctive pajama look of the unemployed. "I'm glad you contacted me, Damon."

"I need you to go see that detective."

"Sanderplaatz?"

"Yes. I have some information. Bring it to him."

Sam bristled. "Well, I've tried to appeal to him, Damon, but I don't think he trusts me."

"Tell him I think I was murdered by Reginald Cooke."

"Well, I certainly think everyone is a suspect now."

"No, no, Sam. Listen. The person who killed me smelled exactly like Cooke's cologne."

"Cologne?"

"Grey Flannel."

"I hate Grey Flannel," Sam said.

"I don't think this is a coincidence. The killer smelled like wet wool."

"The same odious smell as Grey Flannel..."

"Exactly," I said. "Exactly!"

"I'll get right on it," Sam assured me. "And thanks for getting in touch."

"No problem."

"How is everything where you are, Damon?"

"So far, so good. But everything is so new to me."

"Hmm. I'm sure it is."

Then I moved on.

I decided to phone a few others.

First, Louise: "Hello? Is anybody there?" she asked. "Hello?"

Then, Karl: "Hello? Hello? Hello? Who is this? The least you could do is breathe heavy, say something dirty..."

Louise again: "Hello? Aw, c'mon, man, I don't have time for this bullshit."

And Claire: "Good afternoon, Now Voyager Travel. Hello? Anybody there?"

273

It was wonderful to hear their voices. I only wish they could have heard mine.

✦ ✦ ✦

A few weeks went by, and I saw no progress with my Grey Flannel theory. Settling into heaven, meanwhile, was a blast. Literally and figuratively. Lots of joyous explosions up here. Fireworks of celebration. And the music, my God, the music is exhilarating. From where it comes I do not know. But it is magical.

On Earth I could see Richard Neckingham cursing me in a special way. He loved me and hated me but had to deal with me even in my death because the Donna Donovan–Damon Fitzgerald team report had forced him to reopen the investigation into Gina Parr's murder. This did not mean freedom for Roberto Cruz; he still languished in jail while the wheels of pretrial justice creakily jump-started. Meanwhile, Raleigh Dean puttered around town with a shit-feasting grin, his eyes just waiting for the signal to jump out of their sockets...the signal that Berger, Berger, Cooke, or Langham had been arrested for murder.

Raleigh Dean dreamt about me. Or, I should say, I paid him a visit in his sleep and he gave me a high five. Which made me think of Johnnie and Donna and how they had high-fived the expectation of an Emmy (*my* posthumous Emmy!) and I paid them a visit and found that, indeed, they were fucking. But they were fucking like new fuckbirds so I do not suspect that Johnnie had lied when I had asked fairly directly before my death if they were fucking. They were hunger-fucking, can't-get-enough fucking. Sweat poured from their bodies and soaked the sheets. We are not able to see the fucking of everyone from up here. Some greater being normally protects the privacy of those fucking on Earth by sending out a star stream of gauzy light that shields the fuckers like a blue dot on the televised faces of protected witnesses.

But there was a reason to see the fucking of Donna Donovan and Johnnie Fanahan. This vision was granted to me for a reason. And so I studied them closely as they turned Donna's bedroom into an athletic arena and fucked each other into oblivion. Donna hopped out of bed first, lit a cigarette, and ran the water for a bath.

Johnnie snoozed for a few short minutes, rose, and raided the fridge for a beer.

She bathed. He drank. They reunited shortly thereafter, she in a robe, he in his BVDs. He lamented my death. More so than she could comprehend. After all, Johnnie Fanahan had discovered my lifeless body—twisted there at the head of my bed—when he had been sent to look in on me after I had failed to show for work. He had enlisted the help of a neighbor. The neighbor, a quiet, timid old woman named Mrs. Haberman, called the superintendent. He had unlocked the door to my apartment, deferring there at the threshold to Johnnie's request.

"Go ahead," the super said. "Go in and see if he's home..."

Mrs. Haberman covered her mouth and turned her shell-shocked face away. That was not unusual for her. She always seemed terribly alarmed at something, life in general, whenever I would run into her.

I wish I could say Johnnie's reaction was heroic or romantic or, in the classic sense, Shakespearean, but it wasn't. He simply shook me once or twice, felt my neck for a pulse, and stared at the walls of my room. He then uttered "shit" and "fuck" a few times each, picked up the phone, and called 911.

Now, postcoitally, Donna hushed him, told him they would have to learn to let go.

"Do you think they've rented his apartment yet?" Johnnie asked his lover.

"Oh, my God, Johnnie! You can't honestly be thinking of renting it. How morbid!"

Johnnie laughed. "No, I'm not thinking of renting it."

"Good," Donna said.

"But I do feel kind of weird (*weehd*) because I lent Damon a lot of CDs and I'd really like to get them back. I mean, I feel bad about it, but I don't want his family to think they can just take them for themselves."

Donna rolled her eyes. "How many, Johnnie?"

"Probably a dozen."

He was wrong. I had borrowed closer to two dozen. I found his predicament amusing.

"They haven't rented his apartment," Donna told him.

"How do you know?"

"Because Neckingham told me. They're preserving the crime scene."

"Huh? It's been over a month, Donna. That's ridiculous."

She leaned forward and caressed his shoulders. She relieved his hand of its beer and took a swig. "Okay, well, maybe not *preserving*," she conceded. "But protecting. You've got to figure the same person who killed Gina Parr killed Damon as well. Both crime scenes are inextricably connected now."

"You think?"

"I'm sure of it," she said, pausing for another swig. "And we all know it wasn't Roberto Cruz. 'Cause he's been locked up the whole time."

"Would it be offensive of me to ask for my CDs?" Johnnie asked her.

"No, of course not."

"You don't think it would be...tacky?"

"Now you sound gay."

He gave her a tender slug in the arm, the way straight men do when they don't truly know the avenues of affection. "Come on," he said. "I suppose I should call the D.A. and ask if I can get in there."

"To Damon's place? Fuck the D.A.," Donna said. "I can get you in there."

"Legally?"

"I don't see why not. There's still a key in Damon's desk."

"Oh?"

"Yeah, I had to rescue him one day when he locked himself out."

"Oh, good. I don't want to bother his old neighbor again."

54

RICHARD NECKINGHAM WANTED TO WASH HIS HANDS OF THE whole mess. That's essentially what he told the partners of Berger, Berger, Cooke, & Langham when he met with them on that warming March afternoon in the privacy of his office.

"Look, Don, I have three people at Channel 11 who witnessed you tell a lie about the murder scene. One of those witnesses is dead, but the other two will give me sworn statements of that lie. You didn't ID the body that night. Why would you have lied like that?"

The lawyer chuckled. A pompous, arrogant, white-collar laugh of haughtiness, indifference, and pure disdain. "I wanted those morons at that TV station to know who they were dealing with..."

"And who were they dealing with, Reggie? Two shitheads whose alibis don't really check out? To think I had given you the benefit of the doubt."

"Excuse me, Richard, but are you suggesting my partners need representation now?" Walter Langham asked.

"No one is reading them their rights," Neckingham retorted. "If that's what you're asking."

"Then what are you getting at?" Langham demanded.

"I'm getting at this: You boys fucked up. You lied about your whereabouts that evening and now I've asked my men to truly check your alibis. There were no trips to Florida," he said firmly. "Not for anyone in this room."

Langham cleared his throat. "Well, actually," he huffed, "I was playing golf in Palm Beach."

"You don't count," Neckingham told him. "You checked out years ago, Walter. You hang around that firm because you have nothing else to do. You're oblivious."

Walter was elderly. Not frail, but certainly not spritely either. He wore a pinstripe suit. His white hair swooped to the front of his head like the crest of a wave bound for shore. His voice was deep and his words drawn out when he spoke.

"I resent being spoken to this way," the old man told the district attorney.

"Well, I suggest you clean up the mess you have in your own house before you expect any more favors from this one."

The old man with the deep voice rose to his feet. His body seemed to unfold in stages but his posture, once it composed itself, was regal nonetheless. "I think our business is through here."

"Maybe not," Neckingham said, not acknowledging the attempted exit. "When you return to your offices, gentlemen, you will find that my investigators have secured a search warrant."

The old man's hand went to his heart.

Donald Berger jumped to his feet. "Walter! Easy now..."

Walter Langham steadied himself and leaned over the district attorney's desk, meeting the man squarely face-to-face. "Richard, you better know what you're doing. Every *i* dotted, every *t* crossed. My firm will not be brought down by you or anyone else."

They filed out of Neckingham's office, the younger attorneys behind the elder figure, like a very serious episode of *My Three Sons*.

In the car on the way back to the firm Walter Langham turned to his ducklings and said, "I don't like this one bit and nobody better be fucking with me." And the car was quiet for the rest of the ride.

❖ ❖ ❖

A nearby star explained it rather simply. An unresolved death like mine allows for the spirit to linger. The spirit does not have to linger, but it may. Those who die more conventional deaths tend to cross over far more quickly, efficiently, and with a lot less drama. "I like the drama," I announced proudly to the other souls of heaven. They dismissed me with a sneeze of stardust, but truly I meant what I said. The opportunity to observe this way is precious. Kind of makes up for the violence of the murder and that whole "life cut short" thing.

❖ ❖ ❖

The search of Berger, Berger, Cooke, & Langham turned up no physical evidence to speak of, but (and this is a very big and important "but") the investigators were able to get the fingerprints of all the partners off their everyday work materials. They were perfect prints because they belonged to fingers that belonged to brains that had apparently not anticipated this search warrant. The prints came from telephones, computer keyboards, assorted paperwork, the toilet handles in the private gilded bathroom. Bet these stuffed shirts never thought they'd be betrayed by their own defecation.

It was about a week before the results came back and Richard Neckingham had a positive match. Actually two positive matches.

The fingerprints of Donald Berger and Reginald Cooke both matched prints found in Gina Parr's apartment. Her home, of course, had been thoroughly dusted for prints during the initial investigation of her murder.

"I promised myself I would not make a move until we had some physical evidence," Neckingham told the head detective of CPAC. "Now you can bring them in for questioning."

"Voluntary?" the detective asked.

"Let them volunteer. If not, arrest them. For murder."

The detective nodded soberly—as if he understood the torn feelings, the conflicting loyalties of the district attorney—and walked away.

✧ ✧ ✧

The panic below was somewhat satisfying, vindicating even, possessing, it seemed, the same frightening beauty of a churning, erupting volcano.

It was too damn late. At least for Donald Berger.

He had told Reginald Cooke that he was going to confess and clearly implicate Cooke in the crime. He was going to make a deal with the prosecutor to plea for a lesser charge. "This wasn't my idea," he cried. "None of this was my idea. You pushed the New England Savings thing on me. And then Gina Parr. I told you this thing would blow up in our faces but you wouldn't listen. You think you know everything about everything. Walter was right. Young does equal stupid. Both of us were stupid but you're younger than me and more stupid than me and this fucking mess proves it."

Cooke approached him slowly. "Look, you knew what was at stake all along. You just got greedy. And you couldn't say no to New England Savings. I had nothing to do with your greed. You came by that on your own."

They were standing on the stone walkway leading down to the sea from Berger's lavish North Shore home. They had come out of the enormous manse and had started for the ocean, freezing in midpath to wrestle each other's psyches. Neither looked particularly tough or daunting. Both strained to intimidate, emasculate, but the posturing was just that, posturing. It rolled too cleanly off them, their machismo falling to the ground like thick Rolex watches slipping from their thin, dainty wrists.

"Who do you think has the New England Savings files?" Berger asked.

"They've been turned over as evidence. Or haven't you been watching the news?"

"Those were Gina's copies. I have the original files. I've had them all along. And I never kept them in the office, Reggie. Now, *that* would have been stupid. The search warrant would have turned those up and you and I would be facing an indictment right now."

"We are, aren't we?"

"Yes, but I'm going to take those files to the D.A. and show chronologically who was involved first. You, not me. You were well into this for months, maybe even a year before I got involved. I've got the leverage, buddy. And I'm going to make a plea."

That's when Reginald Cooke pulled out his gun and, like the pop of a firecracker, shot his colleague in the head. Cooke then turned the gun on himself and was just about to pull the trigger when a small army of men burst from the sides of the house and told him to freeze.

"Let me do this," he screamed to the men. "Let me do this with dignity."

He then broke down to the ground in sobs, unaware apparently that he and his dignity had parted ways long ago. The gun languished in his hand; it dangled there underscoring his helplessness, it seemed. He heaved more heavy sobs as the officers handcuffed him and walked him across the manicured grounds to a waiting car in the circular drive.

Stunning, really.

55

THANK GOD FOR DONNA DONOVAN. SURE, SHE HAD upstaged, undermined, backstabbed even the ghost of me—but she had done her job. She had made the right connections and she had taken them to the district attorney. It was she, after all, who related my suspicions to Richard Neckingham about the firm's visit that Friday morning to Channel 11. It was she who related Reggie Cooke's claim that he had identified the body.

That lie proved to be pivotal in the psyche of Richard Neckingham.

That lie had taunted him, had itched at his conscience like a wool turtleneck at a freshly shaven face. Wool...my killer wore wool. Smelled like damp wool...and I felt the itch of wool against my neck as the rope pulled me tighter toward my death.

"Will you be checking the fingerprints taken at Damon's place for a match?" Donna asked.

The district attorney's office had sent out a press release announcing the arrest of Reginald Cooke on charges of first-degree murder. The press release also included a brief mention about Roberto Cruz: The D.A.'s office would be moving to have the state's case against Mr. Cruz dismissed.

I roused Raleigh Dean from a light slumber of alcohol at Kelly's Toe and whispered the good news into his ear. He, of course, couldn't hear me. But the whisper had its purpose and its power just the same. The whisper jolted him just in time to see the special bulletin airing on the TV set suspended above the smoke-infested bar.

"We interrupt this program for a Channel 11 Special Report..."

I wanted to offer a heavenly high five, but all I could do was enjoy the public defender's triumph vicariously.

And then, off I went, through the TV, into the microwaves of transmission, into the circuitry of signals and receivers, and back into the newsroom of Channel 11. That's where I found Donna Donovan now, on a call with the district attorney.

My spirit twirled its way into the phone cord and listened in.

"Yes," the D.A. was saying. "We will naturally check the prints in Damon's apartment for a match to our suspects."

"Would it be premature to say the person or persons who killed Gina Parr most probably perpetrated the crime against Damon Fitzgerald?"

"Premature," Neckingham replied, "and awfully technical, Donna. You might say that we're looking at any evidence whatsoever and are highly interested in whatever evidence could link Damon's murder to another crime."

"I may speak too technically...but you, Mr. D.A., speak too rhetorically."

"We'll be in touch. And, I don't know if I've said this, but I'm sorry for your loss. Damon was a great reporter."

"And a great guy," my former colleague said.

My spirit almost melted right there in the phone cord.

✧ ✧ ✧

I thought it was rather ballsy that Johnnie would actually infiltrate a crime scene to recover his CDs. But, then again, an audiophile like Johnnie could be rather anal about his music collection. He had, in fact, etched his initials into the corner of each plastic CD holder. "Just in case," he had once told me.

"Just in case of what?" I had challenged him. "I start selling your music on the black market?"

He simply gave me a you-wouldn't-understand shake of the head. I had borrowed music from the audiophile arbitrarily. He would play me a sample, and if I liked it, he would eject the disk and hand it to me, not unlike a librarian checking out a book.

And so, now, as he gathered his CDs on the floor of my living room, he insisted on checking every one.

"Would you please hurry?" Donna urged him. "It's not like we're supposed to be here..."

"I thought you said it was not a problem."

"Well, I never got the chance to ask the D.A."

He dropped the short stacks of discs on the floor. "We're here illegally?"

"Well, technically, maybe, yes," she said.

He shook his head, disgusted, and began to stuff CDs quickly into a duffel bag. "You're too much," he said to Donna.

"C'mon, honey, I was just trying to help you out," she purred.

Honey?

They were calling each other "honey" now?

I wanted to react with the afterlife equivalent of vomit spew but, you'll be pleased to know, there is no such thing as an upset stomach on the other side.

"Then help me now," Johnnie insisted. "Go through those

CDs in the bookcase, look for my initials, and give me the ones that are mine. Or just dump them in this bag."

He scooted the bag at her without taking his eyes off the task at hand. She backed away, offended for a moment, but then acquiesced and went to the bookcase.

They were probably ten minutes into the CD hunt when the door to my apartment creaked open and two men appeared at the threshold.

One of the men cleared his throat and bellowed, "Can I help you folks?"

Donna spun around not unlike a startled poodle who had just piddled on the carpet.

Johnnie looked unconcerned. I could tell what he was thinking (and I must admit I got a kick out of it): This broad got me into this mess, she's gonna get me out of it.

Donna walked toward the man and extended a hand. "Good to see you again, Raul." She then turned to Johnnie. "Do you know Detective Sanderplaatz? I suppose you can say we're old work buddies."

Sanderplaatz stepped out of the doorway and into the apartment, and as his figure and its shadow came forward I could see the man behind him. It was Karl. How my spirit fluttered!

Johnnie, still on the floor, acknowledged the detective with a nod. "Aren't you the one who came by the station to take statements from everyone?" he asked.

"Almost everyone," the man said with an ironic laugh. "And, Donna, you of all people should know the media has no access to this home right now."

"But it's not still a crime scene, is it? Technically speaking?"

"The media has no access to this home right now," he repeated to her.

She gestured to Johnnie Fanahan, who was still kneeling there in a circle of compact discs. "We're not here on professional business, so to speak. We were both friends of Damon.

Good friends. We just thought we should come by and gather some of our things."

"Things?" the detective asked.

"Well, yes," Donna said solicitously. "Things. You know how friends will leave things at your house now and then. Johnnie came for his CDs. I came for my wok. Damon was constantly borrowing stuff."

"Damon didn't cook," Karl interjected. "Didn't know how. Didn't want to learn."

"Well, what are *you* here to collect?" Donna asked my best friend.

"Photographs," he replied.

"Photos? Damon borrowed photos from you?" Her eyes were pure steel again.

"No," Karl told her. "I had a few pictures of us that he really liked. I had them framed for him. But I figured they might get lost in the shuffle, so I wanted them back."

"Oh. Of course," Donna said.

"But the wok," Karl persisted. "Believe me, Damon had no need for a wok."

Love you, Karl!

"Donna, how did you get in here tonight?" Sanderplaatz asked.

Johnnie stood up, wiped his hands on his trousers, and shuffled over to Donna's side. "Look, folks, we meant no harm," he said. "If you don't believe us, you can check the CDs. My initials are on all of them."

Sanderplaatz shook his head. "I don't care about the CDs or about your initials, sir. I want to know how you got in here and why you didn't get clearance from the authorities first..."

"Like *I* did," Karl snapped.

"Please..." Sanderplaatz told my friend. "Donna?"

She stiffened. "Why so formal, Raul? I mean, it's been a few years, but we're old colleagues for God's sake... If you want us to leave, we'll leave. No harm done."

"I want to know how you got in here tonight," he repeated with thinning patience.

"Johnnie had the key," Donna told him.

"I, what—?"

"The key, Johnnie," Donna said, turning to him, clasping his hand. "Didn't you find it in Damon's desk?"

"Uh...yeah. In his desk, I think."

"But you're not sure?" the detective asked.

And neither was I.

And neither was Raul Sanderplaatz.

56

No sign of forced entry.

Believe it or not, that mantra started to haunt me. That's right, a ghost haunted by the ghost of words.

No sign of forced entry.

I watched with great interest as Sanderplaatz maneuvered his way through the court system and secured warrants to search Channel 11, particularly the news vehicle driven by Johnnie Fanahan and the office of Donna Donovan.

My murder, after all, was no different than any other; everyone was a suspect. And some more so than others.

Meanwhile Johnnie and Donna were fighting, well, like Berger and Cooke had fought just before one of them had ended up dead behind the beachside mansion.

"Why did you make me lie for you?" Johnnie asked her, panicked.

"I didn't *make* you do anything," she snapped.

They were outside the station, in the back, hidden by the huge arsenal of live trucks. "I didn't even know he had a key in his desk."

"So?"

"So, what are you hiding, Donna? What do you know? Are you that desperate for the big story?"

"Shut up, Johnnie. Just shut up."

Sanderplaatz found nothing at Channel 11, though his men did dust for fingerprints. Next, he moved on to the Fanahan home in South Boston, where Johnnie's mother begged the cops not to arrest her boy. She followed them wild-eyed throughout the small Irish home, pleading with them to have mercy on her son. I wish I could have grabbed her by her dainty apron and held her quivering hands in mine and told her not to worry, that Johnnie had nothing to do with this, that her son had not strayed from her heart and her faith in God, that he had not betrayed his family in the eyes of God and had not disgraced them in front of the neighbors. Johnnie was a good boy, I would have told her. A sweet boy with a heavenly heart. I would not mention that, like most men, he was guided by his prick and it was his prick that got him into this mess and nothing more.

Officers dusted for fingerprints.

And they did so again at Donna Donovan's house in Dorchester. She lived on the top floor of a triple-decker. Naturally, I beat them all upstairs. They came and dusted and seized evidence.

Yes, evidence.

When Sanderplaatz found an unusual stash of accelerants in a shed behind the house, he made a call to the detective investigating the torching of Donna Donovan's automobile.

"Where is it?" Sanderplaatz asked the detective.

"What's left of it is in the Charlestown impound lot."

"Do we still have the Fitzgerald car?"

"Yeah. But it's in another lot. East Boston, I think."

"I want my guys to go through it for evidence. The guy is dead and we happen to have his car. What luck. I want those cars on the same lot," he said. "Side by side. I'll perform a fucking autopsy on both cars if I have to."

✧ ✧ ✧

Turns out, with the help of an arson investigator, Sanderplaatz was able to determine that Donna Donovan most likely torched her own automobile.

She had had two motives. One, to create a sense of danger, a bit of misdirection to make the public think she was the target of criminals—nice try at deflection. Two, to hide the evidence that it had been she who had run me off the road that night on Memorial Drive. The dents and scrapes on her automobile matched precisely the contusions on mine.

Wow.

But there's more.

Fibers from a wool sweater taken from Donna's apartment matched fibers found in my bed. Any number of people would testify that Donna had no more place in my bed than, say, Marie Osmond at a Phish concert.

✧ ✧ ✧

The police made it very clear to Johnnie Fanahan that he was not under arrest. "We just want to ask you about Donna's relationship to Damon Fitzgerald."

He was wild-eyed now, just like his mother. Stunned and pale, he sat there in an interrogation room, his head back as if it had been slapped, or punched at the jawline. I tried to whisper "Don't be scared, Johnnie" in his ear, but, of course, he could not hear me.

"I lied about the key," he told them. "You won't find my fingerprints on it. I didn't find it in Damon's desk. I didn't even know it was there."

"But Donna did?"

"Yeah. She knew. She took the key and let me in the apartment."

"Are you saying we'll find her fingerprints on the key?"

"Definitely."

"Why would she want Damon dead?"

"I don't know. They got along fine. The only thing I can think of is the story. She did it for the story."

"The Gina Parr case?"

"That, and New England Savings," he replied. "You never really know somebody in this business until you see their ego. I think she wanted all the spotlight, or something like that."

Tears started to form in the corners of his eyes and I kissed the back of his neck to acknowledge his honest love for me. He brushed the tickle away but seemed to understand, in that moment, that he was protected. "I don't think she's a jealous person," he continued. "Insecure, maybe. But you won't hear me saying that this is completely out of character for her, you know?"

The detective nodded. They did not really know, but they were obliged to make him think so.

"I'm not saying it was her nature to kill anybody. All I'm saying is you won't hear me saying it was out of character, because the truth is no one really knew her true character. She was distant at times. Sometimes just a head case."

"A head case?" Sanderplaatz prodded.

"Obsessed with her job, her career," he replied and dropped his head to his chest. "Obsessed with being better than everybody."

"We know this is hard for you."

"You don't know how hard. You know I identified the body," he told them.

"Yes," Sanderplaatz said. "The officers told us."

"He didn't show up for work. And we tried calling and paging him. And no one could find him. So I went over there.

I mean, the guy could sleep through a nuclear (*nuke-kley-ah*) attack."

"And that's when you found him?"

"Yes. The place smelled like a county hospital. Don't ask me why."

"Like death."

Johnnie nodded. Yeah, like death. Then he shook his head, unable to reconcile himself to the truth. My death. "I can't believe this," he said. "It was really, really hard for me to go back there, you know."

"So why did you?" Sanderplaatz asked.

"To get my CDs."

"Really?"

"Really," Johnnie replied. "And Donna told me I had to. You know, for closure. I hate that word *closure*. I didn't need *closure. I* needed Damon to ask me something stupid like 'Are you rolling on this, Johnnie?' I *needed* Damon to piss and moan about Gretchen and call her a cunt."

The detective tried not to laugh.

"But Donna talked you into going there?" Sanderplaatz asked.

"Yeah. She said it would be good therapy for me."

"Did it ever occur to you that maybe she wanted you there to plant evidence against you?"

"Against me?" Johnnie asked with a jolt.

"Or at the very least ensure that your fingerprints were scattered around the apartment?"

"No. That never occurred to me," he said. "Jesus."

◇ ◇ ◇

Donna Donovan and Reginald Cooke did not end up in the same prison. But their accommodations were similar. A hard bed, four gray walls, and tasteless food. Donna would serve her time at Framingham State Prison.

Reginald Cooke—a jury convicted him for the murders of Donald Berger and Gina Parr (he was the shooter, they determined)—would sit in Walpole Prison for the rest of his life.

Johnnie Fanahan would make his family proud with his fifth Emmy. We were both named and awarded a statue. Only he, of course, was able to attend the ceremony and accept the golden angel and her beautiful orb of achievement.

I was there. Literally, in spirit. Learning how to be an angel myself.

As for the astonishing debut novel, I suppose one has to do such things for the right reasons. The purest reasons. For love, I imagine. Which may explain the passion Sam Young brings to his writing. I can tell you he is hard at work on a novel. I visit him every so often—by invitation, most times, but sometimes uninvited. Sometimes when he sits staring at the blank screen in front of him, I stare back with ideas of my own.

Why the hell not?

ACKNOWLEDGMENTS

I want to thank Marielle and Chloe who are too young to understand how much they inspire me. And I want to thank my editor, Angela Brown, who knows a thing or two about inspiration. And, last but not least, Pierre, who knows a thing or two about patience.